TORTURED SEASON

A LOGAN FAMILY WESTERN - BOOK 6

DONALD L. ROBERTSON

CM Publishing

COPYRIGHT

Tortured Season

Copyright © 2022 Donald L. Robertson
CM Publishing

Books@DonaldLRobertson.com

TORTURED SEASON

ISBN print: 979-8-9855100-2-7

❀ Created with Vellum

LOGAN FAMILY GENEALOGY

Ethan William Logan, 1779
Married
Rose Isabel Tilman, 1780
CHILDREN
Matthew Christopher Logan, 1797
Mark Adair Logan, 1798
Nathaniel Grant Logan, 1803
Owen Lewis Logan, 1803
Jennifer (Jenny) Isabel Logan, 1812
Floyd Horatio Logan, 1814
Martha Ann Logan, 1816

Matthew Christopher Logan, 1797
Married
Rebecca (Becky) Nicole Doherty, 1810
CHILDREN
William Wallace Logan, 1834
Callum Jeremiah Logan, 1836
Joshua Matthew Logan, 1840
Katherine (Kate) Logan, 1851
Bret Hamilton Logan, 1852
Colin Alexander Logan, 1854

1

———

Will Logan stepped from the saddle and stretched. He felt good. He had spent a week helping Josh, Callum, and the boys with the cattle, and now he was on his way back to Pueblo and his wife, Deborah. She had wanted to go with him to see the family, but her uncle, Dr. James, needed her help with a surgery. Will missed her, but it was nice to see Ma, the family, and Josh's boys.

He patted Buck on the neck and ran his hand through the horse's mane. Buck was a sandy-colored buckskin, with black legs, tail and mane. The horse stomped and turned his head to look at Will.

"All right, boy," Will said, "we'll be on our way, but I want to swing by Mrs. Ketchum's place just to make sure she's doing fine."

The horse, as if to say hurry, tossed his head, flipping the black mane. With that response, Will swung back into the saddle, bumped the buckskin in the flanks, and started down the trail. The sun had slipped well past its zenith.

They rode through the foothills of the Greenhorn Mountains rising to their left. It was a warm July day, and, with no clouds, the sun beat down on rider and horse. Reaching a trail that turned north from the main trail to Pueblo, Will took the turnoff. The cabin was only a short distance down the path.

Like everyone else in the Logan family, Will usually stopped by Lilith Ketchum's place to see if she needed anything from town or any help. Her husband, Tom, had died recently. Doc James said it was most likely a heart problem, but his dying left his wife alone in the mountains.

Will's uncle Floyd, who had been in the Rockies since around 1830, had met Tom Ketchum in those mountains when they both were much younger. Though never good friends, they'd seen each other at rendezvous several times and trapped together on occasion. Once the trapping gave out, Ketchum went back east to Missouri, married Lilith, and brought her to the mountains. They'd lived in that same cabin, doing a little farming, and hunting as needed. He occasionally guided the army and wagon trains. They'd raised their sons in that cabin and lived a happy life.

Happy, that is, until Tom had the audacity to up and die on her. He left her in the cabin with only memories for comfort. Their five sons were gone. Where, she had no idea. Being men, they had left the nest and been swallowed up by the big country. But she was a strong woman. She'd always said, "This is my home. I've raised my boys here and loved my man. I'll live here until I die," and flatly refused any offer of help to move her to a more populated area.

Detouring by her cabin to see if she needed anything, he thought he might spend the night in her barn. It was a good place to stop on his way back to Pueblo from the Logan Ranch.

Rounding the large boulder marking the upcoming home, the cabin swung into view. The first thing to catch his eye was the body collapsed by the hitching post in front of the house. He kicked Buck into a lope, hoping she had just passed out, but nearing her, he could see the blood surrounding her upper body. The ground was already dry, leaving only dark-brown-stained dust. At her side lay her trusty old single-barrel ten gauge —unfired.

He quickly dismounted, tied Buck, and knelt by Lilith's frail, dead body. Turning her over, he lifted her into his arms and saw a bloody hole in her left breast and a smile on her wrinkled face. The thought struck him, *Don't think I've ever seen a person die a violent death with a smile.* He gently closed her eyelids over the lifeless green eyes and carried her frail body to the cabin porch. He laid her on the timbers of the porch and entered the cabin. Ducking to get his taller frame through the six-foot-high door, he stepped inside to find the cabin torn apart.

She had kept a few mementos of her life, and these were thrown about the room. The doilies she had so carefully embroidered were ground into the rough-hewn floor. Clothing had been ripped from its pegs and tossed about haphazardly. The kitchen utensils had been thrown across the room, knives and forks scattered.

He stood for a moment taking in the destruction. Lilith Ketchum had always been a neat person. Anytime he had visited, everything was in its place. The rough floor she had lived on for all these years was kept clean and as free of splinters as humanly possible. Will could feel cold anger building deep within. *This lady,* he thought, *always lived in peace, never asking for much, but always willing to give whatever she had to help someone. Now she's been murdered by a bunch of coldhearted killers.* His face set in a grim mask, he found an old blanket that was still clean, and stepped outside to the porch. He gently wrapped Lilith in the blanket, carefully covering her face, and carried her to the plot alongside where Tom was buried. She had wanted her husband buried where she could see him from the kitchen window.

From the barn Will retrieved a shovel and pick, stripped off his shirt, rolled up the sleeves of his long johns, and grasped the pick. With long, swinging, overhead strokes, he attacked the hard ground. Through the tight long johns, muscles rippled, and the sleeves stretched around his biceps. The rocky ground made for slow progress, but he was unrelenting. Soon, the hole was deep enough.

He laid Lilith gently in the hole, extended her legs, and covered her with dirt from the mountain she had made a home. Once finished, he removed his hat and spoke a few words from the good book. The afternoon sun highlighted the white streak of hair around his old head wound. Once finished, he slapped his hat back on his head, returned to the barn, and searched through it until he found an appropriately sized board. He carved Lilith's name, the date, and an epitaph into the board. Then, using the shovel, he drove the board into the ground at the head of the grave next to Tom.

After returning the tools to the barn, he reexamined the scene of the murder. Three sets of horse tracks were around where Lilith had fallen. He had no idea what had transpired here, but he knew Lilith never turned people away, so they must have said or done something that closed the normally open door. He picked up the shotgun and returned it to the house and latched the door behind him. The old porch creaked as he lowered his weight into the rocking chair. He removed his boots and replaced them with the moccasins he had brought from his saddlebags. The killers were headed into the mountains, and the soft soles of the moccasins might prove an advantage for him. Determined to find the men who murdered the gentle old woman, he hung the boots over the saddlebags, mounted Buck, and followed the killers' clear trail toward the Greenhorns.

It was easy to follow. They had done nothing to attempt to hide their tracks. Even traveling through the thick pines, where with just a little effort they could have disappeared, limbs were broken, rocks kicked over, and brush torn. He could only figure they thought the cabin was far enough out of the way, there would be no one stopping by anytime soon.

Your tough luck, gents, Will thought.

The men he was following rode in a straight line, never deviating, indicating they had a destination in mind. After the sun set behind the peaks of the Greenhorns, daylight faded in the shadows. When darkness fell, he pulled Buck to a slow walk, but continued in the same direction.

His first indication he was nearing the killers was firelight on a distant slope. Will allowed Buck to continue his slow, careful walk. Finally, when they had drawn within a couple of hundred yards, he pulled Buck to a stop and listened. Then he swung his right leg over the saddle and lowered his foot to the ground, feeling for anything that might roll, scrape, or break. Finding nothing that might give him away, he lowered his weight to the foot. It sank softly into the thick bed of needles.

He took a deep breath, smelling the crisp welcome smell of the pines, his left foot remaining in the stirrup. He waited, alert for any noise, anything indicating the men were aware of him. His big buckskin stood like a statue, ears thrust forward, nostrils flared. Along with the fresh pine, he could smell smoke from the campfire. Occasionally the heat on a resin-filled limb caused a loud pop, echoing through the night. Will shook his head and thought, *How can anyone on the run be so stupid as to light a fire, especially with pine? On a night like this, a man can hear burning pine crackle and pop half a mile away and see the flame farther.*

Voices floated on the light night breeze. With his reins in his left hand, and the Winchester Model 1866 Yellow Boy in his right, he lowered his left foot to the ground and looped Buck's reins over a small patch of sage. He could smell the perfume of the sage blend with the pine.

Drawing closer, he felt the outline of a dried branch through his moccasin. He silently lifted his foot, moved it forward, felt the ground, and lowered his weight back to soft ground, remaining unknown to the killers. *Thank goodness for moccasins,* he thought. *If I'd been wearing hard, leather-soled boots, that branch would've snapped like a pistol shot.*

The men's voices grew clearer as he moved through the trees toward them. Nearing the camp, he kept the trunk of a tall pine between himself and the gang. He couldn't believe the size of the fire the three men had built. He could feel the heat from the thick coals all the way to the tree he hid behind, and the fire's blaze licked high above the ground.

A man's voice, high pitched with a drawl, said, "Blake, you shouldn't oughta shot that old woman. Law's gonna be after us somethin' fierce. They hang a body for such."

A gruff voice said, "Stop yore whinin', Early. Couldn't you see she was fixin' to ventilate Blake with that big ole single barrel. There wouldn't of been enough of him left to feed the buzzards."

Will slipped nearer, his moccasins gliding over the dried pine needles with barely a whisper. With his right hand, he double-checked the leather loop securing his Remington .44 in the holster. Clear and ready. Early summer meant warm in Pueblo, but it was much cooler in these mountains. The night breeze moaned through the pines, sounding almost like a man groaning. The conversation stopped, then picked up again.

The man called Early spoke. "That's a mighty scary sound. It sounds like someone's hurtin' bad."

Now a third voice spoke up, this one with cold authority. "Early, shut your mouth. It's just the wind. I swear, I think you're scared of everything."

"It's haints I'm afeared of, Blake. My uncle's place back in Arkansas had the worst kind. They finally kilt him. It was all-fired terrifying finding him dead on the floor by his fireplace, and bullet holes all in the walls—everywhere. It was like he stood in front of the fire and emptied both his pistol and rifle into the walls. He weren't shot or cut or nothing—just dead— dead for no reason. Course, his empty bottle of corn likker was sittin' next to him, but corn likker ain't never kilt a man. We got him outta there, buried him, and burned that place to the ground. While it burnt, you could hear voices inside, groanin' like we just heard. They finally stopped when it was most burned out."

Will was in a good position to cover all three men. He had the protection of the tree and couldn't resist an impulse. As soon as Early stopped talking, he leaned his head back, so his mouth would be pointed toward the treetops, waited until the night breeze picked up, and let out a low, mournful groan.

Silence. No movement from the camp.

After at least a minute, Early said in a whisper so low Will could barely hear him, "Did you fellers hear that?"

This time the answer wasn't so sure or quick. Finally the gruff-voiced man said, though with little confidence, "Ghosts don't exist, Early. That must have been the wind. You heard it pick up."

Will could hear no movement. The men must be sitting stone still, trying to see into the darkness with eyes blinded by the bright fire. He chuckled and waited, but his smile disappeared with the thought of Lilith Ketchum and how she had been laid out in the dirt, dead, blood all around her.

A loud crack sounded from the fire as a pine limb burst, bringing Will's thoughts back to the killers. He removed his hat and eased an eye around the tree. A tall, gaunt, scruffy-looking man must have just returned from watering the horses at the nearby stream before bedding them down. The other two were sitting on a log, staring into the blazing fire. One of the two, a thick wide-built man, turned his head and said in the gruff voice, "Early, afore you sit, pull another log on the fire."

The tall, gaunt man studied the speaker, his scraggly beard moving as if he were muttering to himself. Finally, he walked to their woodpile, made his selection, and dragged a sizeable log toward the fire. Near the fire, he stood the long log on its end and let it fall. It crashed into the fire. Sparks and burning embers leaped in all directions. The two men who had been sitting jumped away from the fire, cursing.

Watching the sparks rise high into the dark night sky, Early said, "That oughta last us all night," and sat on the log the other two had vacated.

"Early," the gruff man snapped, "whatcha tryin' to do, roast us?"

"Well, shoot, Jesse," Early replied, staring into the settled flames, "my pa always said, 'If'n you want somethin' done a certain way, why, you just oughta do it yoreself.'"

Jesse started toward Early.

"Leave it," Blake barked, stopping Jesse in his tracks.

"Be glad Blake Foster's around, Early. 'Cause if he weren't, I'd take you apart, here and now."

Will watched Early turn his head and eye Jesse from under his floppy hat brim. In his high nasal twang, and through a humorless grin, the man said, "Why, Jesse, I'm yore huckleberry, boy, anytime, anyplace." When he grinned, Will could see, in the firelight, the tall man's jagged and broken teeth.

"Enough, I said," Blake snapped as he sat back down on the log next to Early.

A few moments later the man Early called Jesse sat on the other side of Blake and stared into the fire.

Will watched the three men, then straightened. Now was as good a time as any. He took a deep breath and stepped from behind the tall pine. He was behind the killers. He stood there and waited, the Winchester leveled at the men, no more than twenty feet away.

Blake, a darkly handsome younger man of average height with long, well-groomed hair hanging below his collar, said, "Early, why don't you get that bottle out of my saddlebags. I think we all need a drink."

"Why, Blake, that shore sounds mighty fine to me," Early replied. He stood, turned, stepped over the log, and with one foot on each side of the log, froze. His eyes were glued on the golden reflection of the fire on the Winchester Yellow Boy in Will's hands.

Will rotated his wrist, allowing the reflection to play on the brass of the Winchester's receiver, and in a conversational voice, said, "Mighty pretty, isn't it?"

At the sound of his voice, the two men still sitting on the log jumped to their feet and whirled, both going for their guns. Their hands stopped in midair at the sight of the big muzzle trained on them.

"That's smart, boys. After finding Mrs. Ketchum facedown in her own blood, I'd just as soon shoot you as take you back to the law. You"—he indicated Early with the muzzle of his rifle—"collect their guns and gun belts and bring them to me."

Early looked at Blake. "Boss?"

"Do as he says. Start with Jesse's."

Will could see the calculating look Blake had given Early, because Early had to cross between Will and Blake to get to Jesse.

Will thought, *Does he think I'm that stupid?* He said nothing and waited as Early slowly crossed in front of Blake. Will caught the quick movement as Blake's left arm disappeared behind Early, and shot Blake in the right shoulder.

The .44-caliber ball slammed into the younger man, spinning him around. Blake stepped back, his left heel caught on a branch, and he tumbled, his body twisting into the blazing fire. The other two men stood staring at their leader as he fell, arms flailing for balance, into the flames.

"I'm burning! I'm burning!" Blake screamed, trying to overcome the shock of the bullet and roll from the fire, but he couldn't roll because each of his gang had jumped forward and grabbed him by the boots and were dragging him. From where he was standing when he drew, except for his boots, the rest of his body had fallen across the fire. Dragging him from the fire entailed dragging his upper body and head through the hot coals. His hat had fallen in the fire, and his hair was blazing.

Will saw a bucket of water near and picked it up with his left hand, holding the Winchester in his right, like a pistol. As soon as they pulled Blake from the fire, Will poured the water over the bleeding man's face and burning hair. The man lay on his back, staring up at Will, his eyes coal black in the firelight, filled with pain and hate. With a few exceptions of curled and crisped strands, his hair was gone, and his scalp was bright red with areas of burned black skin. His head must have broken through the burning limbs and landed directly on the hot coals, because the left side of his face and ear had been seared like a steak.

Early looked at his boss lying on the ground moaning, and then up at Will. "You shot him."

"I did. I wasn't born yesterday, boys. Did you think I didn't know he was going to draw when you walked between me and him?" Will shook his head. "He'd be in a lot better shape if he'd left that hogleg in its holster." Will had backed up to put more space between him and the killers. "Now, get those guns and bring them over here."

Moaning, Blake said, his voice small and young, "I need help, please. The pain. It's terrible."

Will nodded. "Reckon that .44 ball you slammed into poor, old Mrs. Ketchum hurt mighty bad. You didn't have much problem living with her pain. Looks like you're just gonna have to live with yours."

Jesse had said nothing. He just stood staring at the gruesome sight of Blake. Early stepped over to him, making sure he stayed well clear of the muzzle of Will's rifle, and said, "Jesse, you'd best give me yore gun."

Jesse looked surprised, turned to look at Early, and then at Will. Without a word, he unfastened the gun belt and handed it to the tall, bearded man. He then turned in the opposite direction, bent over, and began throwing up what appeared to be everything he'd had since breakfast.

Will, while still keeping the others covered with the rifle, glanced back to look at the steaming, red head of Blake. The man's left ear had already swollen to half again its size and was seeping fluid onto the man's burned neck. He shook his head and turned his attention back to Early and Jesse.

Early bent over, unfastened Blake's gun belt, and pulled it out from under him. The injured man moaned from the movement. Early straightened, carried the two gun belts back to Will, and dropped them in the dirt. Then he removed his and added it to the pile.

Will nodded and said, "Get the rifles, and understand, you make the slightest move, I'll shoot, and my next shot may do more than hit a shoulder."

Early nodded, for both he and his partner had been completely demoralized by the sight of Blake, gathered the rifles, and dropped them with the handguns and belts.

"Good," Will said. "Now get some rope and tie up your friends, hands behind their backs, and feet tied."

Early looked at Will and, in his whiny voice, said, "Blake's hurt mighty bad. He needs some doctorin' soon."

"The sooner you get him tied, the sooner he'll have someone looking at those wounds."

Early, almost as tall as Will, but not as big, said, "You're a cold man, mister."

"No, I'm not cold. A cold man shoots down an old woman in her front yard. That's what a cold man does. Get it done, and now."

Will watched as the two men were tied, the younger man moaning constantly. Once they were tied, Will tied Early in a like manner and went after Buck.

2

It had been a long ride back to Pueblo. There had been no trouble from the three killers. Will found it difficult to keep his eyes from the burned man. He'd also found it hard not to feel sorry for him, even considering what the man had done to Lilith Ketchum. Short of hanging, burning was about the worst punishment a man could get, and the killer had definitely been burned.

The man's hat had been destroyed in the fire. Will had an old flop hat he carried in his saddlebags in case something happened to his black Stetson, so he handed it to Foster. The young man had put it on gently. But when he tried to take it off, all of the skin touching the hat stuck to it and pulled from his head. He had screamed from the pain. Riding now, the screaming had stopped, but his low guttural moans filled the air. His eyebrows were gone. Both ears were swollen and cracked, with the top half of the left one starting to droop, like that of an old hound. Fluid, some bloody, mostly clear, seeped from his head. His left ear and cheek, where he had fallen through to the coals, were the worst, but the rest of his face did not escape the blaze. His lips were swollen to twice their size, and Foster, when he looked at Will, no longer had hate in his eyes, only an all-encompassing pain.

Everyone on the streets of Pueblo stopped to stare at the procession. The normal noise and chatter of a busy day quieted as they rode along the dusty street. Wagons halted, and other horsemen moved to the side, pulling up and watching as they passed. The clip-clop of their four horses thudded like heartbeats through the town. The people on foot paused as they passed and spoke in low, indistinct tones. A child of no more than five pulled at her mother's dress, pointed at Foster and said, her voice carrying across the silent streets, "Look, Mama, that man's head is all red and wet, and he don't have any hair?"

Will could see the killer's shoulders hunch at the child's words, like he had been struck a heavy blow. He guided the gang to the hitching rail in front of the sheriff's office and swung down from Buck, his rifle pointed at the killers. "All right, boys, get down. Let's go visit the sheriff."

Early helped Blake Foster down, but Jesse steered clear, keeping his eyes averted from his partner. A boy about twelve years old stood near the sheriff's office, his mouth hanging loose as he stared at Foster.

"You," Will said to the youth.

The boy slowly tore his eyes away from the gory sight and looked at Will, who flipped a quarter into the air toward him. Not so engrossed he didn't see the quarter, the youth snatched it out of the air. "Yes, sir?"

"Go get Doc James, and tell him to hurry."

"Yes, sir," the boy said as he turned and dashed toward the doctor's office.

Will turned back to his three prisoners and waved the muzzle of the rifle toward the door. "Inside."

Jesse went in first, followed by Early helping a groaning Blake Foster through the doorway.

Following the three, Will ducked as he went through the high doorway, a habit developed through years of banging his head. The sheriff had a cell door open and was herding the three men toward it. When he saw Blake Foster, he looked at the man and then at Will.

Will said, "I shot him, and he fell into their fire. Doc's been sent for."

The sheriff nodded and stepped farther back when Foster passed. He closed the jail cell door, inserted the key into the lock, and rotated it. The sound of the bolt, steel on steel, going home had a finality to it.

Will stood his rifle in a corner of the office and looked at the stranger standing by the window. The man nodded and said, "I see you caught up with three we've been looking for, Blake Foster, Jesse Nash, and Early Fisher."

"Will," the sheriff said, "this here is Benjamin Morgan, U.S. Marshal."

Will stepped forward and shook the man's hand. "Howdy. I'm William Logan, Will for short."

"My pleasure. I'm Ben. We've been talking about you Logans."

The door burst open, and Doc James charged in, followed by Deborah, Will's wife. She passed the doctor and ran straight to Will. He grasped her in his arms and said, "Hi, honey."

After a quick hug, she held him at arm's length. "Are you all right?"

He marveled every time he saw her. Her soft brown hair was pulled back in a bun to keep it out of the way. In so many women, it looked severe, but with her it exposed a long graceful neck, reminding him of a doe stretching her neck in search of a wandering fawn. She must have dashed out, leaving her bonnet. Her petite ears complemented the lines of her neck, and he loved the deep brown of her eyes and the strength of her chin. She was well put together.

Her eyes laughed as he gazed at her. "*I said*, are you all right?"

He grinned. "Right as rain, though that young fellow is a bit under the weather." He nodded with his chin toward the cell.

The sheriff had unlocked it to allow Dr. James to enter. The doctor said, "Hello, Will. Glad you're safe. Deborah, come help. We've got a bad burn case here."

"Doc," Will said, "he's also got a bullet hole in his shoulder."

Somewhat testily, Dr. James said, "Thank you, Will. I can see that."

Deborah smiled at Will and shrugged before rushing to assist her uncle. Will couldn't help but notice there was no shock on his wife's face when she looked at the burned man. She had seen so much during the war, little in the way of wounds or injuries shocked her.

While they worked on Foster, the sheriff asked Will, "What happened?"

"I was coming back from the ranch and stopped by the Ketchum place to check on Lilith."

Sheriff Fletcher shook his head. "I wish she'd move into town. A woman her age shouldn't be living that far from town by herself."

Will watched Dr. James removing Foster's clothing to get at the bullet wound. While he worked on the man's shoulder, Deborah began cleaning the burns with a cloth she had taken from her bag. She had wet it with a solution from a bottle, also from the bag, and was speaking in a low, soothing voice to Foster while she worked.

He looked back to the sheriff. "We've all tried to get her to move, but she won't be moving now. I found her lying in a pool of her own blood by the hitching post at the front of their house. She'd been shot right through the heart."

"Those fellers did it?" the sheriff asked.

"That they did," Will replied. He placed his left forefinger under the front brim of his hat and pushed it to the back of his head, bringing into view the white streak along the right side of his head, contrasting with light brown hair now salted with gray.

"I followed them, caught up with them, and in the short fracas"—he nodded to Foster—"he tried to draw on me. I shot him. The shot knocked him back into the fire, and before his pards could get him out, that happened." He turned to look at the man, who moaned in pain as Deborah and Doc worked on him. His brow wrinkled. "Don't regret shooting him, 'cause he was drawing on me, but I sure wouldn't wish that on any man."

Marshal Morgan, a man of striking countenance, with his almost silver hair, neatly trimmed mustache, and deep voice, spoke up. "Save your sympathy for someone who deserves it. I recognized those boys the minute you pulled up out front. They shot a lawman in Denver and robbed a couple of miners in Colorado City. Beat 'em mighty bad. Everybody lived. The lawman said Blake Foster shot him. Said he had about the fastest draw he'd ever seen. He also said Foster liked the girls, but after a few drinks he got mean, and the word was he liked to carve on 'em. The miners said that Jesse Nash and Early Fisher did the beating while Foster kept his gun trained on 'em. One of those miners may never walk upright again, thanks to those boys."

The marshal hooked thumbs in the pockets of his brown vest and turned a steely gaze toward the jail cell. "Like I said, don't be wasting any sympathy on those three, especially Blake Foster and Jesse Nash. Those two are bad hombres."

Deborah had finished cleaning Foster's head. After the cleaning, she applied an oil over all of his burns and then wrapped his head, leaving just enough space for him to see, breathe, and eat. She finished only slightly ahead of Doc James, who was tying the last bandages over the man's shoulder.

Once completed, the doc straightened with a groan. Placing both hands to his back, he said, "I'm certainly not feeling as young as my mind thinks I am. Bending over like that about killed my back." He turned to the sheriff. "You can let us out of here. Either Deborah or I shall return on at least a daily basis to check on our patient."

Deborah closed her bag, picked it up, and started to follow the doctor, but Foster's hand shot out, grasping her wrist. "Thank you, ma'am," he said, his voice almost a croak. "That's the best I've felt since that feller shot me."

She smiled at him. "I'm glad. I'll be back to change your dressings." She patted his hand. "Now, can you release me, please?"

Will had seen Foster grab Deborah. He was to the cell door in three strides, followed by Sheriff Fletcher, who quickly thrust the key into the lock and turned it.

Foster let his hand drop from her wrist. "Sorry, ma'am. I just wanted you to know before you left."

She continued to smile at him. "Thank you," she said, and followed Doc James out the cell door.

She smiled at Will. "I'm fine. He only wanted to say thank you."

Will, eyes narrowed, said in a cold voice, "He can say thank you without touching you. Maybe you should let the doc take care of him."

"Nonsense, Will. I'm a nurse, and the sheriff or his deputy will be here. I'll be perfectly safe."

He relented only slightly, his face softening. "I know men, and he is no good. You come over here only when the doctor can't, and be careful."

The corner of Deborah's soft mouth pursed, and her eyes flashed. "I don't take orders, Will, and I've handled worse. I'll be over here whenever I'm needed."

To the sheriff, Dr. James said, "We'll be back at least once a day until the patient is better, maybe more often, depending on how he is doing."

"Sure, Doc, anytime," the sheriff said.

Dr. James said to Will and Deborah, "Good to have you back,

Will. Come along, Deborah. We still have patients at the office."

Her tense face softened, and she smiled. "See you at home when you're done." She followed the doctor from the sheriff's office.

Will watched her as she passed the office window. *She is such a pretty woman,* he thought, *but she can be as headstrong as a mule.*

"Sheriff," Will said, "if you don't need me anymore, I need to get Buck to the stable for some well-deserved food and water."

Will caught the sheriff's look at the marshal, and he raised his eyebrows, then remembered the marshal's comment about them having been talking about the Logans. The thought drifted through his mind, *Why were they talking about us?*

"Will," the marshal said, "I need to talk to you. How about we go over to the Pueblo Hotel for a piece of pie and a cup of coffee."

"Marshal, that'd be fine. My horse needs to lose that saddle and get something to eat. Give me half an hour, and I'll meet you there." He turned to the sheriff. "Sheriff, I'm headed down to the stable. I can also take those men's horses down and get them watered and fed."

"I'd be obliged, Will. I've got paperwork to do here if you're gonna get your reward."

"What reward?" Will asked.

The marshal spoke up. "Five hundred on Blake Foster, and two-fifty each on Nash and Early, not bad pay for just doing what's right."

The two men grinned at Will. He shook his head. "I'm sure not one to turn down a gift horse. Thanks."

Sheriff Fletcher said, "I'll have the paperwork done, and Ben, here, can bring it to you when he meets you at the Pueblo. Take it to the bank, and they'll pay you."

"Sure thing," Will said, and walked out the door. He mounted Buck, and leading the other three horses to the livery, he rode down the main street of Pueblo. Riding past, he examined the buildings. The town was growing. John Thatcher no longer had the only store, though his was the largest. The town boasted three saloons, attracting all types. When ranch hands rode in, the sheriff and his jail were kept busy. However, Sheriff Fletcher had proven up to the challenge.

Will rode Buck to the trough, and all four of the horses crowded forward. He had to push Early Fisher's roan out of the way so he could dismount. Hearing the noisy drinking, Alton Barber, the owner, walked out the double-wide doors to where Will was untying his saddlebags and pulling the Winchester from its scabbard.

"Howdy, Will. How's everybody out at the ranch?"

"Doing fine, Alton." He indicated the three horses he had led to the stable. "You'll need to take care of these boys, compliments of the sheriff. He said you'd understand."

"Rightly do, Will. I take care of all the stock seized by the sheriff. Don't usually amount to much, but it looks like he made quite a haul. Where'd he get them three from?"

"I brought 'em in and offered to bring 'em to you for him."

"These horses belongin' to them killers what killed Mrs. Ketchum?"

Will had started leading Buck into the barn. He stopped and turned to look at the stableman. "Alton, how the blazes do you already know about that? I just told Sheriff Fletcher shortly before riding down here."

Alton grinned at Will. "Rumors travel like wildfire. Ain't no secrets in a town this size."

Will shook his head and led Buck to his regular stall. Reaching the stall, he started stripping the tack from Buck. He carried it to the tack room, laid the saddle and blanket across the rack, and hung the bridle on a peg. On his way back, he shoveled a scoop of corn from the bin and dumped it in the trough in front of Buck. The horse wasted no time. Thrusting his nose into the trough, he took a quick whiff of the corn and started eating.

Will lifted a worn towel hanging over the side of the stall and started rubbing and drying the big buckskin. When he finished, he picked up a brush and went to work.

"I swear," Alton said, "you Logans shore baby your horses. Don't think I've hardly seen anyone else so particular of 'em."

"Pa raised horses, Morgans," Will said. "He taught us to take good care of our stock. He always said, 'Treat 'em right, boys, and they'll treat you right.'" Will patted Buck on the hip. "I consider Buck a Logan. He's done mighty good by me. So has Smokey, a couple of fine horses."

Finished, he picked up his rifle, saddlebags, and bedroll. "You know where to find me, Alton." He lifted his hand in a wave and walked from the stable.

Entering the hotel, he nodded to the clerk and turned left toward the restaurant. The Pueblo Hotel had been around for several years and was beginning to show a few signs of age. The wallpaper under the last coat of paint was beginning to sag, causing a few small tears. The brown leather on the cushioned armchairs that sat near the entrance of the hotel had cracks, which were widening. So many men had sat in them, they had a permanent dip in the middle of the seat cushion that continued to deepen. But even with its wrinkles, Will liked it. The food was good, the beds were clean and free of bugs, and the people were friendly.

He walked into the dining room to see Marshal Ben Morgan sitting at a corner table, hat in one of the chairs, exposing his thick white hair. On the table and to his right lay several papers. In front of him sat a half-full cup of coffee and a piece of pie. The marshal, his brown broadcloth coat on the back of his chair, waved him over. The silver, circular U.S. Marshal's badge, attached to the left breast of his vest, glistened in the light. "Have a seat, Will."

"Thanks," Will said, pulling out a chair. As soon as he sat, the waitress placed a glass of buttermilk and a piece of apple pie in front of him. He grinned up at her. "Polly, you read my mind."

"I doubt that, but I do know you like buttermilk, and everybody likes apple pie."

"Well, thank you kindly."

She smiled at him and walked off. The marshal took a bite of pie, chewed, swallowed, and followed it with a sip of coffee. Using the end of the cloth napkin tucked into his collar, he wiped his mouth. "Now, that's mighty good pie, and the coffee ain't half bad."

Will nodded, slipped the end of his napkin into his collar, and said, "That's why I eat here when I get a chance, but Marshal, I'm sure you didn't invite me over here to tell me how much you like the pie."

3

W
ill watched the marshal take another bite and chew. *Reminds me,* Will thought, *of an old bear eyeing his prey.* The marshal continued to chew, his steely gray eyes constantly active. Occasionally they would rest on Will.

With his pie half-eaten, he took another swig of coffee, laid his fork down, and waited while Polly refilled his cup from a steaming pot. He nodded his thanks. When she had moved away, he said, "What are you doing these days?"

Will tried to discern what the marshal meant by his question, and why he asked it. After a few moments, he replied, "Not a lot, and it's kind of a long story."

The marshal nodded. "I've got time. Still working on my pie."

Will took a deep breath. "Alright, I'm part owner of a spread in South Texas. They'd had some problems and needed help, so I rode down to help them."

The marshal nodded his silver mane and, with a look indicating he knew quite a bit about Will's history, said, "Sheriff Fletcher told me about that. You had some shootin' trouble down thataway."

Will again remembered the comment about discussing the

Logans back in the sheriff's office. He continued, "I had planned on gathering up a herd to drive to Montana Territory and start a ranch, but it was late in the year, and the drought had killed most of the grass. Cattle would never have made it, so I headed back up here to see my wife."

"See your *new* wife," the marshal added, a gleam in his eyes.

"That's a fact," Will said. "Anyway, I had planned on going back with several of my family and bringing up a herd. That would've been early last year, but it turns out Dr. James was down mighty sick, and my wife felt she should stay and help with his practice, so we spent last year here."

The marshal had finished his pie while Will was talking. He laid his fork across his plate, wiped his mouth again, and said, "Why didn't you go this year?"

"Got a message from my partners. The cattle are still in mighty poor shape. They recommended waiting until next year to make the drive. We're planning on putting together a herd of about four thousand."

"That's mighty big, isn't it?"

"It is. Our plan is to drive them to the railhead in Kansas, sell three thousand head, and then drive the remaining cattle to Montana. If everything works out, that'll give us a herd plus a profit."

"Ambitious. When you planning on leaving for this drive?"

"Not the best time of year, probably early February next year."

"That's a tough time to be traveling this country," Marshal Morgan said. "I've seen the temperature reach well below zero in February. That's cold enough to kill man or beast, and that's not even considering the Comanche and Kiowa. You're choosing some mighty hard going."

"I can't argue with you there, but I've made the trip once, so I have a good idea of the country. Also, I've talked to folks more experienced than me, and they say it can be done."

The marshal leaned forward. "So what are you planning on doing between now and then?"

"I really don't have any plans. I help out on a couple of ranches around here. On occasion, I head out for the family ranch along the Sangre de Cristos. That's how I happened by Mrs. Ketchum's place. I was returning from a week of helping with the cattle out there."

Marshal Morgan frowned. "Sounds a little aimless to me."

Will considered the marshal's remark. He could be offended or just take it for a statement of fact. He had to admit, it sounded that way to him. After a moment, he nodded. "Yep, me too, but it does give me time with my wife. Her uncle has gotten well, but he's getting older and can't get around like he used to. She's helping him more and more. There was some talk of his son coming out from back east, but he's in high demand back there."

The marshal leaned forward. "Will, I like the way you brought those men in. You could have shot all three, and there'd be no question, but you elected to bring them back. I'm looking for a good man I can depend on. I'm offering you the job of deputy U.S. Marshal. You'll work in the Colorado Territory, but you'll have jurisdiction in any territory or state."

Will took a long sip of his buttermilk, wiped the residue from his upper lip with his napkin, and leaned back in his chair. He took a minute staring at Morgan. He had never considered being a lawman. It took a lot from a man and didn't give much back, at least that was what he saw.

Before he could speak, the marshal continued, "Look, Will, you like to help people. I've been asking around. About the only folks who don't like you are the ones who wouldn't like me either. Those types either I or the sheriff might end up arresting anyway, so they don't count.

"You're helping out at the different ranches. Shoot, you rode all the way to South Texas to help your friends. I even heard about how you got your medal rescuin' those soldiers." He lifted a hand and pointed a thick finger at Will. "You *are* the man for the job."

Will thought about Deborah. *She's taking on more and more duties with Dr. James. How will she feel about me accepting the job of U.S. Marshal? She's in the business of helping other folks. I imagine she'll understand and be fine with it.* "Alright, Marshal, here's what I'll do. I've got that cattle drive I have to make next year, but I have some time on my hands between now and then. I'll take the job, but I'll only commit until February of next year at the longest. Then I'm done."

"Understand," the marshal said. "Aren't you interested in the pay?"

"Sure I am."

"You'll be getting two hundred a year."

Will grinned. "Not overpaid, huh? The sheriff makes more than that. Shoot, a regular cowhand makes around three-fifty a year."

"I ain't done yet. The two hundred is a base salary. Then you get three dollars for an arrest and a buck fifty for serving papers."

"Marshal, like I said, I'm your man until as late as February of next year, then I'm headed south."

Will tossed two bits on the table and shoved his plate aside. He had finished the pie while the marshal talked. He emptied his glass of buttermilk and stood. "Got to be heading home. How do we do this?"

Marshal Morgan stood and said, "Meet me at the judge's office at eight in the morning. We'll get it done all nice and legal."

"See you in the morning," Will said, and strode from the hotel. He felt a little tingle of excitement. He'd never been a lawman. He had a good idea of the dangers of the job, but if he could help folks, he didn't mind. It wouldn't be the first time he had been shot at. He made his way down the main street, turned right on a cross street, and walked to the small white house on the first corner. He could see a light in the kitchen window and knew Deborah was home. His pace quickened.

In four long bounds, after closing the gate, he was on the porch and through the door. He had no sooner closed it than she rushed into his arms. He had longed to feel her warmth. Her clean sweet smell filled his nose as he pulled her close, feeling the softness of her lips. Enjoying their long embrace, he raised his head at the same moment she stepped back.

"Mrs. Logan," he said, "you are a fine sight for these tired eyes."

"You're not so bad yourself, cowboy." She smiled up at him. "You hungry?"

"Hungry enough to start chewing on that table leg."

She gave him a happy laugh. "Well, you just come sit down, and let me see what's hiding in the pot."

A large pot sat steaming on the cast-iron stove. Claw feet supported the heavy black box. The heat from the stove warmed the kitchen and sitting room, which felt good. Though it was summer, once the sun went down, it cooled quickly in the high desert.

Deborah bent and, using a hot pad, opened the oven. She brought out a large pan of golden brown biscuits. At the sight of the biscuits, Will felt his mouth instantly start to water. He swallowed and said, "Beautiful."

"Yes," she set them on the side of the stove top, admired her work, and flashed a wide smile at him, "they are, aren't they."

Will grinned, feigning surprise. "Oh, yeah, the biscuits are, too."

Her smile widened as she grasped the sides of her dress and curtsied—"Why, thank you, sir"—and turned back to the stove.

"Honey," he said, becoming serious, "I am a lucky man."

She slipped the pot to the side of the stove, farther away from the heat and near the biscuits. Once she had it in the correct position, she turned and glided to her husband and dropped into his lap. Putting her arms around his neck and clasping her wrist, she said, "I love you, Will Logan. I am the one who is lucky. Now what do you have to say to that?"

He waited a few moments, leaned forward, and whispered into her ear, "When are we going to eat?"

She frowned at him, jumped up, and slapped him across the arm with the potholder. "You might be looking for a place to sleep tonight."

He grinned at her. "I know where *I'm* sleeping."

She leered back at him. "Don't be too sure, fella."

They both laughed. She ladled a plate with chicken and dumplings, set it in front of him, and placed the biscuits on the table. After sitting, they said grace, and he made short work of supper while she talked about the happenings around Pueblo for the time he'd been gone. She made it a point not to ask him anything about the men he'd brought to the sheriff.

"That was really good, honey," Will said. "It tasted just like Ma's."

"It should," Deborah said, "it's her recipe."

He picked up another biscuit and took a bite. Half the biscuit disappeared. After swallowing, he said, "We need to talk. Why don't I help get this kitchen cleaned up, and I'll tell you the news."

With water already heating on the stove, it took little time to clean and put up. They moved to the leather-covered settee and sat.

"So tell me," she said. "What's the news?"

"First, let me give you the bounty money on those three I brought in." He winked at her, her face showing surprise as her dainty hand reached for the envelope. Before she could say anything, he continued, "And you saw Ben Morgan, the U.S. Marshal, when you were in the sheriff's office?"

"Who could miss him? He isn't as big as you, but he still is an impressive-looking man."

He grinned at her. "Should I be jealous?"

Deborah punched him on his arm. "Don't be silly, Will. You know better than that."

"Well, that impressive man offered me a job."

Her smile dropped as she studied his face. "Doing what?"

"Deputy U.S. Marshal."

"Did you take it?"

"Sort of."

"I thought we were moving to Montana Territory."

"That's still the plan. I work for him only until next February when we trail down to South Texas. He was fine with it."

"He was fine with you working for only eight months and then quitting? That doesn't strike you as peculiar?"

"I hadn't thought of it, but when you put it that way, it does seem a little funny."

"Will, that's a dangerous job."

He looked up at the ceiling and thought, *Everything's dangerous in this country,* but decided not to say it. "Honey, I was just riding home and, out of the blue, had to shoot someone. That was dangerous, too."

"But you weren't looking for it. You didn't leave here looking for those men. You acted after finding poor Mrs. Ketchum. As a marshal, you'll be hunting men down, and they'll know you're after them. That's dangerous."

"There's a lot more to it than just chasing crooks. When called on, a marshal sets up courts, arranges for furniture, deliver subpoenas . . . They don't always chase criminals."

"But Will, they mostly do, and I've heard of them collecting taxes, too. Sheriff Fletcher has to do county taxes, and he's said it's the most dangerous part of his work. I don't want to ever again see you hurt like you were when we first met. You almost died, and you lost your memory for so long."

Deborah reached out and ran her fingers through his hair around the scar, the wound that had stolen his memory for years.

She gazed at him intently, her eyes filled with concern. "Are you sure you want to do this?"

"Sure, it can be dangerous, but that's life. Buck could step in a gopher hole when I'm chasing a wild cow, and I could break my neck when I fall. Yes, I'd like to take the job. It's a way I can work and help people over these next few months. You remember how you reacted when I told you not to visit Foster? Are you telling me not to take the job? You know I'd be an asset, just like you are to your uncle."

It was her turn to think. He watched the wrinkle lines appear across her forehead. The lines were always visible when she was thinking hard on something. He waited.

Looking up, she reached out and ran her hand over his stubbly cheek. Her hand felt soft, warm, inviting.

"I can't say I like you taking the job, but I won't tell you no. You're a lot like me in one way. You help people. I've found that all of your family has that trait. That's one of the things that attracted me to you. I guess it isn't my place to try to change the very quality I love."

She took a deep breath. After exhaling, she said, "I'm not happy with the prospect of staying up at night worrying about you, but, not that you need it, you have my blessing."

"Good," he said, and drew her to him. Speaking into her hair, he said, "I'll be careful, honey. Now that this is settled, are you ready for bed?"

She leaned back in his arms. "I am definitely ready, husband."

He grinned at her, slipped one arm behind her back and one under her thighs, and stood. She let out a little shriek and then laughed. He walked over to the table, and she blew out the lamp. Then he moved to the lamp in the sitting room, again close enough for her to blow it out.

In the darkness he turned toward the bedroom. She pushed the door open with a foot, and after they were through, using a hand, she swung it closed.

4

W ill and Deborah entered the small, new court office of Pueblo. It was a tiny building squeezed between a store and a saloon. The front door opened to the right side of the main room. This room took up most of the building's space. It was arranged with several rows of chairs, with two desks, side by side, at the front of the chairs. An additional desk sat on a raised stand, facing the two desks and chairs. Behind and to the left of the raised desk, another door opened into a small office space. It was from there Marshal Morgan called, "Come on back here, Will." Upon seeing Deborah, he removed his hat and said, "Howdy, ma'am. It's mighty fine seeing you again."

She gave him one of her big smiles and extended her hand. "Good morning, Marshal. It's nice to see you." After shaking hands with the marshal, she turned to the judge, who, though behind his desk, stood at her entrance. Rewarding him with a similar smile, she said, "Good morning, Judge Bolton. It's good to see you. I didn't realize you were in town."

He gave a slight bow of his head, took her hand, and said, "Why, thank you, Mrs. Logan. It is very nice to see you. I might add you are looking quite radiant this morning."

Her smile broadened. "Thank you." She leaned forward and whispered into his ear, "How's your gout? Are you following your instructions from Dr. James?"

He smiled at her concern and said in a strong voice, "The gout's mostly gone, but I find it difficult to stay away from an occasional evening toddy."

She straightened, lost the smile, and said, "I don't think an *occasional* toddy will hurt, but, along with Dr. James, I recommend not imbibing every day, or you might find yourself in such pain you'll not be able to ride circuit."

The judge straightened, looked at the two men, who were both grinning, cleared his throat, and in a more officious voice, said, "Ah, yes, ma'am. Thank you, but we have some business to take care of."

"Yes, we do," Marshal Morgan said. "Will, if you'll step forward." He picked up the Bible from Judge Bolton's desk. The judge cleared his throat again. "Place your left hand on the Bible and raise your right, Will." The marshal, holding the Bible in the palm of his right hand, extended it to Will, who followed the judge's instructions.

The judge nodded. "Fine. Now repeat after me."

Will listened and repeated after the judge. "I, William Wallace Logan, do solemnly swear that I will support and defend the Constitution of the United States against all enemies, foreign and domestic; that I will bear true faith and allegiance to the same; that I take this obligation freely without any mental reservation or purpose of evasion; and that I will well and faithfully discharge the duties of the office on which I am about to enter. So help me God."

"That's it," the judge said, extending his hand. Let me be the first to congratulate the newest member of the U.S. Marshal Service."

Will took the offered hand. "Thanks, Judge. Never thought I'd be taking that oath again."

"Glad to have you," Marshal Morgan said. He reached into a vest pocket and pulled out a badge similar to his. The badge was a flattened, silver, circular band with Deputy engraved on the top portion and U.S. Marshal on the bottom, and a star set in the center.

Will took the badge, glanced at where the marshal had his pinned, and pinned it to the left side of his vest. Deborah pulled him down as she stood on tiptoe and gave him a kiss on the cheek. "I've got to get to the office. Dr. James will be wondering where I am." She glanced at the other two men, said, "Gentlemen," and left the office.

The three men watched her go. Once the door closed, the judge said, "You have yourself quite a woman, Marshal Logan."

"Thank you, Judge. She certainly is." Then he grinned. "Marshal Logan sounds ... new."

"You'll get used to it, Will," Marshal Morgan said. "Now let's leave the judge to his work. We can talk out here in the courtroom." He turned to the judge. "Thanks, Your Honor. Your being here made it mighty convenient."

"Glad it worked out. There's not much more for me to take care of here in Pueblo, just papers to sign. I don't think those boys Will brought in are likely to be ready for trial anytime soon, so I'll be moving on to Trinidad after dinner. Supper will be on the trail. I'm getting too old for this circuit riding."

The two walked into the courtroom, closing the judge's door behind them. The marshal said, "He's been doing this a long time. He's gotten bullet holes from thieves attempting to rob him, and arrow scars from Indians trying to scalp him. But nobody's managed to stop him. He'll die on the circuit before he'll retire." He pulled up a chair, sat down, and indicated a chair across the aisle for Will.

Will grabbed the indicated chair, spun it around with the back facing the marshal, swung his legs over it, and sat with his arms folded atop the back. "So tell me. I know you've got something on your mind. You seemed awful anxious to get me signed up."

"You called it. Did you hear about the stage robbery near Denver about four days ago?"

"Can't say as I have. I've been out at the ranch."

"Right. We had a deputy U.S. Marshal murdered on the stage between Denver and Colorado City. He was Farley Osborne, and he'd been with the service for three years." He removed his hat and combed his silver hair back with his fingers, then shook his head. "I knew Farley mighty well. He was a good man. He didn't deserve to die by some two-bit thief's gun."

Will waited in silence, watching the marshal process his anger.

Morgan put his hat on a chair next to him, shook his head one last time, and said, "It was also carrying fifteen thousand dollars. The description of the bandit sounds like Ambrose Cooper, a worthless no-account. I've talked to several people between Colorado City and here who claim to have seen him heading south. If he keeps moving in that direction, it'll take him through New Mexico and right into Texas. I know he has family down there, but he also has some friends in Trinidad, and I think he's got an uncle in New Mexico, Las Vegas, I think. If he stops in Trinidad, you might have a chance to nab him quick, maybe New Mexico, too, but if he makes it to Texas, he'll have family around, and it'll be a lot harder taking him." He rubbed his forehead with a scarred knuckle. "I'd like to bring him in myself, but I've got to be back in Denver for a trial. The other deputies are already working on cases. I got approval to add one more, and you're it."

Will nodded. "You have anything else on him?"

"I've got this." He pulled a paper from his inside vest pocket and unfolded it. "Here's a wanted poster on Mr. Ambrose Cooper. He's already wanted for an attempted robbery on a Cheyenne, Wyoming, bank. That was almost his last mistake." The corners of Morgan's eyes crinkled only a little, with what Will figured was the marshal's expression of humor. "He hit the bank just as they were closing. Guess he figured they'd be packed with money. What he didn't figure was those Cheyenne bankers weren't your average, run-of-the-mill bankers. Every soul was armed to the teeth. The minute he stepped through the door with his gun drawn, they opened up, no questions, no howdy-do. They just started firing."

At the thought, Morgan chuckled. Will, picturing the bandit standing in the door, gun drawn, expecting everyone to throw up their hands, only to be met with a hail of bullets, laughed out loud.

"Yeah," Morgan said. "That fella was mighty lucky. Those bankers may be quick on the draw, but it appears they can't hit what they shoot at. Not a bullet clipped Cooper. One creased a bystander just passing the bank, but he was all right. The report quoted one of the bankers as saying, 'That thief disappeared faster than a cowhand's money on payday.' It looks like he likes stealing other folks' money, and he doesn't mind killing, so we need to stop him. The way I see it, sooner's better than later."

"Is that it?" Will said.

"That's about it. Take this." He handed Will the circular on Cooper, a warrant for the man's arrest, and a document stating Will was a deputy marshal. "This will cover you should you have any difficulty from local law."

Will stood. "I'll get packed and be on my way."

"One other thing," Morgan said. "Since you're headed for Trinidad first, why don't you ride along with the judge. That'll give him some protection at least that far."

"Sure," Will said, "it makes sense. I'll be ready when he is."

Morgan stood. "I'll tell the judge, and, Will? Bring Cooper back. We'd like him alive, but do what you must. We can't let murderers like him escape."

Will nodded and walked out the door into the bright July sunlight. He looked up and down the busy streets of Pueblo. It probably wouldn't make sense to most people living their everyday lives, but he had to admit to himself. He felt alive. There was a feeling of excitement in the air. Was he the only one who could feel it? *Ambrose Cooper,* he thought, *I'm on your trail, and I won't stop until I've found you.*

WILL WAS RELIEVED to be entering Trinidad. He had thought his uncle Floyd's friend Shorty was a talker, but the judge had him beat hands down. The older man was pleasant enough, but it was like he couldn't abide silence and had to fill it with words. Will's ears were tired. What he hadn't known before about Trinidad, he knew now.

The pastureland near the town was covered with grazing oxen from the wagons traveling along the mountain route of the Santa Fe trail. Trinidad sat directly on the route. The rich valley grasses along the Purgatory River provided an excellent resting point for the traders after crossing the rugged Raton Pass and before venturing east onto the Great Plains.

"Thanks for the company, Will," Judge Bolton said. "I'll be staying here for a while. I've several cases that need my attention. Wish you were staying. I could use your help." As Will started to respond, the judge held up a hand. "No, no, it's no problem. I know you're after Cooper, and I don't want to delay you from catching him. Good luck. If you do, try to bring him back alive. I'd sure like to see him tried before he gets hanged."

"I'm expecting to be on my way pretty quick, Judge. But if you need me, let me know." Will guided Buck to a hitching rail by a watering trough. He stepped from the horse, gave him enough slack to drink when he tied him, and walked into the nearest saloon.

Stepping into the saloon, after a pause to allow his eyes to adjust from the bright sunlight, Will walked to the long bar that ran along the right side of the crowded room. The light from one of the large chandeliers glinted off the shiny badge he wore.

The bartender wore garters on his sleeves to keep his cuffs pulled up, and a long dirty apron. He was busy wiping down the bar with a dingy towel but stopped and said, "What can I do for you, Marshal?"

"I'll have a buttermilk if you have it," Will said, and reached into his inside vest pocket, drawing out the wanted circular. He unfolded it and laid it out on the bar. After wiping a big hand along it to flatten it out, he said, "Have you seen this man?"

The bartender took a close look at the picture and said, "Ambrose Cooper? Sure. He was in here two or three days ago." He raised his head and called to a patron sitting at one of the tables reading a newspaper. "Hey, Rayford."

The man lowered the paper and, through a thick pair of glasses, squinted back at the bartender. "Yeah?"

"Weren't you talking with Cooper the other day?"

"Yeah."

"The marshal, here, is looking for him."

"What for?"

Will turned toward the man and leaned against the bar on his left elbow. "He's wanted for robbing a stage and killing a U.S. Marshal."

While Will was speaking, the bartender stepped quickly to the back. Moments later he returned with a glass of buttermilk, placed it down by Will's elbow, and stood listening.

The man laid the newspaper on the table and continued, "I knew it. I told Ambrose years ago if he didn't straighten up, he'd be stretching a rope." He shook his head, paused, as if thinking, and continued, "Last I saw of him, he was heading down south, New Mexico or Texas. I know he has relatives in both places."

While he had been talking, Will examined the speaker. He was of average build, probably in his forties, maybe a little thick around the middle, obviously not a cowhand from the way he was dressed. Neatly cut black hair, graying over the ears and near the temples, covered a large blocky head. "How do you know him?" Will asked after taking a sip of his buttermilk.

"I'm Rayford Browning, Marshal . . ."

"Logan, Will Logan."

"Marshal Logan. You any kin to the Logans ranching between the Sangre de Cristos and Greenhorn Mountains."

"Yep."

Browning waited for a more detailed response. When it wasn't forthcoming, he cleared his throat and continued, "Yes, well, as I was saying, I am Rayford Browning. I'm a sometimes schoolteacher, newspaperman, and writer. It just so happens that, oh, about seven years ago I had a teaching job in El Paso. One of the boys in my class was Ambrose Cooper, a bright lad. Very promising, except he was always getting into fights. It's a real shame. He had a beautiful singing voice. I do believe he could have become extremely successful performing on the east coast, but his father wouldn't hear of it."

Will took another sip of buttermilk. It was good. He wiped his mouth with his sleeve. "Does he have any other friends in Trinidad?"

Browning thought for a moment. "I wouldn't really call them friends, more like drinking companions, and not very good citizens at that. Almost a gang. Three of them, about his age. They are part-time cowhands. They work until they get the urge, then quit, come into town, and get drunk. I don't think a one of them is over twenty-two, if that old."

"Where could I find them?"

"If they're still in town, they hang out at the Red Dog Saloon. A lot of miners hang out there too. Many of the miners are Irish and not too fond of lawmen."

"I've got a bit of Irish blood in me myself," Will said. "Maybe I can parley that into more information."

Will couldn't help but notice the skeptical look Browning

flashed at him. "Then I wish you the best of luck, Marshal Logan, for you will be needing it."

Will nodded, finished his buttermilk, tossed a nickel on the bar, and returned to the sunshine, blinking for a moment. When his eyes readjusted, he saw the Red Dog at the other end of town, near the livery.

"How'd you like some corn, Buck?" he asked as he swung into the saddle. He turned the buckskin south toward the livery and examined the Red Dog Saloon as he rode past. Several miners began to enter, but stopped, spotting the badge glistening on his chest. They glared at him until he passed. He touched his hat to the men and pulled up to the livery. After requesting feed and a good rubdown for his buckskin, he explained to the man at the stable that he would probably be needing Buck later in the afternoon. Before stepping outside the stable, he removed the leather loop securing his .44 Remington in the holster.

Walking to the Red Dog, he rubbed the scar on his left wrist where the rattlesnake had bitten him while he was in Texas. It occasionally itched. He paused again after stepping into the dark saloon from the bright Colorado sun. After a moment, his eyes adjusted, and he strode toward the bar. A pale blonde latched onto his arm and swished along with him, her ruffly skirt brushing against his leg.

"Hi, Marshal," she said, looking up at him. "I don't know you, and I *know* all the men in Trinidad."

Will touched his hat. "Ma'am. You know Ambrose Cooper?"

They reached the bar, and she dropped his arm, now placing one finger against her painted cheek. "Let me see, Marshal . . . Ambrose Cooper. I'm awfully dry. I find it terribly hard to think when I'm dry. Don't you, Marshal?"

Will motioned to the bartender. "Give her whatever she's drinking."

The bartender reached beneath the bar and pulled out a bottle of amber liquid. He filled a glass and slid it to Will's companion. She caught it deftly and in one easy motion lifted it to her lips, emptying the glass. She slammed the glass on the bar and said, "Another."

The bartender started to reach across the bar with the bottle, but Will covered the glass with his hand. "Not yet. You drank, now talk. If I like what I'm hearing, then I'll consider another."

The blonde extended full lips in a bogus pout. "Why, Marshal, you'd refuse a girl a drink?"

"Nope. I'd refuse a girl a second drink if she doesn't talk. Now what do you know about Ambrose Cooper?"

The soft pout disappeared, replaced by a brassy stare. "Who wants to know?" she replied.

"The man who controls the bottle right now. What about Cooper?"

She looked out the door, then said, "He left yesterday."

"Where was he headed?"

After watching Will for a moment longer, her features softened. "He was heading for New Mexico, Las Vegas I think, at least that's what he told me. Now can I have my drink?"

"What's in Las Vegas?"

Using a wheedling tone, she said, "Marshal, I'm really thirsty."

"Answer my questions and I'll get you another one, but questions first. Now, what's in Las Vegas?"

"His family. I think it's an uncle. They're close. Coop goes down there just about every time he gets in trouble. So, now answer my question. Why do you want him?"

Will watched her closely. "He robbed a stage and killed a U.S. Marshal."

The woman's act fell away, and a hand jerked to her mouth. "Oh my goodness. He'll hang for this, won't he?"

"Likely."

She looked up at Will, her blue eyes pleading. "I really do need a drink, Marshal."

Will nodded to the bartender, who, still holding the bottle, reached for the glass. She jerked it away, saying, "Give me the real stuff, Bernie, rye, and a water glass."

The bartender gave her a dirty look and took a bottle from the shelf behind him. He picked up a water glass, set it on the bar next to the woman, and poured a shot of rye into it.

When he stopped, she said, "More."

He poured until the glass was half-full and looked at her. She nodded, picked up the glass, and drank the contents in three swallows.

The bartender said to Will, "That'll be a buck."

Not willing to argue over the cost, Will pulled a silver dollar from his vest pocket and tossed it to the bartender, who trapped it with three fingers of the hand holding the cork. He shoved the cork back into the bottle and deposited the bottle on the shelf where it had been sitting. He turned back, dropped the dollar into a pocket, and moved down the bar.

"Feel better?" Will asked.

"No," she said. "I can't imagine Coop killing anyone. He likes to pretend he's fast with a gun, but he's never hurt a soul."

"He has now."

"He plans on quitting, he's told me so."

"I wouldn't bet on it. I understand he has three friends he hangs out with."

"He does, unfortunately. They're worthless trash. Not one of them deserves to walk in Coop's shadow."

"Were they around when he was here?"

She shook her head. "They weren't here when Coop came through. He left without seeing them. Said he needed to be heading south."

"You know where this uncle lives in Las Vegas?"

The girl nodded, blonde curls bouncing on her forehead. The bouncing curls gave her a girlish look. "He's got a ranch east of town. But, Marshal?"

Will had started to turn for the door, and the woman caught him by the arm. "Yes?"

"Marshal, that man loves Coop like a son. He'll fight for him, and the cowhands who work for old Mr. Cooper like him. They'll fight for him, too. If you go down there and try to take him, they'll kill you."

"Thanks," Will said, and started for the door.

She grabbed him again. When he stopped and looked around, there were tears in her eyes.

"Marshal, please don't kill him. I've known him since we were kids. His pa was really hard on him, and he got mixed up with the wrong crowd. He's not really a bad man once you get to know him."

With her face turned up to him, Will could see the sadness and concern in her blue eyes. As kindly as he could, he said, "Ma'am, he's tried to rob a bank. He's robbed a stage and killed a marshal. He's not the young fella you remember, but I'll try not to kill him. Mostly, that'll be up to him. Now, I really do need to go."

He reached down to the hand gripping his arm and gently pulled it away, leaving her staring hopelessly at him. Glad he had gotten out without any problem from the miners, he turned for the door.

"Hey, Marshal," a deep voice called.

5

W ill turned to the voice and saw nothing but a huge fist coming at him. He managed to move enough so the blow didn't land full on his left jaw. From the size of the fist, he knew a solid blow to the jaw from that club could very well break it. Still, the blow knocked him through the swinging batwing doors and into the street. He landed on his back, dust exploding around him. He could see stars shooting in front of his eyes, and his ears rang with the sound of a thousand bells. Fortunately, he remained conscious enough to see the big man stomping toward him.

Dressed in miner's garb down to the huge boots, he was covered from head to toe in coal dust. Instead of a hat, he wore a cap similar to a logger's and had it sitting to the back of his head, as if he had a minor job to do and had no fear of losing it. Will shook his head again and scrambled to his feet just as the miner arrived with an uppercut that buried deep into his belly. He felt the wind explode from his lungs. He managed to stay on his feet and erect as he stumbled backwards. Staying vertical was almost an impossible action. His body cried for him to bend over and draw air back into empty lungs, but he knew he had to stay erect so he could keep an eye on the man who was attacking him.

The miner swung a long looping left. In his confused and weakened state, he couldn't react fast enough to dodge the blow, but was at least able to move his head back. The glancing blow caught him on his right forehead, leaving a deep gash from the ring the man was wearing. The cut immediately gushed blood, as head wounds do, blinding him in his right eye.

Finally, he managed to draw a full load of air into his empty lungs. He took a quick swipe at his bloody eye, clearing it for a moment. At last he got a good look at his assailant. Behind the coal dust stood a man at least as tall as him, but who carried an additional thirty pounds. There couldn't be an ounce of fat anywhere on the man's body. He was built like a triangle, tiny feet, narrow hips and wide shoulders, with a big head sitting deep into those shoulders, almost no neck.

The miner was confident. He had sucker punched Will and landed several telling blows. Will could see the man was striding in to finish him off. Will tasted blood from the first blow, spit, and having regained his air, grinned at the approaching miner. He could only imagine how grotesque the grin must appear, with blood running down the right side of his face and blood covering his teeth and mouth. He was not at all surprised to see the miner pause in his stride toward him.

"What's the matter, fella," Will said, "am I wearing you out with my face?"

The man frowned and stepped forward. "You can be making your jokes, funny boy, but it's time I put you down for good."

For the first time, and surprising his opponent, Will stepped forward and popped the man with a straight left jab, smashing his nose. Will grinned again as the man's nose erupted in blood. The miner kicked out, striking Will in the knee. His leg collapsed, and he dropped to the ground.

When Will dropped, the miner instantly rushed him, raising

his heavy boot to drive it down onto and crush the lawman's rib cage, but Will straight off started rolling. The big man's foot missed him by inches, and then he was under the two horses tied to the saloon's hitching rail. Both horses began pulling at their reins and bucking. The miner tried to reach him, but the bucking horses kept him away. Will quickly rolled out the other side of the horses and was on his feet. His knee was sore but useable, and it was time to take care of the miner.

A large crowd had gathered, and as Will moved forward toward the boardwalk, the crowd scattered, leaving a path open between Will and the miner.

Will stepped up onto the boardwalk, and using his momentum from the step, he drove his right fist deep into the miner's belly. The big man made the mistake Will had not, and doubled over. With deliberate care, Will brought his knee up hard to meet the man's face. Bone crunched, and more blood flew from the man's face. With a loud gasp, the miner caught his wind, inhaled and straightened, but too late. Blood in his eyes, he was turning his head like an owl, trying to locate Will, when the lawman unleashed a powerful right. It struck the miner on his left temple, and his arms dropped to his sides. He stood staring at nothing and then slowly toppled over backward and lay still.

Will stood gasping for air. His head throbbed, his right hand hurt from colliding with the miner's hard head, and his body ached all over. "Get the doc," Will said, pointing at the miner.

A gruff voice from the crowd said, "I'm right here, but I don't know which one of you needs my services the worst, Marshal, you or him."

Without answering, Will turned and, through eyes partially blinded from flowing blood, carefully made his way to the horse trough in front of the livery. Once there, he thrust his head into the water, submerging it to his chin. He shook it under water, rubbed the dried blood until it dissolved, and raised his head from the water to take a breath.

He heard the same gruff voice. "Turn around so I can get a good look at you."

He turned to see a middle-aged man looking up at his face.

"I'm Marcus Fisher, town doctor." He pressed the cut's edges on Will's forehead. "That'll leave a scar." Then he bent over and felt Will's knee. "Knee'll be fine, but you need some stitches in that cut on your forehead." Feeling Will's right hand and wrist, he released it, nodded, and motioned for Will to walk with him. "Come on, I'll fix you up in my office. They've already taken O'Rourke up there. If he recovers from your last blow, he'll be a lucky man. His lesson has been a long time coming. By the way, your hand feels fine. I don't think you broke anything, though that surprises me, as hard as you hit him."

Will felt like someone had drained every ounce of energy from his body. He had been in fights before, but never had he been this tired. *Age,* he thought, *I'm getting too old to be fighting in the street. I need to leave that to the young pups.* He followed Doc Fisher up the stairs to his office and apartment. *Why is it,* he wondered, *all doctor's offices are up a long stairway? As tired as I am, I'll be lucky to make it to the top.*

Reaching the landing, he found the doctor had gone inside his office and left the door open. Will followed, closing the door behind him. Stretched out on a bed was the man who had attacked him, still out cold. The doctor was holding the man's wrist.

Moments later Doc Fisher said, "He's still alive, no thanks to you."

Will looked at the unconscious man for a few moments, then shook his head. "I don't know him. I have no idea why the fella attacked me."

"Humph," the doctor said, "I do. He doesn't like the law. His name is Bailey O'Rourke, from Ireland. The story goes, he had to leave Ireland because of the law, and he came to America through New York City and also had trouble with the law there.

He doesn't like lawmen, and when he gets a little liquor under his belt, he gets the bug to fight a lawman. You just happened to draw the lucky card today. The town marshal just knocks him over the head, takes him to jail to sleep it off, and the next morning, after fining him five dollars, turns him loose."

"Wish I'd thought of that," Will said dryly.

"You didn't have much chance. He caught you by surprise, and you had to fight him. When he gets like this, he's downright mean. Now come over here and sit down so I can sew up that cut."

As the doctor pushed the needle through the first section of skin, the office door opened, and the judge walked in.

"Well," Judge Bolton said, "you are alive. I had tremendous doubt when you came sailing out into the street."

"So did I," Will said, his voice rough.

"Yes, I can certainly imagine." The judge nodded to Doc Fisher. "Doc, is O'Rourke going to live?"

"I feel sure he will. Right now he's reaping the just rewards of his sins. He's got a pretty severe concussion from the blow to the head he received from . . . I just realized I don't know your name, Marshal."

"Will Logan."

The doctor nodded. "Are you one of those Logans who live east of the Greenhorn Mountains?"

Without nodding, Will said, "Kin."

"Makes sense. I've heard those are some tough folks."

"That they are, all born and bred in Tennessee."

The judge moved forward as Doc Fisher pulled the last stitch tight, tied the knot, and clipped the thread.

"Why, Doc," the judge said, "that's mighty pretty work."

"Thank you, Judge Bolton." To Will he said, "Let me take another look at those hands."

He took each of Will's hands in his, going over them, pushing, prodding, and feeling each digit. "There's a lot of swelling, and there'll be more. You'll need to soak them, especially the right one. I have an excellent solution that should reduce the swelling and tenderness. You can soak them here to start with, then at least twice a day for a week. By then the swelling should be down enough where you can use that." He nodded toward Will's Remington. It had stayed in the holster throughout the fight.

Will flipped the loop back over the hammer and said, "Doc, I might need to use this a lot sooner than a week."

Dr. Fisher frowned. "You shouldn't. That right hand, though not broken, is in pretty bad shape. You've some strained tendons and damaged tissue that needs to rest and heal. The swelling, even with soaking, will take at least a week to go down, and then they'll both be stiff for another week." He looked up at Will. "You know you're not as young as you used to be. You don't heal as quickly.

"Mandy," Dr. Fisher called.

A woman at least ten years younger than the doctor came into the room. "Yes, Marcus?"

He handed her a bottle he had taken from the shelf above his head. "One tablespoon to a pan of warm water. Please take Marshal Logan into the dining room and let him soak his hands for fifteen minutes."

"Yes, Marcus," she replied. "Come, Marshal, we'll take care of those hands."

"Yes, ma'am," Will said. As he was leaving the room, he heard a moan from O'Rourke.

The judge followed him into the dining room. "Will you be able to pursue Cooper?" he asked.

"I don't see how this changes anything, Judge. I'll stay on his tail. Before that O'Rourke fella tried to coldcock me, I found out he has an uncle in Las Vegas. That's where I was headed before this happened, and I see no reason to change my mind. These hands will heal with me sitting here doing nothing, or on the road searching for Cooper, makes no difference. So I reckon I'll continue after him."

The judge nodded. "What if he elects to draw on you?"

"Judge, I've got my rifle, and I'm thinking on buying me a shotgun. That might come in handy, at least until my hands heal."

"Good idea, Will. Do that, and put it on the expenses. I'll authorize it."

Fifteen minutes passed quickly. Whatever the solution was, it worked. His hands felt much looser. Mrs. Fisher handed him a towel, and he dried his hands. Passing it back to her, he said, "Thank you, ma'am. You've been most kind."

She smiled at him and said, "You are most welcome, Marshal Logan. I hope your hands do not give you any problems at all."

"I appreciate that, ma'am. I'm sure they won't. Now I'd best be going." Will stood and followed the judge back into the doctor's office.

O'Rourke was waking when Will walked back into the doctor's office. The judge looked at the man as Doc Fisher worked on him, and said to Will, "You throwing him in jail where he belongs?"

"I'm thinking about it."

The beating had partially sobered O'Rourke. "Judge Bolton, I'd take it as a real favor, for sure, were you to not put me in the jail. Me bonnie wife would not look with kindness upon me if I could not report to the mine for duty tomorrow."

The judge glowered at the still bloody man. "It is not my decision Mr. O'Rourke. If it were, I assure you, this has happened too often, and I would throw you in jail and let you sit. However, it is the decision of Marshal Logan. I believe he was the individual you sucker punched."

O'Rourke was having a difficult time breathing through his flattened nose. He turned his bloody and swollen head toward Will. His attempt at a grin through split lips was almost comical.

"Marshal, dearie, could you see it in your heart to be forgiving the likes of a poor Irishman?"

"O'Rourke, I'm half Scottish and half Irish. Don't be trying to sweet-talk me after nearly knocking my head off. I've a good mind to send you to a federal prison for assaulting a United States Marshal."

The grin vanished from O'Rourke's face, and his brow wrinkled with worry. "Marshal, I'll be asking you straight from me heart not to do that. I've got five little ones and the missus who depend on me putting beans on the table. If I go to prison, I'm not knowing what will be happening to them."

Will tried to frown, but the burning in the stitches across his forehead increased dramatically when he frowned. "You should have thought of that before you threw your punch."

"Aye, you speak the truth. Sometimes when I get too much of the whiskey, Beelzebub gets ahold of me."

"I can attest to that," Will said.

"Turn your head to face me, Mr. O'Rourke, and stop talking," the doctor said.

O'Rourke turned his head and looked at the doctor. Doc Fisher eyed the man's nose, then gently ran his index fingers along each side. O'Rourke tried to follow the fingers with his eyes as they slipped up and down his sore nose. He was about to say something when, with his right hand, the doctor suddenly grabbed the man's nose with his thumb and forefinger and squeezed while pulling. O'Rourke let out a quick yelp of pain, and just as quickly the doctor was finished.

"There," he said, "all done. It won't be the prettiest nose in the world, but you'll still be able to breathe through it."

"Doc," O'Rourke said, "that hurt worse than when the marshal hit me." He took a deep breath through his nose and gave his sideways grin. "But it seems to be working mighty well. I thank you."

Doc Fisher finished stitching the side of O'Rourke's head,

cleaned the man's face, staying well away from his nose, and said, "That's it. You're done and free to go."

The judge looked at Will. "So what do you want to do with him?"

O'Rourke's big head turned toward Will.

Will gently rubbed his knee where O'Rourke had kicked him. "Tell you what I'm going to do, O'Rourke. First, I'll not ask you to stop fighting. That, I'm afraid, is in your blood, but this I'm not asking. I'm telling. I am letting you go." At O'Rourke's brightening face, Will raised a finger. "Wait. There's more to it. If I ever hear of you attacking a lawman of any kind again, I personally will ride to Trinidad, no matter where I am or what I'm doing. I'll arrest you, take you before Judge Bolton, and have you sentenced to five years in prison for attacking a federal officer. Am I making myself clear?"

Though wincing from the pain of smiling through smashed lips, O'Rourke's worried countenance broke into a wide smile. "Aye, Marshal, you are making yourself as clear as a morning after a spring rain. It is another chance you have given Bailey O'Rourke, and I'm thanking you for it. You'll not ever again hear of me fighting a man of the law. Never."

O'Rourke stood, still a little wobbly, grinned at the judge and thrust his hand out to Will. Will looked at the big hams that had, only a short time ago, brought excruciating pain to his body.

"I'll shake your hand, O'Rourke, but if you squeeze too hard, I swear I'll still take you to jail."

The Irishman laughed as he took Will's hand gently in his. "It is a promise I make to you, Marshal. I owe you a big one. Feel free to call on me at any time day or night."

Will found it difficult to remain stern. "Just stay out of trouble."

"Why, Marshal, I'll be the angel of Trinidad, so help me." He grew serious. "Thank you, Marshal Logan."

"Get out of here, O'Rourke," the judge said. "Go home to your wife."

O'Rourke waved and walked unsteadily toward the door. He opened it, flashed a wide grin to everyone, and pulled it closed. His uneven steps could be heard as he made his way down the stairway to the street below.

6

The sun was drifting toward the west, and Will was headed south, out of town. He held the reins in his left hand. Though his left hand was swollen and sore, it was nothing like his right. Only a few hours earlier, Mrs. Fisher, the doctor's wife, had soaked them both, but now the right hand was again swollen and tight.

He tried to make a fist, but could barely flex his hand. Pain shot through the back of it and into his fingers.

Glancing up, he noticed he was passing Thatcher Brothers' Company Store. The pain in his hand reminded him of the shotgun he had mentioned to Judge Bolton. He laid the reins over and guided Buck to the hitching rail. Stepping down, he said, "I won't be long, boy. Stand easy."

Will walked to the counter and examined the rack of rifles and shotguns behind it on the rack against the wall. A man nearing thirty came from the back, stepped behind the counter, and asked, "Can I help you, Marshal?"

"Hope so. I'm looking for one of those newfangled breech-loading shotguns."

"I can certainly help you. Not only do I have the shotguns, but

I have the cartridges to fit them." While he talked, he had turned to lift a long-barreled side-by-side from the rack. "You just push this lever here on the side, and the breech opens up." He shoved the lever down, and the shotgun did exactly as he said it would, opening and allowing easy access to the breech. "Once open, you can quickly reload, and you're ready to go." He handed the shotgun across the counter to Will.

Will opened and closed it a couple of times. "Mind if I shoot it?"

"Not at all." He reached to a shelf beneath the counter and took out a handful of brass cartridges. Then he picked another shotgun from the rack. "While you're out there, you can try both. Just take the door at the end of the counter. It'll open onto the back. We have some targets for shooting back there."

Will did as directed, with the man behind him.

"Logan's the name, Will Logan."

"Marshal Logan." The man nodded. "Yes, I saw you and Bailey O'Rourke going at it. Quite a fight. I thought he had you there at first."

Will closed the door after the clerk, who had both hands full with the shotgun and shells. "I was a little concerned myself, but luck won out."

"No, sir," the clerk said, "the way he hit you by surprise? That would have finished just about any other man. That was pure grit. Bailey's had that coming for a long time. Here you go." He handed Will a couple of shells.

After dropping them into the chambers, Will picked a can about twenty yards away, threw the shotgun to his shoulder, and pulled the trigger. The blast tossed what remained of the can ten feet into the air. Waiting until it reached the top of its arc, Will let his finger drift back to the next trigger and fired again.

The first load had shredded the can, leaving only tiny threads of metal holding it together. The second load of shot tore those shreds into three separate sections, which arced higher and finally fluttered to the ground like a dying bird.

"Shoots mighty fine," Will said, examining the detailed engraving that covered the receiver. He opened the breech and pulled the two empty brass cases from the chambers.

"Try this one. You'll find the breech release inside the trigger guard."

Will first handed the empty brass to the clerk, then traded shotguns and pulled the curved latch sticking down in front of the triggers. The shotgun fell open, ready to receive the loads. The clerk handed him two more shells, which he dropped into the chambers, and he snapped the weapon closed. In one fluid movement, he shouldered the shotgun, pulled the trigger, and then pulled the other, again keeping a can airborne.

"I have some more shells if you'd like to try them out a little more."

"No. I'm satisfied, and I've got to be on my way."

Walking back inside, the clerk asked, "Did you decide which one?"

"I did. The first one is real nice and a fine shooter, but with all that fine engraving, I'd be real hesitant to do what I need to do to it."

"What do you have in mind?"

"That barrel is fine for most hunting, but the kind I'm going to be doing, I need it shorter, and it would be a sin to saw off a fine-looking shotgun such as that one."

"I understand," the clerk said, laying the engraved shotgun on the counter under the rack. He turned back to Will. "So you'll be taking this one?"

"Yep. How much do I owe you?"

"This is a fine, sturdy weapon, not as pretty as the other, which is a Clabrough, but a solid shotgun. It'll be thirty dollars, and Marshal, we have a gunsmith who works here. If you'd like for him to shorten the barrels, it won't take him long. He'll make it look like it came that way, front sight and all."

"How long, and how much?"

"Just another two dollars, and it will take him less than twenty minutes. If you need any supplies, you could pick them out, and by the time we're all settled up, it'll be ready."

"I'd like that," Will said, "but tell him to leave the front sight off. I don't want anything up there but smooth barrels, and I'll also need a scabbard for it."

The clerk took the shotgun and, turning toward another door, said, "You go ahead and look around, and I'll be back shortly."

BUCK TURNED his head and looked at Will as the big man slid the new scabbard next to the rifle scabbard. "It's alright, boy. I'll fix this so's you won't even know it's there." He untied the reins, moved to the other side, and swung into the saddle. Then he tried the feel of the new bulge and practiced drawing the double from the scabbard. "Easy as pie, Buck." He slid the shotgun back into the scabbard, turned Buck, and headed toward the pass.

Once out of town, he rubbed his right hand with his left. Gripping the forearms of the shotguns, the recoil of the four shots had been more punishment than his right hand deserved. And he was paying for it now. The hand throbbed as he rode, but gradually, as Buck began slowly working up the trail, the ache subsided. It got to a point where he started exercising the fingers, but soon stopped. *Maybe later,* he thought.

Deborah came to mind as he rode along the trail. The last time he had left her for any appreciable length of time was his trip to the Double R in South Texas, near Dog Town. He had vowed he would never leave her again, and here he was, not only riding farther away from her, but wearing a badge that would guarantee this would happen as long as he wore it. "I sure miss her," he said to Buck. The horse's ears pricked, as if he was listening closely to what Will was saying. "You know, boy, I was really lucky to find her after all those years. It just don't make sense to take a job that makes me ride away from her."

Will rocked in the saddle as Buck slowly made his way up the slopes of the Sangre de Cristos. Though the day was coming to a close, there was still enough daylight for him to make out the dark green of the tall pines in the distance, interspersed with patches of the light green aspens. Come fall, the aspen leaves would turn golden, making the hillsides, from a distance, appear to be painted with gold.

They came to a small stream making its way down the mountainside. From the road, Will could see the stream turn and disappear into the piñon and cedar trees. He turned Buck and followed the stream. They could probably make Uncle Dick Wooton's place before dark, but rather than answer questions about his head and hands, he decided to stay on the hillside. "It's not like we haven't slept under the stars before, is it, boy?" At his voice, Buck picked up his pace, moving quickly over the broken, rocky ground.

Following the bend of the stream, they came upon a small grass-covered meadow. It was hidden from the well-traveled road. "Looks like we've found a place for the night, Buck." Will dismounted, slipped his rope over Buck's head, and stripped the tack from the animal. He pulled some grass and dried the sweat from the horse's back, led him to a likely area where he would be in the grass, close enough to the stream to drink from it, and near the camp and fire. He drove in the stake, patted the horse, and moved to his camp.

He worked quickly, for daylight was rapidly disappearing. With the fire going, he pulled a log near, so he would have a place to sit, and spread his bedroll. At the store in Trinidad, while waiting for the shotgun, which for good measure, he had laid near him, he had purchased several cans of beans and peaches.

From his bag, he retrieved one of each and a couple of hard biscuits. He opened both cans with his knife and poured the can of beans into his skillet, setting it close to the fire to warm.

Once the beans were heating, he picked up the can of peaches and took a small sip. He loved peaches. His mind drifted back to his ma and the houseful of aunts peeling and cutting bushels of peaches to dry and can. The smell of those peaches cooking outside in the big iron pot filled his mind. He had another sip. Using his knife, he lifted a half section from the can and let it slide into his mouth. He smiled with the taste, shook his head in determination to save the peaches until after the beans and bread, set the can down, and glanced over at Buck.

The horse wasn't alone. Sitting next to it was a huge wolf. The animal's eyes were glowing green from the firelight. What shocked Will more than the wolf being there was that Buck wasn't kicking up a ruckus to get away, kick, or attack. The horse just stood there eating. Will could see the wolf's eyes watching him as he slowly eased his hand toward the shotgun. When he picked it up, the wolf whirled and was gone.

Will sat staring into the darkness. He had made a cardinal error. He had relaxed and had been staring into the fire while he dreamed of the past. That was one of the first things Pa had drilled into his boys. He could hear him now, "Never stare into the fire. It ruins your night sight and can get you killed." He had gone over it time after time. Keeping his eyes diverted from the fire, he carefully picked up the steaming beans and moved them farther from the fire. He continued to check the perimeter of the camp. Buck, relaxed and unconcerned, chewed contentedly on the grass.

He laid the shotgun against his saddle, within easy reach, and picked up the skillet. *What was I thinking,* he thought, *picking up that shotgun. I had no reason to shoot the wolf unless it was rabid, and it certainly didn't show any signs of having rabies. Anyway, even if it did, I couldn't have shot him with the scattergun. I would've hit Buck with some of the shot.* He shook his head and looked at his horse. There was the wolf again, sitting right next to Buck.

Surprise gone, this time he examined the animal as closely as he could. The light from the fire reached Buck and the wolf, but only faintly. The wolf's glowing eyes had a tinge of green. The animal just sat watching him, his tongue lolling out to one side. It was a big wolf, really big. *I don't think I've ever seen one that big. Why is it so relaxed?* Then the thought hit him. *Could it be a dog?*

At the thought, Will broke a biscuit in half and tossed it about halfway between him and the animal and waited. Moments passed. The wolf, or dog, eyed the biscuit, sniffed, moved closer, smelled it again, and gulped it down in one gulp, then sat watching Will, as if asking for more.

How about that, Will thought. He tossed the other half to the animal, again about halfway between them. The animal sat looking at it, turning its head first to one side and then the other. Then, making up its mind, it stood and walked to the biscuit, smelled it, and made it disappear.

With the second toss, the animal moved close enough for Will to clearly identify what he was. "You're a dog, aren't you, boy?"

The dog's tail started wagging against the ground slowly. First to the left, then right, only a couple of times. "What's your name?" Will reached into his bag and pulled out some jerky. He tore a strip in half and tossed it to the dog. Without any hesitation, the dog reached down and grasped it in what Will could see were strong white teeth. He started chewing. After about three chews, he swallowed the jerky and sat down, closer.

Buck had been watching the dramatic events, but as if it was of no importance, he reached down for another mouthful of grass and began chewing again.

Beneath the dog's long white hair, Will could see it was lean, almost skinny. There was no telling how long he'd been lost in these mountains, but it hadn't been so long that he'd forgotten his closeness with man. Will tossed the other half of the stick of jerky, and the dog snatched it out of the air, chewed a couple of times, and swallowed.

"How long have you been out here, boy?" The dog watched him. Will made a sucking sound with his mouth. Back home, when he was a boy, he had used that sound to call the dogs close.

At the sound, the dog's ears perked up, and he turned his head slightly to look at Will. Trying it again, he watched the dog's tail start wagging again. "Come on, boy. You can do it." Will took another piece of jerky from his bag. This time he didn't throw it, but held it out to the dog. "Come on, fella. I know you're hungry. You can trust me." He made the sucking sound with his mouth, and the dog lay on the ground, looking first at the jerky and then at him. Slowly, it crawled on its belly, closer, paused, and closer. Will could see the saliva dripping from the dog's tongue.

"Come on, boy. No one's going to hurt you. You can have this and more. All you have to do is get up the nerve to take it." Slowly, one leg forward and then the next, the dog crawled closer. Finally, he stretched his neck and gently took the piece of jerky from Will's fingers.

Before the dog had swallowed it, Will pulled another piece from the bag and held it out. The dog edged closer. This time close enough for Will to scratch the animal behind the ears if he took the jerky. Almost without hesitation, the dog stood, walked forward, and took the jerky. He didn't try to retreat when Will put his hand on his head, but stood there, looking at Will, chewing. Will rubbed the big head for a minute, then slipped his fingers behind the dog's ear and started scratching. That did it.

The dog moved up next to him and sat staring into his face, while Will, using both hands, worked on the ears, then moved his hands down the dog's sides.

"Been a while since you've had a decent meal, hasn't it, boy." He could feel the ribs standing out on the sides. "But you've been staying alive." He picked up a foot and looked at it. There were healed cuts and scratches, and the pads felt thick. Will had eaten a fair portion of the beans. They had been sitting well away from the fire and had cooled down. He leaned over, picked up the skillet, and set it in front of the dog.

The animal looked at the skillet and then at Will. After a few moments, Will considered the dog might be waiting for permission. Will said, "Alright." The dog's head shot down to the skillet, and in no time it was cleaned of every little speck of bean or juice. Will scratched the dog behind its ear one last time and said, "I think that'll do it for tonight. You're welcome to stay with us if you like."

It was getting chilly in the mountains. He made sure the fire was well banked, slid down into his bedroll, and leaned back against his saddle. It had been a long and eventful day. He'd received information on where Ambrose Cooper might be heading, darned near gotten whipped, and found a dog. He hadn't owned a dog since he was a boy. Pa had always said you never own a dog, the dog owns you. "Well, mutt, I guess we'll just have to wait and see if you like it here."

He thought about Deborah. How did she feel about dogs? He had no idea. Will slid farther into his bedroll, glanced one last time at Buck, who had walked to the stream and was drinking. He pulled the blanket up around his chin and thought, *When the fire goes out, it's going to get mighty cool tonight.* As if in answer, he felt the dog make a couple of circles near his back and drop to the ground against him. The warmth was welcome, and it was comforting knowing he had both Buck and the dog guarding camp. He closed his eyes, and his last thoughts were of his wife back in Pueblo. He hoped she liked dogs.

7

The morning cold pulled Will from a deep sleep. The first thing he noticed was his missing back warmer. *Oh well,* he thought, *I guess he likes going his own way.*

He eyed the cold remains of the fire, decided it wasn't going to get any warmer with him lying there, and threw back the blanket. He turned his boots upside down and beat them together. An angry scorpion dropped to the ground and dashed for cover. "Did you see that scorpion, Buck? He would've surely livened up my day had I slid that boot on." Buck, one ear turned toward him, ripped up a mouthful of grass and continued chewing.

Will pulled his boots on and stood, picking up his gun belt in the process and swinging it around his waist. He flipped the loop from over the hammer and checked the loads. The five chambers looked dry and ready. Dropping the Remington back into its holster, he picked up a stick and dug through the fire. Finding a few live coals, he raked them together, picked up kindling he'd gathered the night before, and laid it across the coals. The warmth from the coals felt good to his aching hands. In moments the kindling was aflame. Adding a few larger limbs, he left the fire, moved to the stream, and kneeled on one knee at the water's edge.

Using his left hand, he quickly washed his face. His right already ached from the cold. The last thing he wanted was to shove it into the near freezing water of the mountain stream. He dipped another handful of water and rubbed it through his hair. The cold sent shivers down his back. Finished, he slapped his hat back on his head, feeling the warmth from the felt, stood, and flexed his injured knee—pretty good. He was surprised it was working so well, and with minimal pain.

Daylight was coming quickly, as it did in the mountains. Will looked around, thinking, *It seems like it takes daylight forever to arrive, and then, boom, it's here.* As he turned back to the fire, his evening companion was sitting there, a rabbit dangling from his mouth.

"Well, I'll be," Will said. "I didn't dream you up, huh, fella? You're for real, and you've brought breakfast. I'll cook some bacon, and we'll fry that rascal in bacon grease. I bet that'll be the best rabbit you've eaten in a while."

He walked over to the dog, wondering how the animal would react when he took the rabbit. The dog did nothing, only opened his mouth and let it fall into Will's hand. "What am I going to call you, boy?"

Will took the rabbit to the side of the camp and quickly dressed it. After rinsing it in the stream, he shook off the excess water and laid it across the log next to the fire. The dog sat watching. "You hungry, boy?" Will walked to the stream again, leaving the rabbit on the log, and washed out the skillet. The dog never made a move toward the rabbit. Once back, he sliced off several thick slices of bacon and dropped them into the skillet now sitting on coals he had raked to the side of the fire. In no time the bacon was sizzling.

While the bacon cooked, he cut up the rabbit and dug out four more biscuits. Once the bacon cooked, he laid it out on the log and dropped in the rabbit. Bacon grease popped and sizzled as the wet meat of the rabbit hit the greasy hot skillet. Will leaned away from the splattering grease and glanced at the dog. The animal's tongue was dripping with drool, but he didn't move toward the bacon. Will laid two strips of bacon near the dog and said, "Alright."

Instantly, the big jaws opened and snapped tight around first one and then the other of the two pieces. Will scratched the dog behind an ear. "Was that good, boy? Well, you just wait a minute. I think you'll like this rabbit."

Will made sure the rabbit was seared on all sides and then forked half of it onto the log. "Alright, boy, have at it." The heavy jaws clamped down on the rabbit, and bones crunched. Before Will's rabbit had finished cooking, the dog had devoured his portion. "Just wait, boy, there's more coming."

Will forked out the rabbit onto his plate alongside the bacon, broke the four hard biscuits open and dropped them into the remaining grease in the skillet. Using his fork, he pressed the biscuits firmly into the skillet, browning them and forcing the hot grease into the bread, turned them over, and did the same to the other side. When all of the grease was gone, he slipped on a glove and forked four halves on the log. The dog watched him, waiting. This time he just nodded to the animal, and before he could take his first bite, the dog had devoured all four halves of the steaming biscuits and was looking at him.

Will laughed. "That won't work with me, boy. You had your share. Now I get mine," and he started eating.

As if he understood, the dog stood, walked to the stream, and drank for a long time.

"Yep, that bacon grease and those dry biscuits'll make you thirsty every time. Reckon I'll be doing the same here shortly."

Will finished eating, cleaned the utensils and the camp, and packed up. All the while, the dog sat watching. While Will saddled and loaded Buck, the dog hadn't moved. His head followed Will's every move.

Will ensured the fire was completely out, filled his canteen, and mounted Buck. The dog still sat watching. "You want to go with us, boy?"

The dog turned his head and gazed at Will.

"Well, come on. Let's go."

The dog stood, and as Will clucked at Buck, the three of them followed the thicket out to the road and headed for Las Vegas.

The sun was well up when they came to the old mountain man Uncle Dick Wooton's house and his toll road. Will pulled up Buck and stepped down from the saddle. The front door opened, and a fine figure of a man stepped onto the porch.

"Get down and sit a spell," Uncle Dick called.

"Morning, can't stay long," Will said as he stepped up onto the porch. From his vest, he had taken two bits, and he held it out for the mountain man.

Uncle Dick took the twenty-five cents, and a long look at Will. "I swear, if you ain't a Logan, I'll eat my hat. Why, you look so much like Floyd Logan it's scary."

Will grinned at the older man. "Will Logan, Mr. Wooton, it's a pleasure to meet you. Floyd's my uncle. He's spoken of you many times."

"Come on in, boy. I can tell you some tales about that uncle of yours."

"I imagine, he's told some pretty good ones about you."

Uncle Dick chuckled. "I just bet he has."

"I'd love to sit a spell, but I'm on business—"

"I figured as much." There were several chairs sitting outside. "Pull up a chair and take a load off. Maybe I can help you. I see most everyone who passes by. You thirsty? Can I offer you a cup of coffee, water, buttermilk?"

At the mention of buttermilk, Will nodded. "I never turn

down a good glass of buttermilk. I could also use some information," Will said, taking a chair.

Uncle Dick called into the house for coffee and a glass of buttermilk. In no time, a handsome young girl came out with the drinks.

Will, taking the buttermilk, smiled at her and said, "Thank you, Miss."

She returned the smile, gave Uncle Dick the cup, and scurried back into the house.

Will took a long pull on the buttermilk. "Mmm, that's mighty fine."

"From our own cows. Now what can I do for you?"

Will pulled the circular from his inside vest pocket, opened it, and gave it to Uncle Dick. "Have you seen him?"

"Ambrose Cooper. He was by here two days ago, heading for Las Vegas. He has an uncle there by the name of Mott Cooper. You after the boy for the stage holdup and killing of that U.S. Marshal?"

The man's response surprised Will. "How did you know about the stage robbery?"

"Son, the Barlow and Sanderson stage comes through here all the time. They keep me pretty well up to date on what's happening, plus they bring me newspapers."

Will nodded. "It was Farley Osborne. I didn't know him, but understand he was a fine fella."

Uncle Dick shook his head. "I knew him. He'd been by here several times. From what I saw of him, you're right." He paused, staring out across the high mountains. "Ambrose Cooper never had a chance. That boy was destined to be a killer. His pa is no good and treated that boy like a slave, beat him unmercifully. It's a wonder Ambrose didn't start his killing on him, but he didn't." Uncle Dick looked over at Will. "You should hear that boy sing. Has a voice like an angel and a heart as cold as ice. His uncle tried to help him, but by the time he got him away from his pa, it was too late. The boy was already set in his ways."

Will finished his buttermilk, set the glass down by the chair, and stood. "I thank you for the information, Mr. Wooton. I'll be seeing you on the way back."

Uncle Dick stood. "Make sure there is a way back, boy. Mott Cooper's a hard man, and he loves that young feller. He'll fight you tooth and nail. He'll not let that boy be taken, not to prison, and especially not to a hangman's noose."

Will shook the mountain man's hand and said, "I'll be careful, and thanks for the buttermilk."

Will turned and headed for Buck. The big white dog was lying next to the horse, watching his approach.

From the house, Uncle Dick called, "So the shadow has latched on to *you*. I'm glad he's found someone. Come winter, the wolves would've killed him."

Will turned and said, "The what?"

"The shadow. That's what I've taken to calling him. He shows up, and then he's gone. He was a cattle dog for a while. Heard he was a good one, but the folks who owned him had to go back east, and for some reason they didn't take him."

Will shook his head. "I can't imagine that. He seems like a real fine dog."

"Does to me too, what little I've seen of him. Those folks left him, and their neighbor, Ned Fairburn, everybody calls him Nasty Ned, 'cause I swear he's never touched a bar of soap, took him. He beat the poor animal until the dog finally got fed up and turned on him. If Nasty Ned hadn't made it into his house, I reckon that dog might have killed him."

Both Will and Uncle Dick looked up the road at the sound of horses, leather creaking, and coach rattling.

Uncle Dick went on as Will swung up into the saddle. "Anyway, he come out with a shotgun, but the dog was too far and only got burnt a little by the birdshot. I guess that's when he took to the trail."

The stagecoach loomed over the rise, slowing as the driver pulled the panting horses to a trot.

"Been nice talking to you. I've got to be feeding those folks on the stage." Uncle Dick waved and said, "Good luck."

Will waved back and held Buck to the side of the road. The coach pulled up next to him. The driver leaned past the shotgun and said, "Howdy, Marshal. You heading to Vegas?"

"I am."

"Road's clear. Had no problem coming through. You after the Cooper boy?"

I guess everybody knows, Will thought. "Yep. Have you seen him?"

The shotgun rider spoke up. "Sure did, Marshal. He's in town spoutin' off as to how he killed one marshal, and he can surely kill another one."

Will smiled. "I guess this is still a free country. A man can say what he feels like, as long as he can back it up."

"Reckon," the shotgun said.

"Looks like you picked up the shadow," said the driver.

"I think he picked me up," Will replied.

The driver nodded and popped his whip over the horses, moving them forward.

Will bumped Buck, and the man, horse, and dog headed for Las Vegas. Will looked down at the dog trotting alongside Buck. "Fella, I think we have your name. Since it seems like everyone's calling you the shadow, how would you like Shadow for a name?" The big white dog looked at Will and back down the road. Will gave a firm nod of his head. "Yep, I think you like it. Shadow it is."

LATE AFTERNOON of the third day, Will stopped Buck on a rise overlooking Las Vegas. As soon as the horse stopped, Shadow, trotting alongside, sat and looked east toward the ranching country. Will could see open land dotted with cattle, some grazing not far from the outskirts of the town. *Is that Mott Cooper's land?* he thought. He turned his attention to the town. *Seems most build up near rivers,* he thought. *Pueblo has the Arkansas, Trinidad the Purgatory, and now Las Vegas is right on the Gallinas River. It's a wonder they don't wash away with the spring snowmelt.*

While examining the town, he removed his badge and slipped it into his vest pocket. "I think it's time we travel incognito. They'll be looking for a marshal. Maybe we can fool 'em for a while."

Buck was ready for a barn with grain and water. It had been a long three days. They'd traveled a lot of up-and-down country, and they were all a little worn. Will patted Buck on the neck. "I figure you're looking forward to a good rubdown and a bit of corn. I can tell you, you've earned it. We've been pushing hard, and I know you must be plain tuckered out."

He looked down at the big white dog. "Shadow, you've hung in there pretty well. How are you doing, boy?" Leaning from the saddle, Will patted the big dog's head. "We'll all get some rest in just a bit." He flipped the leather loop from over the hammer of the Remington, moved the weapon up and down in the holster, and clucked the buckskin forward.

Like many western towns, saloons were the gathering places of men. If you wanted to find something out, you could read a newspaper if the town had one, or you could head for a saloon. Will headed for the closest one. Pulling Buck up at the hitching rail, he swung down, tossed the reins around the hitching post, and watched Shadow lie down alongside Buck. Satisfied they were safe, he turned and headed into the saloon. Stepping inside, he looked around the busy establishment, hoping he might be lucky enough to find Cooper here and save some time. No such luck.

Behind the bar, a mirror traveled the bar's length. *That cost a pretty penny,* Will thought.

The bartender caught him staring at the mirror. Typically dressed in a dingy apron, he strolled up and said, "Nice, ain't it. Hauled it up here myself, all the way from Albuquerque. That's the longest mirror in this here country."

Will nodded. "Pretty thing. Bet it was tough getting it here over those mountains."

The bartender snorted. "Mister, you don't know the half of it. Why, that there mirror came all the way from San Francisco. That's the third one I've ordered. I tried one from St. Louis and one from Denver City. When both of those were broken in the shipping, I gave San Francisco a shot. They said they'd send it to Albuquerque, but I had to get it here. They did, and I did." He turned and cast an admiring look at his mirror. "Ain't she a peach."

"How long have you had it?"

"Two weeks. It's nice and solid up there. The carpenter who installed it said it would never break."

Will tossed the man a skeptical look. "That seems like a mighty chancy thing to say." He looked around, then back to the mirror. "Especially in an establishment such as this."

The bartender nodded, then reached beneath the bar and pulled out a sawed-off shotgun similar to Will's. "See this? I picked it up in Albuquerque when I got the mirror. Used to have an old single-barrel muzzle loader, but this breech loader is mighty nice, isn't it?"

Will looked it over. "It sure is. Looks like it should get the job done."

"Yep," the bartender said, examining his scattergun. "It does, doesn't it." Then he looked up at Will. "I've let every one of these rowdy cowhands know that whoever breaks that mirror gets a load of buckshot, no discussion."

Will nodded. "I can see where that might lower the chances of your fine mirror getting broken, but what about strangers riding in?"

The bartender smiled. "I explain to everyone who comes through those swinging doors what will happen should they break my mirror. It seems to work pretty well." He gave Will a meaningful look. "Understand?"

"I sure do," Will replied. "Clear as a church bell."

"Good, I'm glad we understand each other. Now what would you like to drink?"

"I could go for a buttermilk if you've got one handy."

The bartender nodded. "One buttermilk coming right up."

Using the bartender's mirror, Will gazed around the room. He felt sure, from the wanted circular, he would be able to recognize Cooper if he saw him. The boy was not in this saloon. *I like buttermilk,* he thought, *but if I have to go to every saloon in town today, I'm going to be drowning in it before the evening's over.*

The bartender returned with his glass. "That'll be a nickel."

Will tossed a quarter on the bar. "Nickel for the buttermilk, twenty cents for some information."

The bartender looked him over. "Mister, the information you want must not be very important."

"It's important. I'm just broke."

"So what do you want to know?"

"Any ranches around here that might be hiring?"

The bartender took the quarter and dropped twenty cents back on the bar. "For that kinda question, I'm not gonna take a down-and-out cowhand's money. There's the Lazy Y, the C Bar, and the Bar 3."

"Much obliged. Who owns them?"

"The Lazy Y is owned by Fran Young, the C Bar by Mott Cooper, and the Bar 3 by Trace Tanner."

"I take it Fran Young is a woman?"

"She is that, and a mighty pretty one at that, but don't think because she's a woman, she can't run that ranch. She's doing a bang-up job so far. Her husband was shot by some no-account yellow-belly. Shot him in the back and then in the head. Fran's a brave woman. She stepped in, took over the ranch and its running, and her hands respect her. Can't ask for much more than that."

"Nope, you can't," Will said. "What about the other two?"

The bartender was about to answer when a ruckus of yelling, growling, and stomping took place just outside the swinging doors.

8

W ill ran to the saloon door to see what was going on. Two men, one average sized and the other about six feet, were trying to corner Shadow.

The average-sized man looked as if he had never had a bath. The six-footer was dirty, but nothing like his partner. The smaller man had a club in his hand and was trying to move into position where he could smash Shadow in the head, but the dog was having none of it. He had backed up to where he was almost directly under Buck's belly, and was displaying a fine set of teeth.

Will came out just in time to hear the smaller man, whom he figured was Ned Fairburn, the same man who had attempted to shoot Shadow, say to his partner, "Git around on t'other side of that buckskin. That'll drive my dog over to this side, and I'll take care of him."

The bigger man never made it to the other side of Buck, for when he ran behind the big horse, Buck kicked with both hind legs, sending the man airborne. He screamed and hit hard in the middle of the busy street. A wagon had to swerve hard to keep from running over the moaning man, and its rear wheels slipped inside the front wheel of a parked feed wagon. The first wagon jerked to a halt, and the horses were yanked around and up on the boardwalk, where they began to kick at their harness.

While the excitement in the street was happening, Fairburn raised his club to smash Buck. Will drew the .44 and, to be heard above all the commotion, yelled, "Drop the club, mister!"

The club froze in midair, and the man turned a dirty, anger-twisted face toward Will. The din of the collision quickly subsided as men regained control of their horses.

Since the man was still holding the club, Will said, in a lower tone, "I said drop the club."

The man, seeing the big .44 Remington, dropped the club like it was the wrong end of a branding iron, but he was still angry. He pointed at Shadow. "That there is my dog. You can't tell me what to do with my dog."

Will dropped the big Remington back into its holster. "You must be Ned Fairburn."

"That's right," he said, his head bobbing up and down, "and everybody knows that's my dog, and I aim to take him."

"You'd best aim in another direction. You tried to kill that dog, so whatever claim you might have had is gone. For good. Now step away from the dog, and be on your way."

Fairburn aimed a long dirty finger at Will. "Mister, I ain't knowin' who you might be, but that's my dog, and I aim to take him."

Will looked at Fairburn, then at Shadow, estimating the weight. Fairburn couldn't have more than ten pounds on Shadow if that much. "Alright, Mr. Fairburn, you go ahead and take him. If you can take him, he's yours. Otherwise, he's mine. Does that sound fair?"

The man looked at Will skeptically, trying to see the catch in the deal. Finally, he turned to his friend, who had limped up to his side. He said, "Go around t'other side, like I said. Only was I you, I'd give the back end of that buckskin a wide swing."

The man started to turn, and Will said, "No, sir. I didn't say anything about you and your gimp friend getting the dog, I said you. You get him, he's yours. Go ahead, just walk up and grab him. If he's yours, I'm sure he'll go peaceably with you."

"Mister," Fairburn said, breaking out in a sweat, "that there is a dangerous dog. I might need some help."

"No help."

Fairburn looked at Shadow. The big white dog sat watching him, his mouth open and his tongue hanging out, as if nothing had happened. Then he bent to pick up the club.

"No club," Will said.

Fairburn turned to Will, his face drawn up in exasperation. "Mister, I told you he's a dangerous dog. How about if I rope him? I can rope him, right?"

"Wrong. No rope."

The man's hands went to his hips as he faced Will. Then his look of exasperation turned back to anger, and he pointed the dirty finger at Will again. "You don't want me to take him. You want him for yourself. I've already told you, that there is my dog."

Will shook his head. "Fairburn, we had a deal. Looks like you can't live up to it, so get away from the dog."

Will glanced at Shadow. The dog was sitting calmly watching Will. "Come on, boy," Will said.

Shadow leaped out from under Buck, under the hitching rail, and onto the boardwalk next to Will, and sat gazing up at him. Will placed his hand on the dog's head and rubbed behind his ears. "I think the dog has made a decision. He can go where he wants and do what he wants, and obviously he doesn't want to have anything to do with you."

Fairburn's red face looked as if it would explode. He started to raise the finger at Will again, and Will said, "Mister, don't point that filthy thing at me again. I might take offense, and I sure wouldn't want to do that."

It looked as if Fairburn was seeing the man standing in front of him for the first time. Will, like most of the Logans, was an imposing figure. Standing in his boots, he was nearing six feet and four inches, with shoulders and hands to match. Fairburn stared at Will for the longest time, then said, "This ain't over, big man." He turned to his friend, who had been keeping one eye on him and the other on Buck, and said, "Come on. You ain't been no help." The two walked down the middle of the street, Fairburn angrily waving at the irate mule skinners who had to turn their wagons to keep from running over them.

The saloon had emptied to watch the show, and the bartender stood next to Will. Once the onlookers saw the entertainment was over, they headed back into the saloon or continued along the boardwalk.

The bartender turned to Shadow and said, "Thanks for the show, Toby." At the sound of his name, the dog started wagging his tail. The bartender stepped over and patted Toby on his head. "Come on back in," he said to Will, "and I'll tell you about your dog, and bring Toby. Shoot, he'll class up the place."

Will followed the bartender, who was laughing at his own joke. Toby stayed at Will's side. When he reached the bar, a woman who had been working in back brought a plate loaded with stew out from the kitchen and set it on the floor next to the dog. He looked up at Will, who said, "Alright," and Toby grabbed a mouthful.

"That's a good dog," the bartender said, placing another glass of buttermilk in front of Will. "The owner, when he came to town, used to stop by for a drink and would bring him in."

"So you knew the owner?" Will said.

"I did. A man by the name of Latham Henderson. Wife's name was Alveda. They had a small cattle ranch east of here. They were actually doing pretty well. The problem was she never liked it out here. He did, and his son, Eli, really took to it, boy of about fourteen. Toby followed the boy everywhere he went. They brought him out from back east, the dog that is."

The bartender stretched to look over the bar at Toby, who had finished eating and was lying quietly on the floor. "The woman named him. Some Roman name, I think, Tab . . . Tib . . . Tiberius. That's it. Tiberius. Henderson said he let her name the dog, hoping she would take to it. She never did. Of course, everybody shortened it to Toby."

At the mention of his name, Toby looked up expectantly. Will reached down and scratched his head for a moment while the bartender continued the story.

"So Toby here is a fine cattle dog. I've seen him work those ornery critters. He's mighty good, and he's big enough to make any wolf think twice before tackling him. I think Henderson called him a Great Pyrenees. Never heard of the breed myself, but he's always been a good dog." The bartender wiped a spot where a beer mug had been sitting, moved down the bar and served a cowhand, then came back to Will.

"It was a mighty sad thing. Henderson's wife hounded him all the time to go back east. Finally the man just gave up. Sold his ranch to Mott Cooper, loaded everything, and headed back east." The bartender shook his head. "It about broke their son Eli's heart. He loved it out here, and when Henderson's wife made him leave the dog, I thought the boy was going to stay. Many a lad younger than him has left home, but his ma controlled that family. The dog got left, and the boy headed east."

Will finished his buttermilk, set the glass back on the bar, and said, "Much obliged. Too bad the boy didn't stay. Now I know the dog's name. That'll help. One other thing you can do for me is direct me toward the headquarters for those ranches you mentioned."

"Sure will. Take the road east, along the Gallinas. The first branch to the right will take you to the C Bar, the second the Lazy Y, and if you stay on the main road, it'll take you to the Bar 3. Ask for any of those folks I mentioned. Don't know if any are hiring, but it don't hurt asking."

Will saluted the man with a finger to the brim of his Stetson and headed for the door, Toby right behind.

He stepped outside and looked around. All quiet, and still no Ambrose Cooper in sight. His mind on the job at hand, he untied Buck and turned him toward the end of town. Nearing the livery, Buck pulled toward it. Will let him go. He could see the horse was headed for the watering trough. He swung down, and as Buck drank, Toby eased up beside him and started drinking.

Will patted the horse on the neck. "Sorry, Buck. I should've brought you here so you could rest up. In fact, I think I'll do just that."

He waited until the buckskin finished drinking, and led him through the wide door into the barn. Seeing no one around, he led the horse into a stall, forked some hay into the feed trough, and began removing the tack. Once the gear was removed, he set it across a rail along the opposite wall and started looking at the horses.

"Howdy, stranger," a voice called from a door in the office at the back of the barn. A young fella of no more than sixteen walked toward Will, carrying a broom. "Just doing a little swamping. What can I do for you?"

"I'd like to leave my horse with you for a couple of days. I'll be needin' to rent one of yours."

"Sure," the young man said, "Pa has some fine riding stock in the corral out back. Take a look, and make your pick."

Will walked to the back, the boy beside him. "I don't think I've seen you before, mister. You're not from around here."

Will shook his head. "Nope."

"How long you expectin' to need the horse?"

"Two maybe three days. Mine's just tired. He's done a lot of traveling over the past few days."

They started for the corral, and Will turned to Toby, who had stood to follow him, and said, "Stay." The dog looked at him, then circled a couple of times in the hay and dropped next to Buck.

Will nodded, turned and joined the kid. Reaching the corral, he leaned on the top rail and looked over his choices.

Most of the horses were smaller, probably mustangs origi-nally, or bred from mustangs. It could be a real toss-up as to whether they were good or bad. Another thing he had to think about was their ability to carry his weight and gear. He was much bigger than most of the cowhands, plus with his gear, he was looking at close to two hundred and thirty pounds, a lot of weight for most of those small horses.

He spotted a bay, in the back of the bunch, that stood much higher than most of the horses. The horse acted a little edgy, but it could be that he wasn't good around strangers. "How about the big bay?"

The kid hesitated, then said, "Well, sir, he's a mighty fine horse, and he can carry a load, but he's a little fidgety. He's been known to throw a rider or two, with no warning."

"I'll take a look at him."

"You want I should rope him?"

"No, I'll just walk out there and see how he does. If need be, I'll drop a loop over him."

Will returned to his saddle, untied his rope, and without shaking out a loop, returned to the corral, crawled over a low rail, and entered. The horses milled a little, not familiar with him, but for the most part calm. He even had to push a couple of them out of the way. Nearing the bay, he started talking to him. The bay's ears turned forward, and Will knew the horse was watching and listening. He stepped closer, reached out, and at his hand move-ment the horse jerked his neck up, but didn't run. Will kept talking in the same soft tone. He took several more steps, which brought him close enough to touch the horse.

Again he reached his hand toward the animal, and the horse held its position. He rubbed the horse's neck and spoke softly, noting the clear eyes, strong neck, and thick chest. He rubbed his hand along the front shoulder and down the leg, finally lifting the hoof. The horse was shod, and there was no dirt packed in the shoe, possibly covering a stone wedged between the shoe and the hoof. The shoe was in good shape. He moved around the horse, checking the other hooves, all the same. During his brief inspection, he kept talking to the bay. When he got back to its head, Will laid the end of the rope across the bay's neck. He reached under the horse's neck, grasped that end, and pulled it around and beneath the thick neck, making a loop without having to move anything past the animal's eyes. It wouldn't hold an agitated animal, but a calm one would easily follow him. He then led the bay slowly around the corral, watching him walk. Will nodded to the boy. "I'll take him. How much?"

"Three dollars a day."

Will had never rented a horse for more than two dollars a day and was surprised at the price. "Young fella, I just want to rent him, not buy him."

"Sorry, mister. Pa sets the price. I just do what he tells me."

"Understand. How about opening the gate, and I'll bring him through." The boy swung the gate open and stood watching as Will and the bay walked into the barn. He led the horse to his tack and slipped the bridle over its head. After fastening the bridle, he threw the saddle blanket over the horse's back, smoothed it out, settled the saddle on the blanket, and adjusted the cinch.

He dug nine dollars from his vest and extended it to the boy. "How about a rental agreement so nobody hangs me for horse stealing."

"Yes, sir," the boy said, and dashed to the office.

Will heard hay crunch behind him, followed by, "What's your business in my town, stranger?"

He turned slowly to see the man behind him wearing a town marshal's badge. His mind churned. *Do I tell him, or keep it a secret? If I were him, I'd want to know, but what if he's friends with the*

Coopers? He could tell them, and Ambrose Cooper could take off for El Paso or even Mexico.

"Reaching into my pocket, Marshal," Will said. He pulled out his badge and held it low in his hand.

The marshal wasn't slow. "You're after Ambrose Cooper."

"I am," Will said, returning the badge to his pocket, "but I need to grab him before his uncle's aware I'm in town. I don't want any innocent men killed."

The man nodded. "I understand, but they're my friends. Mott's taken care of that boy since he was barely eight. It'll kill him to see the lad go to prison or even worse."

Footsteps came running up behind them. "Hi, Marshal Snead."

"Bert."

"I'm renting this gentleman a horse, but I ain't got his name."

"Name's Will Logan, boy."

Bert printed out Will's name on the rental agreement, signed it, and handed it to Will.

Will looked it over and saw the value of the horse had been written in as one hundred and seventy-five dollars. He turned to the boy. "Three dollars a day, and one hundred and seventy-five dollars? Boy, this looks a lot like highway robbery."

Bert stared back at Will. "Mister, I told you, Pa sets the prices. If it's too high, go to another stable. See what their prices are like."

"All the same," Snead said. "They got together and set their prices. You'll find you can't rent a horse for less than three dollars a day. If he runs off, breaks a leg, or dies, you'll have to pay one hundred and seventy-five dollars."

Will shook his head. "Not a very hospitable place." Then he thought about Buck. He thumbed toward his horse and said, "How much for him?"

"Fifty cents a day," the boy said, "unless you want something extra, like corn or oats, then it's seventy-five cents a day."

Annoyed, Will shook his head. "Boy, everywhere else it's two bits a day, and that usually includes grain, sometimes maybe as much as four bits, but I've never been asked to pay six bits."

"Sorry, mister, but I don't—"

"I know," Will snapped, "you don't set the prices, your pa does." He pulled a small bag from his inside vest pocket, rummaged around and dug out a buck fifty and tossed the coins to the boy. "That's for two days. If we're here more than that, I'll settle up with you before I leave."

The boy nodded. "Thanks for the business, mister. Come back and see us."

Will shook his head and, with Toby alongside, led the bay through the barn doors to the street. When they were outside, and the boy had gone back to cleaning the office, Will said, "I'd like to keep this quiet, at least until I determine whether or not I can make an arrest without gunplay."

The marshal, walking alongside Will, said, "I can't make no promises. I told you they're friends of mine, and they have a lot of other friends in town."

Will stopped, turned, and looked at the marshal. "Look, if you tell them or anyone else, people could get hurt. If I get shot, they'll send the army down here. You don't want that. Just give me a couple of days. My goal is to catch this kid without shooting him and take him back for trial."

The town marshal shook his head. "But if he goes back for trial, he'll hang."

"Maybe, maybe not. But he's killed a U.S. Marshal and robbed a stage and attempted to rob a bank. It won't be long before he tries something around here, and it'll be your job to clean up the mess. Is that what you really want?" Will stared at the marshal, seeing a man who was caught between a rock and a hard place.

"No, it ain't, but I'll be no help to you. I'll not fire on Mott or his boy. Mott's been good to me and the town."

When Will started to speak, Snead held up his hand. "Just

you wait. I ain't saying I'll run tellin' what I know, and I sure won't let this town get shot up if I can help it. I'm just not going to be a help to you."

Will nodded, thankful, at least, that the man wasn't going to hightail it out to Cooper's ranch. "Guess that's the best I can expect."

"One other thing. You catch him, you take him. He's not going to be locked up in my jail."

Will's face didn't show the frustration he was feeling. His eyes were level, face clear, even a tiny smile pulled at his lips, but only his lips. "You're not giving me much leeway here."

"Nope, I'm not, but I'm not trying to stop you, either. The way I see it, that's a plus on your side."

Will nodded and swung up onto the bay. "I appreciate you being honest with me, Snead, so I'll be honest with you. I'm taking Ambrose Cooper back. I'd like for him to ride back sitting on a saddle, not draped over it, but either way, he's going with me. This is gospel. Don't you or any of your friends get in my way. I won't be stopped, not as long as I'm breathing."

It was the marshal's turn to nod. "Reckon we understand each other, but there's one other thing." He had a thumb hooked behind his gun belt. With the thick rough hand still gripping the belt, he lift a finger and pointed it toward Toby. "You pretty well rubbed Nasty Ned's nose in it today. He may be filthy, but he has a long memory, and he's meaner than a shedding rattler. Only reason he wants the dog is to kill him—get even is what he'd say. Just keep an eye open."

"Thanks," Will said, and clucked at the bay. He rode out of town, his brow wrinkled, brown eyes tight and looking as hard as smoky quartz. *This is shaping up as one of the toughest jobs I've undertaken in a long time,* he thought. Toby trotted quietly alongside.

9

W ill debated his approach as he rode. He could ride into Cooper's ranch, the C Bar, find Ambrose Cooper, and arrest him. Unfortunately, though Mott Cooper was a law-abiding man, from everything Will had heard, the man would fight till his last breath to protect his nephew, and so would his cowhands. Will understood that feeling. Logans would come from miles around to protect one of their own. But there was the matter of the law and the badge he carried. He represented the law, and it was his job to bring Ambrose Cooper back for trial.

The bay walked along the dry road, and Will's mind drifted back to Deborah. *What's she doing right now?* He glanced at the lengthening shadows from the cottonwood trees along the Gallinas. *Probably finishing up with the last patients of the day or straightening the office. Her uncle, Dr. James, likes a tidy office.* Will could see her strong chin, wide mouth, and sparkling eyes.

He patted the bay on his neck and glanced down at Toby, who was contentedly trotting alongside. "Hope she likes you, boy. If she doesn't, we might have a problem, but I think she'll like you a lot."

Several miles had dropped away when Will came to the first turnoff. He pulled up the bay and sat for a moment. This was a tough decision. He had always been a direct man, see a problem and go straight for it. But this was different. He had to be mindful of other folks, more so than usual. Straight to the problem, Ambrose Cooper, or a bit of a ruse? He'd already hidden his true mission from the townspeople. Maybe it could still work.

He made up his mind and rode on, past the turnoff to the C Bar and Ambrose Cooper. Reaching the second turnoff, he swung the bay to the right to follow the road to the Lazy Y. If Fran Young's land ran adjacent to Cooper's, she might hire him on as a day hand, and he could spend a few days scouting around. He didn't like the subterfuge, but if it kept him from having to fight innocent folks, it might be worth it.

The Lazy Y headquarters was much bigger than he expected. The way the bartender had described it, Fran Young had taken over a small spread. If that were the case, a man would expect a smaller house and outbuildings, but when he topped a rise, the huge homeplace loomed into view. A two-story, rambling ranch house with its long deep porch was grand in anybody's book. It was built from neatly sawed and freshly painted lumber, with broad windows looking toward the mountains, and three rock chimneys towering above the structure. The bunkhouse and barn were of the same grand design. All of the buildings were painted a deep rust red and stood out on the plains for all to see.

He walked the bay toward the ranch and corrals. The main corral, adjacent to the barn, was occupied with cowhands leaning or sitting on the rails, while several others were riding the wild horses inside. Will rode up to the main corral in time to see a little black mustang launch his rider into the air. Sitting the bay, Will watched as the man rose high and then plummeted to the ground, dust flying. The rider jumped to his feet, dusted himself off, and headed back toward the rangy, little black mustang. The rider pulled his hat low and tight on his head while the mustang stood watching him.

Will couldn't help but notice that one of the hands, sitting on the top rail of the corral, was a woman. She wore pants shoved down into a pair of expensive but worn boots whose heels were hooked over the second rail. Blonde hair slipped out from under her gray Stetson, which sat level on her head.

At the sound of his horse, everyone turned to look at him, their eyes taking him in and then dropping to Toby alongside.

She said, in a firm voice used to giving commands, "Hello, stranger. What can I do for you?"

When she turned her face toward him, he noticed she had the same color of striking blue eyes his sister, Kate. "Riding the grub line, ma'am."

All heads, including hers, turned back to the corral as the cowhand's body described a perfect arc from the back of the little mustang to land in the dirt at the woman's feet. She looked down at the hand, who had propped himself up on his elbows and was shaking his head. "Have you had about enough, Dusty?" she asked.

"I'm gettin' danged close, ma'am. Figger I might give it one more try."

"Hold on a second." She turned back to Will. "You feel like earning a meal?"

"Always feel like it, ma'am," Will said.

"Good. How about you riding that black mustang?"

Will glanced again at the horse, whose eyes were wide as it strained at the reins held by another cowhand. "Ma'am, I'm awfully big for that horse."

Her eyes tightened with a challenge. "If you're afraid, mister, we'll still be glad to share a meal with you."

At her comment the cowhands sitting around her grinned.

Will nodded, feeling the challenge, and some irritation that she would prod him in such a manner. He looked at the little horse and back at her. "I'm not afraid of the horse, ma'am. I just don't want to break him down."

The woman looked him up and down, taking her time. "How much do you weigh, cowboy?"

He wasn't a boy and hadn't been for a long time, and he didn't like the term. Cow nurse, cow wrangler, cowhand, any of those were fine, but he couldn't stand to be called a cow*boy*.

"About one-ninety-five, ma'am."

"That settles it, then," she said. "That *little* mustang can carry over three hundred pounds. You won't be a problem unless you're scared."

There it was a second time. If she had been a man, he would've ridden to the corral rail, dragged him from it, and dropped him in the dirt—but she wasn't. Dusty had gotten up, walked back to the mustang, and made a point of lengthening the stirrups. Once completed, he slid his hat to the back of his head and stared at Will.

Without another word, Will rode the bay to the water trough, climbed down, tossed the reins around the hitching post, and told Toby to stay. He walked to the offside of the horse where a view of him, from the hands around the corral, was blocked by the animal's flanks, and unloaded his vest pockets into his saddlebags. He couldn't take the chance of his badge getting tossed out from the bucking of the mustang. Then he walked to the corral, scratched Toby's ears as he passed, crawled through the rails, and ambled to the mustang. He took the reins from the cowhand who was holding them, and stepped to the stirrups, which looked to be adjusted just right.

"Watch him," Dusty said. "He likes to buck high and twist left while he's coming down. Try to keep your rear in the saddle, or he'll twist right out from under you." Then he grinned. "She can get under your skin, can't she?"

Will grinned back at him. "A mite, but I'm hungry." He leaned forward and patted the mustang on the neck, then rubbed his hand over the animal's front shoulder. "I'm a little heavy, but it's gonna be all right, boy. This won't take long."

One of the cowhands sitting on the top rail of the corral yelled, "You're sure right about that," and the others burst out laughing.

Will swung up, and the horse was motionless except for the trembling throughout its body. "That's a good fella. Now let's get you *walk*—" Walk burst from his mouth as the black launched into the air without warning. Straight up, he went, and sure enough, when Will felt himself starting to float because the horse was headed down, it turned left. Fortunately, with his powerful long legs, he was able to hang on, but no sooner had the horse hit the ground before it was airborne again. Will managed to stay with the bucking animal, but each flight sent him higher in the saddle. On the third leap, he found himself separated from the mustang and headed for the dirt.

His one hundred and ninety-five pounds collided with the ground with a solid thud. This wasn't new to him. He was good with horses and able to retain his seat with most of them, but sometimes one would master the technique of unseating him, and this mustang seemed to be a specialist. He heard his audience laughing, although he could hear one or two saying he had done good to stay that long.

Will rose, dusted himself off, and headed back to the mustang. This time he spent more time talking to the horse and gently rubbing its neck and cheek, careful of the biting teeth.

The same cowhand who had yelled at him earlier yelled again. "You can sweet-talk all you want. It ain't gonna do you one bit of good."

Again, everyone laughed.

The woman called, "You've earned your meal. You don't have to ride him again."

Will waved in response and swung into the saddle.

The heckler was right, all his talking and rubbing had done

no good, and this time the horse didn't wait for him to get seated. While his right leg was still in the air, the mustang flung his body to his right, away from Will and almost unseating him before he ever settled in the saddle. Using what little leverage he had, he threw his weight into the turn, managing to get his leg across the horse's back, his foot desperately searching for the stirrup. He came very close to grabbing the saddle horn, the apple as many cowhands called it, but fought for and regained his balance, his foot sliding home into the stirrup. Just in time.

The mustang launched high and twisted left, but Will, using his leg strength, managed to stay tight in the saddle. He could feel the little horse tiring, for the next jump wasn't as high, and Will was able to hang on.

The cowhands watching could tell it too and began cheering him on. The mustang managed two more leaps, then crow-hopped several times, and finally came to a halt, its sides heaving. Will patted the animal on the neck and nudged him forward, walking him slowly around the corral. Finally he swung down and tossed the reins to a cowhand who was standing near, waiting.

The woman jumped down from the rail, foregoing any assistance from the hands, and strode over to Will. "Good ride."

"Thanks," Will said. "Dusty got him worn down for me. He was already tired when I climbed aboard."

"Not so tired he didn't pile you up in the dirt once, and almost a second time. I was surprised you were able to hang on." She eyed him again. "I guess those long legs come in handy for something."

Will nodded. "I reckon."

"You looking for work?"

At this question Will removed his hat. "Well, ma'am, I left my horse in one of the town stables to rest up. Reckon I'll give him two or three days. Then I'll be moving on. But I could sure use some day work. I can rope, brand, ride, even do handiwork if I have to."

She pursed her wide lips, which caused her petite nose to lift slightly, and said, "We're pretty well set on hands, but we've lost a few head of cattle over the past few months, and I might need a new face looking over the herd, picking up strays, branding those calves that still need it, those kinds of things. Does that interest you?"

"It sure does. If money's are tight around here, I'm not looking for pay. Just some good meals for the days I'm here would suit me fine. I've been eatin' my own cookin' for a little too long."

Her jaw tightened, and her blue eyes flashed. "No man works for me without getting paid. You'll not be the first. Find a spot in the bunkhouse, and wash up. It'll be supper soon, and Cookie doesn't like people coming in late. By the way, what's your name?"

"Will Logan, ma'am."

"I'm Fran Young."

"Nice to meet you, Miss Young."

"It's Mrs. Young. Put your horse in the barn. There's corn and oats in there. Help yourself." She stepped to Toby, whose head rose well above her waist, grabbed the big dog by the face and bent slightly to bring her eyes close to his while she scratched his cheeks and ears. "How'd you find Toby? He's been missing for a while. Heard he ran away from that Nasty Ned Fairburn?"

"Didn't find him, Mrs. Young. He found me at my camp, out on the Pass. He's stuck with me ever since."

"He's a good dog and excellent with cattle. I saw Eli working cattle with him. Take him with you when you work my stock. He'll be a big help. He's been in my house when the Hendersons were here. I don't think the hands will mind him in the bunkhouse, if you've a mind." She straightened and turned toward the house, tossing her head as she turned. "See you at supper."

He took the bay into the barn, Toby following. Will was

rubbing the horse down when Dusty walked in leading a beautiful palomino. Will watched the horse as Dusty led him by the stall. "That's a mighty pretty animal."

Dusty stopped, admiring the fine-looking palomino. "He belongs to Fran, her personal horse. Her husband, Tyler Young, gave it to her for a wedding present. She places a lot of store by this horse." He patted it on the neck, then led it into the stall beside Will's. "You had a good ride."

Will snorted and said, "After joining you on the ground. Anyway, you'd already worn that mustang down before I ever got to him."

Dusty laughed and then said, "That little horse is quite a bucker. I reckon I'll be sore for the next few days. I'm sure glad you came along to finish him up. I didn't hanker to crawl back on that horse's back."

"You mentioned Mr. Young. Usually the owner or the foreman does the hiring. I was kind of surprised a woman was doing it."

Dusty shook his head. "Foreman's off to Denver, and Mr. Young's not around anymore. He died about a year ago. Somebody shot him from ambush. Never any sign of the feller who did it. The boss's horse showed up at the water trough, and we backtracked him. There he was, stretched out by the trail, a bullet in his spine and one in the back of his head."

"You don't say," Will said. "Any suspicions on who might have done it?"

Dusty stopped brushing down the palomino, turned around and leaned against the stall partition. "That's the funny thing. He was well liked by most folks. He and Mott had had a few words over the springs between the ranches, but it weren't killing serious, and there just wasn't enough sign around to tell who it might be." He shook his head. "It sure broke up Fran something fierce. She seriously loved that man, though he was quite a bit older than her." Dusty turned around and went back to work on the palomino.

Will finished with the bay, poured some corn in the trough, and grabbed his saddlebags, bedroll, and weapons. In the process he was conscious of his right hand. Much of the swelling had gone down, but it was still sore. He couldn't make a tight fist with it yet, maybe tomorrow. He picked up the shotgun with his right hand, thought better of it, and put it down while he worked his fingers, trying to get them limber.

Dusty stepped up beside him. "Here, pardner, let me help. Looks like you've been beating that hand against a corral post for fun. Noticed you favoring it when you mounted the mustang."

"Thanks," Will said. "A miner's head tried to break it. He didn't succeed, but he sure stove it up."

"Those hard heads'll do it," Dusty said, taking the bedroll and shotgun. "Come on, let's get cleaned up. Name's Dove Campbell, but everyone calls me Dusty. Bring along Toby, the boys won't mind, but we'd best get moving. It don't pay to be late for Cookie's meals. When he says, 'Come and get it or I'll throw it out,' he's serious."

"Good to know," Will said. "I'm Will Logan."

Dusty nodded and led the way to the bunkhouse. "You'll get along with the crew fine. There's a couple of cusses who talk too much, but other than them, it's a fair bunch. You might watch out for the redhead. He's the one what was hurrahing you at the corral. Thinks he's a tough feller, which, come to think of it, he is. He ain't bad once you get to know him. Name's Bob Fleming, course we all call him Red."

They entered the large bunkhouse. It was nicer than most Will had seen. Instead of just space and pegs against the wall for the cowhands to hang their things, they actually had small cabinets with doors on them, and boards across the top to put a hat or whatever paraphernalia a cowhand wanted to keep up there. Inside the cabinets, near the top, was a shelf, and beneath the shelf were pegs to hang clothes, guns, belts, or whatever a man needed to hang.

Will looked around, saw an empty bunk, walked to it, and dropped his bedroll and saddlebags on it.

Immediately from across the room came, "That one's mine. Pick another."

Will didn't look up or speak. He picked up his gear, turned and dropped it on the next empty bunk.

Again the voice piped up. "That's mine, too."

Will recognized the voice. It was the same one that had yelled at him in the corral. He looked over the top bunk. Across the room, the redhead Dusty had spoken of was lying on a top bunk, reading a dime novel and scratching his thick red hair. "You sleep on a different bunk every night?" Will asked.

"I'm notional," the redhead said.

Will sized the man up. Fairly big, strong with a petulant face salted generously with freckles. The voice and the flame red hair gave him away as Bob Fleming, or Red, as the cowhands called him. "You get that red hair from your ma or pa?" Will asked.

Surprised, the man said, "My pa, why?"

Will nodded knowingly. "You know what that means, don't you?"

Puzzled, Red said, "What what means?"

"The fact you get red hair from your pa. You know what that means?"

"No, I don't know what that means." Red had laid the dime novel on the bunk and swung his legs over the side. He was gripping the edge, ready to jump down if he sensed a slight. Everyone else in the bunkhouse had stopped what they were doing and were listening.

"Humph," Will said, then, almost to himself, "I thought everybody knew that. Folks say it's always better to get your red hair from your ma." He went about unrolling his bedroll. Red said nothing more about the bunk but dropped to the floor. Will started whistling "The Arkansas Traveler" and continued to straighten his bedding. Toby had lain down near the front door.

Red walked over and leaned on the bunk bed next to Will's. "Are you going to tell me?"

Will looked up, as if surprised the man was standing there, though he had known every step he took. "Tell you what?"

With exasperation in his voice, Red said, "Why it's better to get red hair from your ma than your pa."

Will just stood there looking at the man, face blank, waiting. Then he said, "Well?"

Red's face turned red, and his voice grew louder. "Well, what?"

Will took a deep breath and said, "I thought you were going to tell *me* why it's better to get red hair from your ma than your pa. You're the man with the red hair. You should know."

Red looked around the room at the other men in the room, all listening closely and working hard to suppress grins.

He turned back to Will, who had gone back to making his bed. "Mister, you'd best not be hoorahin' me."

Will shook his head while he folded a blanket across the bunk. "I wouldn't fun a man about something so important. If you're serious you don't know, I'll be glad to tell you."

Red let out an exasperated sigh. "How many times do I have to tell you, *I don't know.*"

Will straightened and turned to the frustrated man, whose freckles seemed to glow on the red face. "Well, Red, can I call you Red?"

Red gave an impatient nod of his head. "Sure, you can, now go ahead."

"Well, Red, now this is according to a wise gypsy I met in my travels, so I can't attest to the truth of it." Will paused for a second, looked around the room at the other cowhands. "But we all know the gypsies are known for their knowledge and fortune-telling."

Every cowhand nodded knowingly.

The wait was long enough for Red to jump in. "Alright, alright, a wise gypsy, keep going."

Will leaned closer to Red, speaking softly. "She told me it was always best for children to get their red hair from their ma, because it grew normally. You know, out, like all hair grows. But if a child gets red hair from its pa, the hair not only grows out, but it also grows in, toward the skull and brain. It gets down into the skull and itches. It'll near drive a man crazy with itching."

Red had scratched his head a couple of times after leaving his bunk. His eyes narrowed, and he canted his head slightly, staring hard at Will. Then first one hand, then the other jerked to his head and started scratching.

"See," Will said, shaking his head, "growing the wrong way. You mind if I use this bunk, Red?"

"What?" Red said, preoccupied with his head. "No, go ahead." He stood at the end of Will's bunk, his fingers digging deep into the thick red hair.

Will shoved his saddlebags under the bed just as the triangle, signifying supper was ready, started ringing, accompanied by a loud voice. "Come and get it, and make it quick!"

He pushed past the flabbergasted man, quickly stepped outside to the washbasin, Toby on his heels, and washed his face and hands. Then shaking his hands off in the dry air, he joined Dusty, and they and Toby headed to the main house.

Walking across the yard, Dusty leaned over to Will, his face serious with the mystery of gypsies, and said, "I hear them gypsies can sometimes tell a man more than he really wants to know."

Will gave his companion a sideways grin and said, "So I've heard, Dusty."

Will opened the door and let Dusty go in ahead of him, told Toby to stay, and stood back as the other hands came in. Mrs. Young was sitting at the head of the table, and each of the men took his seat. There was an open seat next to her, and Will started for it. Dusty, who had waited next to him, shook his head. "That seat's for Art Ramsey, the foreman. Remember, I told you he's gone to Denver."

"When's he supposed to return?"

"Anytime now. Everyone's anxious for him to get back so we can find out what the cattle market's like and hear the latest news." Dusty motioned to seats near the opposite end of the table. "Here we go. We can sit here."

Will started to sit next to Dusty, and Fran said, "Mr. Logan, would you join us up here, please," and she motioned to Art Ramsey's chair next to her.

10

"Thank you, ma'am," Will said, moving to the place Mrs. Young had indicated. The cowhand next to him slid his chair over to make extra room for Will's size, which started a chain reaction down that side of the table, chairs scraping until everyone had repositioned.

She said nothing more, but filled her plate with beans, mashed potatoes, and stew. She made a point of swiftly taking a bite, and all the cowhands began helping themselves. Will followed suit and loaded his plate. The stew smelled good. He took a big bite, along with some of the mashed potatoes. *Not as good as Ma or Deborah makes,* he thought, *but mighty good.*

"So, tell me, Mr. Logan, where did you come from?"

Caught with his mouth full, Will thumbed back over his shoulder.

She nodded and said, "Well then, where are you heading?"

He pointed in front of him.

"You're not very talkative, are you?"

He finished chewing and said, "No, ma'am, I'm really not, especially when I've got my mouth full."

"It's not full now."

The other cowhands were quietly eating, so they could hear the exchange between the blonde owner and Will.

"Been a lot of places. I fought in the war and did a little traveling. Fact is, I'm still traveling, not ready to light."

A voice Will recognized as the redhead's said, "Fight for the rebs?"

"With my Tennessee accent, it's probably a safe bet to think that. But nope, I fought for the North. My brother fought for the South. There were good folks on both sides."

"Yes, there were," Fran said. "That was a horrible war, pitting friends against friends, and families against families."

"Can't argue with you there," Will said. "Lot of good men, women, and children died. Let's hope it never happens again."

"What do you do, Mr. Logan?"

"I've been known to work cattle now and again. Also raised a few horses in Tennessee, and cut a little sugar cane in Cuba."

"My, my," she said, "you have done some traveling. How'd you like Cuba?"

"Well, ma'am, there's a lot of turmoil down there. At least there was when I was around. It's been a while. I wouldn't recommend it."

He hated to bring up the subject, but he was curious as to who Fran Young thought had killed her husband, and it was his job. "Dusty was telling me about you losing your husband. Has the sheriff found anything out about who did it?"

She stopped eating for a moment. With the exception of Dusty, all of the other cowhands gave Will a hard look for bringing up the subject.

"Sorry, ma'am. Maybe I shouldn't have mentioned your husband. I imagine his loss is still a mighty tender subject. Just forget I asked."

The kitchen was silent for a while, even Cookie ceased banging pans or slamming oven doors. The men quietly ate, sensitive to their boss's sadness.

Will thought, *I really stepped into it now. All I wanted to know was if the sheriff had any suspects. Deborah's right, I'm not the most tactful person in the world.*

After a minute, which seemed much longer, she spoke. "I'm sorry, Mr. Logan. I should not be so sensitive. It has been a year since my husband was killed." She took a deep breath and plowed on. "I'm sorry to say the sheriff has not come up with any evidence or ideas, and he searched all around the place where Tyler was shot."

"Has there been anyone else killed?"

"No, I'm not aware of anyone else."

A younger fella, down the table, spoke up. "Ma'am, you may not remember, but there was that stranger who got shot over by the west spring."

"Thank you, Bliss. Yes, I do remember now, but that's been over three years ago. From the way he was shot, the sheriff said it didn't look like an ambush. In fact, there had been signs of two horses, like maybe they had been riding together."

"Yes, ma'am." Bliss spoke up again. "The sheriff said it looked like those two fellers had a disagreement and got into it. That feller came out on the losing end of the deal."

Will thought while he chewed. He swallowed and said, "Both shootings were on the west side of your land?"

"Yes, Mr. Logan, but they were unrelated. They happened at least two years apart, and the first man was a stranger. If I remember right, he was young, probably no more than eighteen or nineteen, but he wore his gun like a gunfighter." She looked down the table at Bliss. "Is that what you remember?"

Red, his left hand scratching his head, jumped in. "That's a fact, ma'am. I remember the sheriff saying the young feller had his gun holster all tied down and everything. If he weren't a gunfighter, he was sure playin' at it." He grinned across the table at Bliss. "Guess he weren't too good at playing."

Bliss was frowning. It appeared he wasn't too happy with the interruption and spoke quickly. "Yes, ma'am, what *Red*, here, said is true, but the sheriff also said the young feller had a couple of notches on his six-gun, so I reckon he played pretty good with somebody else." He gave a short nod at Red.

"This spring you're speaking of," Will said, "is it near the C Bar? Isn't that the ranch just west of you?"

"Yes," Fran Young continued. "Our land joins. Of course, most of it is open range. Our cattle mingle, and we separate them during roundup, but yes, the ranch to the west of us is the C Bar, owned by Matt Cooper."

Red spoke up again, his large teeth showing in a wide grin. "Yep, and I think that nephew of his, Ambrose Cooper, has his eye on you, Fran."

The other cowboys' heads turned to give Red a hard look, for it was obvious to Will the cowhand had stepped over an invisible line, then their heads swung back to the ranch owner.

Her jaw and eyes tightened. All of the conversational friendliness disappeared, her voice sharp and commanding, as she said, "Red, do not start unfounded rumors."

Red's grin vanished. In its place was the face of a young man who might have just been scolded by a favorite aunt. His head made a small turn and dropped slightly while his eyes looked down at the table. He mumbled, "Yes, ma'am, sorry."

Will watched her expression soften. He looked around at the cowhands, realizing these tough hardscrabble men would do just about anything for their ranch owner. He was looking at a perfect example of riding for the ranch.

She threw Red a smile. "Thank you. I know you didn't mean any intentional harm. It's just that those types of rumors can get quickly blown out of proportion."

The rest of the cowhands were nodding their heads in agreement. Red's face brightened, and a small smile crossed his rough face. "Yes, ma'am. I understand, and I'm sure sorry." His left index finger was busy scratching above his ear.

She returned his smile and, in a tone indicating his remark had been forgotten, said, "Thank you." Turning her face toward Will's, she continued, "Let me take a moment to explain. Ambrose Cooper is the nephew of Mott Cooper, the owner of the Bar C. He is much younger than I am. He is trying to find his place in this world. He has a beautiful voice, and since I have a piano and can play, I help him with his singing. I believe he has already reached a professional level, and on several occasions I have suggested he go back east to perform. Unfortunately, he's fallen in with a wild crowd and hasn't visited recently. He is a nice young man. I would hate to see him, because of the crowd he runs with, get into any serious trouble."

"Yes, ma'am, I—"

She held up a small hand, stopping him. "Please, those who work for me call me by my first name, Fran. In turn, I address them by their first names. Is that acceptable to you, Will?"

Will looked at the young, attractive, smiling blonde sitting next to him, and said, "Well, Fran, I reckon that would be a sight easier."

"Good," she said. "Now, you were saying?"

"I was just going to say that's mighty nice of you helping a young fella like that out, but you can't always judge a horse by how pretty it is. There's some mighty pretty horses that'd just as soon take a hunk out of you as look at you."

Her brow wrinkled in a frown. The cowhands around the table, finished with their eating, were listening intently and nodding. She asked, "What are you trying to say, Will?"

"I'm saying that if this young fella is running with a wild bunch, it's not too far-fetched to expect him to be wild himself."

Dusty piped up, "Fran, that's what we've been saying. There's a lot of talk going around that Ambrose is not just in that bunch, but he's leading it. If that's the case, then most of the happenings we're hearing about are his ideas. Ma'am, you just have to be careful around him, pretty voice or not. I've never trusted him, and just because he's gotten older doesn't mean he's grown up and changed."

Will followed her questioning look. She peered at each of the cowhands around the table. As her eyes locked with each one, he would give a sharp nod. *They're worried about her,* Will thought. *Knowing what I know, they have a right to be.* He watched her turn back to him.

"I guess most of my men agree with you, Will. I know my fore-man, Art Ramsey, agrees with you. He's asked me several times to stop inviting the young man over except for when there are cowhands around the house." She made a small fist and banged it lightly on the table. "But I just know. Ambrose Cooper couldn't really hurt any man."

"Fran?" Dusty spoke up again.

She looked down the table at him. "Yes, Dusty?"

"The sheriff told me there was a witness who said he *thought* he saw that stranger who was killed over by the springs riding out of town with Ambrose."

Fran jerked back like she'd been struck. "Dusty, that can't be true, or he would have arrested him."

Dusty took a sip of coffee, swallowed, and shook his head. "He said the fellow who saw them couldn't be positive. He was pretty sure, but couldn't swear to it."

"Well," she said, leaning back in her chair, "there you have it. There's no proof, and I refuse to think bad about someone until it's proven."

"Fran," Will said, "I don't think the boys are trying to get you to think badly of Ambrose Cooper. I think they're just asking you to be cautious. You know, if you want to invite him over, make sure there are some hands around. Don't invite him onto the ranch when you're by yourself. That's not thinking bad of him, that's just being smart."

Several of the hands nodded in agreement.

She let out a sigh. "Boys, I'll have to think about it. I understand what you're saying, and I appreciate your concern, but I do truly love to hear him sing."

"That's all we're askin', Fran," Dusty said. "Just think about it." Then he grinned. "We don't want anything to happen to the boss who pays us."

That brought a smile to her lips and a few chuckles from around the table.

THREE DAYS HAD PASSED since Will had arrived on the Lazy Y. The second evening he returned the bay to the livery and picked up Buck. Will wanted his horse, but he also didn't want to pay the exorbitant rental fee any longer than necessary. The remainder of the time, he and Toby had been busy working cattle on every portion of the sizable ranch except near Mott Cooper's land. One thing he had learned was that Toby was an excellent cattle dog. With the dog's size and speed, even an ornery cow with a calf was no match for the dog. Having Toby made the work go much faster.

Today, he, Toby, and Buck, along with Red, were headed out to the west side to check on calves and brand those who were at least a couple of months old.

Will watched Toby race ahead of them, then turn and race back. He grinned, watching the animal. He'd not had a dog since he was a boy, but now, as the two of them rode out to do a day's work, it felt good having the big, white dog with him. He and Toby were a lot alike. Both loved these early mornings. Though it was nearing the end of July, the mornings were crisp and cool. In only an hour or so, the heat of the day would start to build, but the morning air was invigorating.

"He's putting on weight," Red said.

"Yep," Will replied. "The fact Cookie has taken a liking to him hasn't hurt. I think Toby's gettin' fed better than we are."

Red grinned, lifted his hat with his right hand, and scratched his head with his left. "Yep. If we got fed as good as that dog, we'd be fattenin' up too."

The two horses walked slowly through the scattered bunchgrass. A badger lay near its den, head turning to keep its black eyes trained on the riders as they rode past.

Red nodded toward the small animal. "He's a regular here. I've been on this ranch goin' on four years, and that badger's had his hole right there for as long as I've been here."

The white stripe, running from between the badger's eyes to its tail, glistened in the early morning sun.

"We don't seem to bother him," Will said.

"Nope. He's used to horses and riders. You're not gonna believe this, but I've seen that badger out hunting with a coyote."

Will grinned at Red. "Now you're pulling my leg."

Serious, Red shook his head. "No, sir. I've seen 'em huntin' together. Call me crazy, but that's what they was doing."

They rode on in silence, gradually moving west toward the spring. Throughout the morning, the two cowhands, when spotting an unbranded calf, halted and built a fire. They then heated the brand, roped the calf, and while Toby ensured the mother maintained her distance, branded the calf.

Practiced at what they did, the work went quickly, and by ten they neared the spring.

"Not difficult to spot," Red said.

In the distance, a thick stand of oak bore testimony to the spring's location, the oaks trailing to the east for about a hundred yards. Also, a sizeable bunch of cattle stood chewing on the grass, or lay sleeping in the sun, their jaws working on the grass.

Nearing the spring, Will saw five horses grazing among the oaks. "Looks like we have company."

Red saw the horses at the same time. "It's unusual for that many of the C Bar boys to be riding together unless during roundup."

Will flipped the leather loop from over the Remington's hammer and made sure the shotgun was loose in its scabbard.

Red caught the movement and frowned. "Those are most likely riders of the C Bar. We won't have any trouble."

Will nodded and said, "It's the *most likely* that bothers me. You'd best be ready."

He watched Red shrug, then ready his own revolver. They continued to ride. They were almost to the spring when a melodic voice called from the oaks, "Hold up there."

"Who's that?" Red called. "Is that you, Coop?"

A long silence followed, then the voice said, "Red, what are you doing out here? And who's the big stranger?"

Red glanced at Will and, in a low voice, said, "It's Ambrose Cooper. We call him Coop." He then turned toward the oaks and raised his voice. "He's Will Logan, a new hand. What's going on, Coop?"

The man still hadn't shown himself. He was at the spring, but well hidden in the dark green oaks.

"You boys oughta be riding on. This ain't a good stop for you right now."

Will looked around. They were in the open. There were a few ironwood bushes and a couple of tumbleweeds, but the closest cover was a low rocky ridge twenty feet to their left. "Horses need water," Will called.

The response from Ambrose to Will was short. "Tough."

Will could tell Red's ire was rising. "Coop? That's the Lazy Y's spring, and we'll water our stock at it when we want. You'd best be friendly or ride along. Makes me no never mind, but we're comin' in, and we see five horses. Who else is here? That's a big bunch of C Bar riders to be in one place."

Ambrose stepped out from behind the oaks. "Now, Red, no need for you to get riled," he said.

This was Will's first look at Ambrose Cooper. The young man was of average stature, well dressed for a cowhand, with an expensive, low-crowned Stetson set at a jaunty angle above thick black hair. He showed a cool smile, exposing even white teeth. Greenish-yellow eyes stared out from under the Stetson, similar to the color of a cougar's eyes.

Ambrose continued, ignoring Will, "You just ride on to the water hole south of here. It won't be no problem for you. Maybe I'll see you when I come over to see Mrs. Young."

Red shook his head. "Can't, Coop. I see Lazy Y calves over by that water what need branding, and I aim to be doing what I'm paid for."

Will caught the glint of metal from inside the oak thicket. Whoever they were, they had weapons drawn and pointed toward him and Red. This was a no-win situation for them.

11

"Red," Will said, "why don't we move on. You can show me where the next water hole is. Odds are we'll find calves there, too. Once we take care of them, we can come back here and tend to these."

Red turned a surprised look toward Will. "Whatd'ya mean ride on? We got calves to brand right here."

Will knew Red hadn't known him long enough to trust him. It took time to build trust, but if Red drew his gun, they'd both be holier than Grandma's sieve. Using the tone he'd used so many times in the army as first sergeant, he said, "Leave it, Red. Move on." He nodded to Ambrose Cooper, who eyed him suspiciously, and turned his horse, noticing Red, mad as he was, followed him.

They rode in silence until they were well out of sight.

"Hold up," Red said. "It ain't your place to go ordering me around, mister. I don't back down for no man, and I ain't startin' now."

Will was tired of the deception. It was time he represented who he was and why he was here. Ambrose Cooper was only a short distance away, and he aimed to catch him while he could, and if possible get him out of the country before his uncle could find out. He reached into his vest pocket. From it, he extracted his badge and pinned it on his shirt, beneath his vest.

Red's eyes grew wide, moving from Will's face to the badge and back. "You're a U.S. Marshal?"

"I am. I didn't tell anyone sooner because I was hoping to grab Cooper before his uncle was aware, and get him out of the country. Ambrose Cooper is wanted for a stage robbery, the attempted holdup of a bank, and the murder of a U.S. Marshal."

Red was still staring at the badge. "Then you're not a cowhand?"

"I am a cowhand, but I'm also a marshal. I pulled you away from your little set-to with Cooper because there were guns pointed at us from the oaks. If you had even started to draw, we would've been cut to pieces."

Red's head bobbed up and down as he nodded. "Those other horses we saw. They must be his gang."

"Yep, that's what I'm thinking. If I can slip back there and surprise them, I can be out of here with Ambrose before Mott Cooper has an inkling. I've heard how fond he is of his nephew, and I'd hate for anyone to get hurt trying to free the boy."

Red nodded. "But you ain't gonna stand a chance by yourself. Even with that scattergun, you're goin' to need help. I'm fairly good with a gun."

"I was actually hoping you'd say that, Red. I'll deputize you and make this legal, then we'll slip back and surprise our killer and little group of thieves."

Will changed into moccasins and tossed Red a pair. "They'll make our going a lot quieter and easier."

Red nodded, pulling his boots off and slipping the moccasins on. "Never liked these things. They're not tight enough." He tried wiggling his toes. Then from the boulder he sat on, he stretched his feet toward Will. "See, you can see my toes wiggling. I prefer boots that hold your feet tight. That's good support."

Will grinned at him. "Whatever makes you happy." His face grew serious. "Alright, raise your right hand."

Red did as he was told.

"You swear to uphold the law and the Constitution?"

"I sure do."

"Good. You're deputized." Will turned to his horse, pulled the shotgun from its scabbard, broke it open, and checked the loads. Then he pulled a handful of shells from his saddlebags and dropped them into his vest pocket. After closing the shotgun, he checked his Remington and dropped it back into the holster and turned back to Red.

"Here's the plan. If we stay behind this little ridge of rocks, it'll get us pretty close to the stream. If we can get to the stream where it flows out of the oaks, then the brush should be thick enough to hide us until we get to their camp. I'd like to try to get in close and hear what they're saying."

"Yep," Red said. "The rocks will take us about midway up the stream. The water only runs for about a hundred or so yards, then it goes back underground. So that'll leave us thirty or forty yards from their camp. With all the brush and shinnery, we should be able to get right up in their lap."

"Good. Don't shoot unless I do. I'm here to arrest Ambrose, but if we can listen to their conversation, maybe they'll give us enough evidence to arrest the others." Will paused and looked at Red. "You're sure you want to do this?"

"Shoot, yeah. I'll be able to talk about this for years."

"Alright, let's go."

As soon as the men had swung down from their horses, Toby had dropped flat to the ground, his big head watching them. When Will stepped off, he stood and started to follow.

Will stopped and said to the dog, "Stay, Toby." The big dog sat and then lay down again, watching him.

"You think he'll stay?" Red asked.

"Don't know. Hope so. I'm concerned that big mass of white fur might catch their eye."

Toby watched a moment longer, then laid his head on his big paws.

Will led Red, and they eased along the rocky ridge, watching for thorns, goatheads, cactus, and rattlers. The sun was easing toward late morning. The ground was heating, but the big rocks had not yet gotten so hot the snakes were chased into their cooler retreats deep in the hidden clefts. They might still be out sunning. Will glanced at the scar on his left wrist. It was a reminder left for him from one of the deadly serpents. His eyes left his wrist, searching ahead, ensuring each step was safe and quiet.

He glanced back at Red. The man's casual grip on his Winchester indicated familiarity with his rifle. *I hope he can shoot straight,* Will thought, moving forward.

Slowly, they made their way along the loose rocks. The last thing Will wanted was to roll or scrape a rock, alerting the gang. Here was an opportunity that had fallen into his lap, and he meant to take full advantage of it. After slipping along the low rock ridge, they reached the point where it disappeared into the countryside. Between the remainder of the ridge and the stream were scattered ironwood and sage. Bending low, using the sparse brush as cover, the two armed men moved slowly from the low ridge to the brush along the stream. Will knew any rapid movement could attract the attention of the gang, and though it seemed smart to clear the opening as quickly as possible, the smart move was to cover it in a low, slow stoop.

Reaching the brush along the stream, Will straightened slowly. With the water to feed their roots, the brush had grown head high, and the gnarled oaks taller. In the lead, he slipped from brush to oak, waited and listened to the murmur of voices, and eased closer.

There was a small opening inside the oak patch, large enough for the gang to build a fire and brew coffee. Ambrose was regaling his crew with tales of the stage robbery while he passed around a bottle.

"That stage was carrying close to a thousand dollars, boys. I knew I had to get that money for us. That'd give us two hundred dollars apiece. When's the last time you saw two hundred dollars what was all your own?"

One of the men spoke up. "Shoot, Coop, I ain't never seen a hundred dollars all at once." He pulled a wad of money from an inside vest pocket and, eyes wide, gazed at it trancelike.

"You've seen it now, Finn," Ambrose said.

"We sure have," one of the others said. "It's mighty generous of you, Coop. You didn't have to share."

Will crouched behind a spreading salt cedar and thought, *He didn't share the other fourteen thousand with you boys. He's investing the thousand for your allegiance.*

The one called Finn said, "Tell us again how you took care of that U.S. Marshal, Coop. I love hearing about it."

Will and Red, both back in the shadows of the trees, were well hidden, but could see and hear everything that was going on. Will watched a slow smile envelope Cooper's face. His eyes glinted with pure pleasure.

"There isn't much to tell, Finn," Cooper said, playing up to his audience. "I beat him at his own game. You'd think a marshal would be fast, but he was slower'n molasses. I'd put two bullets in him before he ever cleared leather. He was a sight. It was like he thought he was this big bad marshal and was going to scare poor little ole me into dropping my gun." Cooper pulled his revolver from the holster and spun it a couple of times.

Looking to be the youngest, another spoke up. Still in his teens with blond hair falling over his ears, and thin, barely visible blond whiskers scattered over his face and chin, he said, "He sure didn't know who he was a-messin' with, now, did he? Why, he was going up against Ambrose Cooper, the Las Vegas Kid."

Cooper looked over at the boy who had spoken. "Abel, I like that. The Las Vegas Kid. Yes, sir, it has a real ring to it."

"I like it, too." Another spoke up. He was short and stocky, his face covered with pockmarks. "But what I like most is all this money. Now we don't have to rustle cattle for a long while. I figure that's why Red and the new hand was out here. I bet Blondie is catchin' on to her missing cows."

Will could see the laughing face of Cooper turn to a scowl. He stepped toward the last speaker. "You don't speak of Mrs. Young like that, Levi. We may be taking a few of her cattle, but I don't want to hear her spoken of disrespectful like. You understand me?"

The man he'd called Levi ducked his head. "Sure, Coop. I ain't meant no harm. We all know you're sweet on her."

Cooper had drawn close enough to reach Levi. Will watched as Cooper poked Levi in the chest with his trigger finger. "I ain't *sweet* on her. I like her, that's all."

The biggest and oldest of the group was squatting near the fire, pouring himself a cup of coffee. He snorted. "You like her alright. That's why you plugged her old man. No sweet young thing like her deserves to be married up to a geezer like old man Young."

Will glanced at Red, whose eyes had narrowed, and wrinkles of anger coursed across his brow. He looked back at Will and mouthed, "Now?"

Will shook his head and held up a finger. He wanted to make sure Red hadn't given away their location after hearing the last remark. When he looked back at the rustlers, Ambrose Cooper had stepped close to the last speaker.

"Otis, we agreed to never speak of that," he said, his face cold and grim.

Will watched Otis stand. He was taller than Cooper, with

wide shoulders, at least fifty pounds heavier than the young killer. Though he was older and bigger, he ducked his head. "Didn't think it'd cause much harm." He looked around their camp, then back at Cooper. "We be all by our lonesome out here, and we all know about it."

"Just the same, I don't want it mentioned."

Otis glanced at the others, as if looking for support. "Alright, Coop, I'm mighty sorry. You're the boss."

At the last words Will nodded to Red, and the two of them stepped into the opening. The only one directly facing them was Finn. He saw them instantly, and his jaw dropped. Will could see the man's eyes centered on the muzzle of his shotgun.

The others were engaged in the conversation between Otis and Cooper.

Finally Finn blurted out, "Coop, Red!" and pointed.

Four sets of eyes followed the pointing finger, registered Red first, then immediately jerked to the shotgun muzzle, drawn like steel shavings to a magnet.

Will smiled. "Howdy, boys. U.S. Marshal Will Logan. I reckon you all know Red. Thanks for clearing up the murder of Tyler Young. I'm sure Mrs. Young will be happy to know who killed her husband."

Cooper attempted to hide his slow hand movement toward his holster, but a low threatening growl came from beside Will.

"Young fella, right now, you might stand a chance at a trial, but I can promise you, this buckshot will end all of your chances." He reached down with his left hand, holding the shotgun like a pistol, and patted the big white dog's head. "Thanks for catching that, Toby. You don't mind well, but you sure come in handy."

Will kept his eyes on Cooper, ensuring the man's hand halted its movement.

Cooper turned slowly. Seeing only Will and Red, his face

broke into a sneer. "There's five of us." Then to his gang. "Get ready, boys."

Will shook his head. "That'd be a really bad idea Cooper, 'cause I promise you, the first load from this twelve gauge is for you, and at this range it won't hardly spread at all. It'll tear a hole through your middle big enough to shove a fist through."

Will moved the muzzle so it covered Cooper. "Now drop your gun, and do it nice and easy. That goes for all you boys."

The five young men's weapons hit the ground shortly after Will's instructions left his mouth, with the exception of Cooper. Slowly, he unfastened the belt and laid the belt and weapon gently on the ground.

Stepping to one side, so he could remain clear, Will motioned for Red to pick up the guns. All except Cooper had white faces and wide eyes. Will could smell their fear. Cooper was different. He watched Will and Red like a wolf, waiting for the right moment to pounce. There was no fear on his face or in his eyes. The boy was calculating even with a loaded shotgun pointing at him. *He's dangerous,* Will thought. *I'd best keep a close watch on him.*

Will waited until after Red had finished picking up the guns and dropping them at his feet. He looked each man over, then said, "Red, grab some piggin' strings and tie these fellas up."

Red walked to the horses and pulled five piggin' strings from the saddles. When he returned, Will said, "Tie Cooper up first. Make sure he's good and tight. Next, I want you to tie the big fella and then the rest. Take your time. Just make sure they're tight."

Red went methodically about his business. When he tied Cooper, he yanked the piggin' string especially tight around the killer's wrists.

"Red!" Cooper cried out. "That's way too tight. My hands'll rot and fall off."

Finished with tying him, Red grabbed him by an arm and spun him around to face him. "If it was up to me, I wouldn't be tying a piggin' string around your wrists, you little backshooter,

I'd be tying a rope around your neck." He gave Cooper a hard shove that drove him to the ground.

"I don't think Red likes you, Coop," Otis, who was sitting on the ground near where Cooper fell, said. "Why, it sounds like he'd like nothin' better than to stretch yore neck from the nearest cottonwood. He looked around at all the oak trees surrounding them. "Or maybe he'd settle for an oak."

"Shut up," Cooper said, his voice cold and emotionless.

Red finished tying the rest of the crew and looked back at Will. "Want I should go get the horses?"

"Good idea," Will said. "Check their saddles and saddlebags for guns before you go. Take as many of them with you as you can. Divide 'em between us. That'll even out the weight on the horses."

Cooper spoke up. "You can just leave mine for me, Red."

Will said, "Before you go, why don't you introduce these boys to me, Red. I'd like to know who I'm killin' if I have to."

Finn and Abel turned as white as blanched buffalo bones.

"The loudmouth," Red said, "is Otis Thatcher. You know Cooper." He pointed with his rifle barrel. "That's Levi Edward and Finn Peterson. The one with all the stringy peach fuzz on his face is Abel Rogers. He's the youngest and comes from right nice folks." Red turned back to Abel. "Why are you ridin' with this bunch, Abel? Yore pa taught you to know better."

"You leave my pa out of it," Abel snapped at Red. "He don't need to know nothing."

"Son," Will said, "not only your pa, but your ma's going to find out everything when I turn you over to the town marshal today."

Will watched what little facade Abel Rogers had been able to maintain crumble. The boy, who didn't look to be a day over sixteen, probably more like fifteen, turned even whiter. His eyes widened as he stared at Will. He started shaking his head. "No, sir, you can't tell my ma. It'd just about kill her. I'm the youngest of twelve, and all my brothers and sisters are decent folks. She just cain't find out."

Cooper cleared his throat and, in a mocking, falsetto voice, said, "Please, Mr. Lawman, sir, you cain't tell my mommy."

Heading toward the horses, Red, loaded down with guns, belts, and rifles, stopped. He turned, dropped the guns, and marched straight to Cooper, who sat staring up at him defiantly. He drew his Colt and dropped to his knees next to the prisoner.

"Red," Will said, "leave him be. He'll get what's coming to him."

"He talks too much," Red said, grabbed a handful of Cooper's hair, and rammed the muzzle of the Colt into the killer's left nostril. The sound of a cocking hammer accompanied Cooper's grunt of pain.

"Don't pull that trigger, Red," Will said. "I'd hate to have to shoot you while I still need your help."

The muzzle pressed deeper. Red's face was near the color of his hair, and his jaw muscles stood out like fists on his slim face. Finally he yanked the bloody muzzle of his Colt from Cooper's nose. Close behind the gun barrel came a gush of blood. Red stood and looked down at Cooper, who, in spite of the cascading blood and obvious pain, shot a chilling stare up at his assailant. Red bent over and wiped his gun barrel on Cooper's trouser leg, then shoved the revolver into its holster, and gathered up most of the weapons.

"You cut that pretty thin," Will said, keeping his eyes on the prisoner.

"I was mad," Red said.

"Don't get mad again. I need you calm and ready, not angry and flying off the handle. Cooper's going to Pueblo, and it'll be hard enough without you banging him up before we get on the trail."

Red started off, but halted at Will's call.

"Red."

"Yeah?"

"You understand me?"

"Yep, but I don't like it."

"I don't care if you like it or not. Don't let something like that happen again."

Red took a deep breath. "Alright, Marshal. I'm fine. I'll get the horses."

12

Day was waning, and Cookie was banging on his triangle, calling everyone to supper, when the seven riders rode into the yard of the Lazy Y. Most of the hands were crossing from the bunkhouse to the ranch house.

Cooper's vest, shirt, and trousers were covered with blood, and his nose was swollen twice its normal size. Will watched the hands stop, stare in astonishment, and then start walking toward the riders. Dusty and an older man led the group. When the horsemen pulled up at the barn, the front door of the ranch house opened, and Fran Young stepped out. When she saw Ambrose Cooper's bloody face and tied hands, she lifted her skirt, jumped down the stairs, and dashed toward them.

Will feared she was going to start reaching for Cooper at any moment. In a hard voice, he said, "Hold up, ma'am. That goes for the rest of you," he said to the cowhands. "Ambrose Cooper is wanted by federal authorities for attempted robbery of a bank, robbery of a stage, and the murder of U.S. Marshal Farley Osborne. I'm a deputy marshal, and he is under arrest."

The older cowhand stepped forward. "Red, what the blue blazes is going on here?"

Red pushed his hat back. "Art, it's a long story, but we're tired and hungry. I've found out a few things." He stopped and nodded toward Will. "Guess I should say Marshal Logan and me found out some things that are gonna surprise the lot of you."

Fran looked at Will. "You're a United States Marshal?"

"Deputy, ma'am. But yes, I am, and I'm sorry I had to mislead you. After you hear what I've got to say, I think you'll understand."

A frown replaced her surprise. She said, "Well, get down. You've got a lot of explaining to do."

"I reckon," Will said, then he spoke to his prisoners. "Get down, boys, and don't try anything."

Red had swung from his horse and stood with his rifle covering the prisoners as Will swung his leg over the saddle to step down.

During the transition, Ambrose Cooper said to Fran, "Please, Mrs. Young, don't listen to the lies they've made up. None of it is tr—"

When Cooper began to talk, Red rushed the man, and grabbing his leg, he lifted hard, thrusting him from the saddle. Cooper landed in the dirt at Fran Young's feet. Before he could get to his feet, Red was around the horse and kicked the young man so hard in the ribs the blow lifted him from the ground.

Will, right behind Red, with Toby on his heels, grabbed the big man by his arm and spun him around. "I told you to keep your head."

But Red had given in to rage. When Will grabbed his arm, he spun and swung his rifle, both hands on the barrel, aiming for Will's head. Expecting some such move, Will stepped into his attacker and, using the butt of the shotgun, buried it in Red's belly, driving the wind from the big redhead. Will stepped back to let his friend catch his wind.

Fran yelled, "Stop it! Stop it, I say. I want an explanation, and I want it now."

The cowhands stood watching, not knowing what to think or do. Art Ramsey, the returned foreman, stepped forward. "Red, you heard Mrs. Fran. Stop it. Pull yourself together, man. You don't want to be attacking a U.S. Marshal. Cool yourself down."

Red straightened up from Will's blow. Leaned way back and took a deep breath and nodded toward Cooper. "You wait until you hear what this useless excuse for a man did. Then you'll be with me." He looked at Will. "Marshal, I don't think you'll be taking Cooper from this ranch. Not alive anyway."

Fran stepped into the fray. "Red, I like you. But I will not have this kind of abuse of anyone on my ranch, nor this talk. You either calm down or draw your pay."

Red, stung by her statement, turned to look her directly in the eyes. He pointed at Cooper, who, favoring his left side, had stood, and was calmly brushing the dirt from his clothing. "You want to know who killed Mr. Young? That's him. That's the man who shot him. We heard him talking about it to the rest of this gang. How he ambushed him because he wanted you."

Will watched as Fran's hand flew to her mouth, and her green eyes, wide, stared in disbelief at the bloody boy whom she had spoken of only a few nights before. She had told how he sang so sweetly, so innocently of the plains and young love and tenderness.

"That's right." Red's voice was flint, brittle and hard, when he continued, "That sweet-voiced boy first shot your husband in the back and then stood over him and blew Mr. Young's brains out."

There was a general murmur from the cowhands. For the first time, Will saw something in Cooper's eyes beyond indifference. *It almost looks like anticipation,* he thought, *like he wants to die.*

The murmur grew louder, and as one, they started forward. Will took a step toward the advancing cowhands, earing both hammers back on the shotgun. "Dusty, Bliss, Tyrus, all you boys. You've been kind to me. I don't want to be forced to shoot any of you. But these fellas are my prisoners, and I am to see them to jail unharmed. The only way you'll get to Cooper or any of these men is through me. Maybe you'll get me, but some of you are going to be sucking your last wind. And I'll tell you this, if you kill a U.S. Marshal, you'll never be able to rest. They'll hound you, catch you, try you, and send you to the hangman. You think long and hard on that fact."

The murmuring had stopped. Art, the foreman, stepped alongside Will. "Boys, we're going to hear what happened, then we're going to let the marshal take his prisoners. We might even help him with 'em. But we'll have no lynching on the Lazy Y, not as long as I'm foreman. Now get on inside and eat your supper."

Cookie had been waiting. The instant Art finished speaking, he started clanging again on the supper triangle. "Git on in here and eat up. I ain't in the habit of waitin' on you cow nurses. Now get movin'."

Dusty and Bliss eased over to Will. Dusty said, "We can help. We can lock these fellers in the smokehouse until you're ready to leave. We'll make sure they get fed and taken care of. Course, we'll take care of the horses, too."

"Glad to do it," Bliss said.

"Thanks, boys."

"I'll help, too," Art said, "and Homer's dependable. Nobody stampedes him."

"Good," Will said, "I appreciate it. Red's worn out. He needs some rest. He's been a big help, but I think Cooper trying to talk to Fran pushed him over the edge."

Art nodded. "Take him inside. It'll help if he can fill his belly. Keep an eye on Fran. This is real hurtful for her. She really liked that boy and wanted to help him. He just misunderstood her interest."

Will nodded, handing Art his shotgun. "Be careful. Otis and Cooper are both bad characters. The rest of the bunch are mostly kids looking for excitement. By the way, I think this will solve your missing stock problem. We overheard them talking about rustling Lazy Y cattle."

Art nodded his head toward Abel Rogers. "This is gonna kill his family. That boy has some fine folks who've done real good by their kids. Guess there can always be a bad apple in the bunch."

Art took Will's shotgun and a handful of shells. "Go eat, and try to explain it to Fran and the boys. We'll take care of this end. Take Toby. Cookie'll fix him up a plate." Art reached a big hand for Cooper, grabbed his arm, and shoved him toward the smokehouse.

"Thanks," Will said. He watched as the foreman and other cowhands herded the gang across the yard toward the smokehouse, then turned for the kitchen, Toby at his heels. Walking to the ranch house, he patted the big white dog. "I can depend on you, boy." The tail wagged, and the long tongue hung from one side of his mouth. The dog followed him to the kitchen porch and lay down, his head toward the door and his nose working on the smells coming from the kitchen.

Fran had seated Red to her right, but was ignoring him. She motioned for Will to sit to her left. Red wouldn't meet his eyes. As he sat, he said to Cookie, "Toby's on the porch, if you've got any scraps you could spare."

"I'll whip something mighty good up for that white dog. Yes siree, I surely will." He fixed a big platter that Will could swear had steak on it, and took it out the door.

During the supper, the rest of the hands remained quiet, listening to Will explain what they had discovered. Will saw the pain in the woman's eyes as she battled to hold back the tears. *She thought this was all behind her,* he thought, *but now the scab's been ripped off, and the pain is like it just happened.* "Ma'am, this is in no way your fault. There are people like this Ambrose Cooper in the world, fortunately not many. I don't know what happened to him as a boy, but he's a man now, and a bad one. You couldn't know it by looking at him or listening either."

"Thank you," she said, "but if I had only listened to Art and the other cowhands."

Cookie spoke up. "Ma'am, you cain't go ablamin' yoreself. I liked him, too. Weren't nothin' better than cleanin' this kitchen and listenin' to you play that piano and that boy sing."

She shook her head, her blonde hair swaying with her movement. "It's so hard to believe."

"Those types of folks are always surprises to most people," Will said. "I'm sure there are folks in this town who would never believe he could do anything wrong."

"Yeah," Red said, "and one of them is Mott Cooper. He's been protecting that boy since he had him. Said his pa treated him something horrible. Mott rode down to El Paso and physically took the boy. I understand he threatened to kill the boy's pa if he ever came around. He must've believed Mott 'cause he's never showed up."

The kitchen door swung open, and Dusty stepped in. "Will, we've got 'em locked in the smokehouse, and all the horses are taken care of. Art said that if you'd like to grab some sleep, we'll ride with you in the morning to take them in to town."

Will nodded. "Thanks, Dusty. Let him know I'll be leaving early. We'll be dropping the other members of the gang at the town marshal's office. I'll head on for Colorado with Cooper. I'd like to get him out of the country before his uncle finds out about this."

Fran nodded. "Good idea. Like we were saying, Mott Cooper thinks highly of the boy. He's gotten him out of several small scrapes, but I'm sure he has no idea of his . . . more serious crimes." She took a deep breath and composed herself. "But he will definitely be after you. You should take several of our men with you to Colorado."

Will shook his head. "No, ma'am. You're already more involved than I wanted. I had planned to catch Cooper alone, truss him up, and have him back to Pueblo before his uncle had an inkling, but it doesn't appear that's going to happen. If you'll just let me have a couple of men to get this bunch to town, I'll be fine after that."

"I'll go," Red said.

Will looked over at the cowhand. "Nope, Red, I don't reckon so. You'll be better off staying here."

The cowhand's face turned red, and he looked up at Will. "I know I've flown off the handle a couple of times, but I promise you, right here in front of Mrs. Fran and the boys. It won't happen again. I swear it."

Will studied the big man. Over the years he had become a pretty good judge of men, and he knew Red was a good man, hotheaded, but a good man. *Can I trust you?* Will thought. *You've burned me twice. By any sense of good judgment, I should leave you behind.*

"I very seldom give a man a third chance, Red, and I may be crazy this time, but alright, you can go. Don't make me regret my decision."

"You won't. I promise you. I'll do exactly what you say. I'll be no trouble. I'll—"

"He said yes, you blamed idgit," Cookie shouted. "Now shut up and let my ears rest."

At that, the rest of the hands broke out in laughter. Even Fran's sad face showed a small smile.

"Ma'am," Will said, "I'd best be checking on the prisoners and then grabbing some shut-eye. I'm leaving early." He stood, picking up his hat. "I'd like to thank you for your hospitality and apologize for the deception."

She too stood and extended her hand. "No apology necessary. I should be thanking you for finding my husband's killer and ridding the country of him."

Will shook her hand, said, "Ma'am," and headed for the door, Red right behind him.

LIGHT from the ranch house and barn cast shadows across the ranch yard, men, and horses. Will checked the prisoners. In the chill of the morning, they huddled close to their horses, gathering what little warmth they could.

Will slid the shotgun and rifle into their respective scabbards and patted Buck on the neck. The buckskin stomped, ready to be on his way.

"Good morning," a female voice said behind him.

He turned to see Fran standing there holding a heavy tow sack. She held it out to him. "Cookie put together a few things to keep the wolf away."

"Thank you, ma'am," Will said. "Tell Cookie I said thanks."

She smiled, then grew serious. "May I speak to your prisoner?"

There was no doubt whom she meant.

"Yes, ma'am." With her, he walked to Cooper, checking the young man's lopsided face. It was possible, even in the dim light, to see the darkening around his nose and eyes. Almost the entire left side of his face had swollen more than twice its size. His left eye was barely open, but in the light, Will could see the malevolence issuing from both eyes. He watched Fran stride up to the young man.

In a firm, confident voice, she said, "Tell me why, Ambrose. You owe me that much."

She was almost as tall as the young killer, and she stood close, staring into those cold, vacant eyes.

All activity had stopped. The hands waited to hear what justification he had for killing someone is such a brutal way.

Ambrose gave her a small lopsided grin. "Because you never loved him. Why else would you invite me, a strange man, into your home when he was gone? I feel the same for you. When

Uncle Mott gets me loose from this bunch, I'll be back, and maybe you and me can go to New York like you talked about."

For a moment she was stunned by his reply. Then, surprising everyone, her right hand flashed, not open, but in a fist. She drove it into the already damaged and swollen nose. Cooper howled with pain, grabbed his face, and bent over, blood flowing from his nose for the second time.

"You ungrateful little pig," Fran spat. "I was willing to help you get to New York and take advantage of your God-given talent. How did you repay me? By killing the only man I've ever loved. Ambrose Cooper, I don't know if they are going to hang you or not, but take this fact with you. I never cared for you in any way other than as an adult helping a talented child, and if I ever see your face on this ranch again, I will personally put a .44-caliber bullet right through those melodious vocal cords of yours."

She turned to Will. "Thank you for catching him. Now please get this trash off my ranch." She turned, her back straight, and marched back to the house. She climbed the stairs to the wide porch and yanked the door open, disappearing inside.

Will watched Cooper closely as he recovered from the pain of the unexpected blow. The boy's astonished look disappeared, and in its place was a look of first despair and then hatred, his eyes tracking the lovely, determined woman across the yard and into the house.

"Mount up," Will said. There was the rattle and squeak of leather and metal as both men and boys swung into the saddle. Will turned to Art. "Let's move this bunch out. I want to be in front of the marshal's office at daylight."

Art nodded and said to his crew, "Let's go."

The cowhands spread out much like they would driving cattle, with Art taking the left swing and Bliss the right. Darcy took the left flank, with Homer at the right, and Will rode drag.

Otis Thatcher rode next to Cooper. He leaned over to say something, but before he could speak, Will said, "No talking.

We'll all be nice and quiet into town. All you fellas understand me?"

The five youngsters in the gang nodded their understanding. Thatcher looked back and grinned, while Cooper never moved other than the constant rocking in the saddle as the horses walked toward Las Vegas.

Toby trotted easily alongside Buck on Will's left side.

Red dropped back and said, "Town'll be up by the time we get there."

"Likely," Will said.

"Think there'll be trouble?"

"Not for the Lazy Y crew. As soon as we get there and drop off the five prisoners, I want all of you to hightail it back to the ranch."

Red bristled. "We ain't leavin' you by your lonesome. If Mott finds out, and he will, he'll come barreling into town like a steam locomotive. He'll have his whole crew. You won't stand a chance."

Will nodded. "So tell me, Red, what's going to happen to Fran when you and Art and these other boys get shot full of lead? How's she gonna run her ranch? Who's she gonna be able to trust?"

Red rode in silence while Will continued, "Something to think about, isn't it? I saw how she looked at you and how hurt you were when she spoke hard to you. I don't know if you two have a chance, but you danged sure don't if you get in a gunfight with Mott Cooper.

"I feel bad enough as it is, dragging the Lazy Y into this. But if I can get out of Las Vegas and make sure everyone understands it was me who came after Ambrose Cooper, just maybe there won't be a range war. Now get back up there and think on what I said."

Red thought on it for a moment, clucked, and bumped his horse. The animal trotted until it reached its station, and slowed to a walk. In the fading darkness, Will could see Red chewing on what he had said.

In the darkness, Buck walked slowly toward Las Vegas. A lone coyote, either an early riser or late hunter, yipped in the distance. Will rubbed his stubble of beard, hoping that after Mott Cooper heard what his nephew had done, there would be no range war between the Lazy Y and the C Bar.

13

S unrise caught them entering Las Vegas. Will pulled out his watch and checked it, seven minutes after six. Businesses should still be closed and most people at home. The town's streets were empty, but Will saw a man step out of the hotel, stop, look at the large group of riders, and rush back inside. Moments later the man was back with several others. They stood gaping as they rode by. Art tipped his hat and said, "Mornin', Mark."

One of the men nodded to him and started walking down the boardwalk alongside the riders. The other men followed. Art guided the riders to the marshal's office.

"Get down," Will ordered the prisoners. Nearing town, he had shucked out his shotgun, and rode with it resting easy across his saddle. A few moments passed before the marshal stepped from his office.

"Morning, Alton," Art said.

"Art, what is this?"

"Reckon you oughta ask Marshal Logan that question. We're just riding along as an escort."

Snead looked over the gang, and his eyes fell on Ambrose

Cooper. "Oh my goodness." He looked up at Will, who was still sitting Buck.

"What have you done to Ambrose? Mott's gonna be fit to be tied when he sees this. And why are you bringing all these boys here? I don't have anything on 'em. They're just local boys. They ain't never been a problem."

"They are now, Snead. They've admitted to rustling cattle from the Lazy Y, and Ambrose Cooper, besides the crimes of robbery and the murder of a U.S. Marshal, admitted to the brutal killing of Tyler Young."

"No," Snead said. "That can't be true."

"From his own mouth, bragging to his gang. Red heard him too."

Marshal Snead looked at Red. "He's speakin' gospel. Ambrose, here, bragged to all these fine upstanding citizens of yours about killing Mr. Young, standing over him and putting a bullet in the back of his head."

A crowd was starting to gather. Will said, "I think you'd better get these boys in your jail before some of those drunk cowhands drag themselves out of the saloons and hear about rustling and murder. You wouldn't want that to happen, would you, Marshal Snead?"

Snead shot Will a nasty look and opened the office door. "Bring 'em on in."

Will swung down, watching the prisoners troop into the jail. He was tying his horse when he heard running steps and a woman's desperate cry. "Abel, is that you, Abel?"

He looked over at the boy and watched as the young fella tried to hide behind Levi Edward. He could see tears in the boy's eyes.

"Abel?" the woman said, slowing as she approached the group of men. She was much like many of the frontier women, thin faced and sun-baked skin, but her bonnet, though obviously put on hurriedly, was clean and crisp, much like her skirt. Her face showed the years of strain and toil, but it was a kind face, with numerous laugh lines.

Shocked, her hand flashed to her mouth when she saw Cooper's bloody, swollen face. "Ambrose? You poor boy. What happened to you?"

The gang leader ignored her and trooped into the jail, but her son Abel couldn't. She saw him, and her hand flashed out, grabbing him by the collar and dragging him to the boardwalk. Her voice was quivering with anger. "Abel Rogers, what is the meaning of this? What is happening here? What's wrong with Ambrose?"

Will stepped forward and touched his hat brim. "Ma'am, I'm guessing you must be Mrs. Rogers, Abel's mother. I'm Deputy U.S. Marshal Will Logan, and your son is in a heap of trouble. Were you aware that he was riding with a gang led by Ambrose Cooper?"

Flustered, she looked from Will's face to the badge on his vest and then to Toby. "What's Toby doing here? I thought Mr. Fairburn had him?"

"Ma'am," Will said, "I asked you a question about your son."

"I'm sorry, what was your question?"

Will needed to get out of Las Vegas with Cooper, and he didn't need to delay. He knew word was probably on its way to Mott Cooper even as he stood here in the street talking to the kid's mother.

"Yes, ma'am, I asked you if you are aware that Abel is riding with Ambrose Cooper's gang?"

"Gang? Why, no, Marshal. They're no gang, just a bunch of boys having fun." She released her son and pulled at her collar. "Are you hot, Marshal? I'm very hot." She started to fan herself with her hand, but after fanning only twice, her eyes rolled to the back of her head, and she would have collapsed to the boardwalk if Will hadn't stepped forward and caught her.

"Mama!" Abel shouted and ran to her, grabbing her arm with his tied hands.

"Move aside, folks," Will commanded and gently stretched her out on the boardwalk. He looked around at the faces staring at him and said, "Get a doctor!"

One of the men spun around and raced back down the street. Abel had knelt down beside his ma and was holding her hand in his. "I'm sorry, Ma. I'm so sorry. I didn't mean to hurt you none at all. Please be all right. I'll never do anything wrong again. I promise. Please be all right." The last was said in a long wail as the doctor pushed through the crowd.

"Good gracious," he said, looking at Abel, covered in tears, and the woman lying on the boardwalk. He picked up her wrist and felt it. Waited a moment and moved his fingers, waiting. Finally he looked at Abel and said, "She's alive, boy, but just barely. Her pulse is weak and thready."

At that moment her eyes opened, and she turned her head to her son. She waited a moment, then said to the doctor, "Happened? Raise my arm . . . umm . . . Raise my arm. I can't."

He patted her cheek. You just relax, Mrs. Rogers. You're going to be fine." He looked in the crowd and spotted two big men. "Jacob, you and your brother take Mrs. Rogers to my office. I'll be right along."

The two men lifted her gently. The crowd parted, and the men carried her down the street.

"Is she going to be alright, Doctor?" Abel asked, through his sobs.

"Son, I'm afraid it's possible your ma has had an attack of apoplexy. I can't say how serious it is right now. She's able to talk, though her speech is a little broken. Hopefully there is no permanent damage. I'll have to give her a good check in order to find out for sure." The doctor looked at the boy's wrists tied together and at Will's badge. "The boy needs to be with his mother."

"The *boy*, Doc, is a cattle rustler," Will said.

"Marshal?"

"Logan."

"Marshal Logan, right now I don't give a good hoot what this boy has done. He needs to be with his mother, not for his sake but for hers. His being there could go a long way toward her coming out of this whole instead of crippled."

Will yanked out his knife and sliced the piggin' string from Abel's wrists. "You go take care of your ma, boy. But when she's better, I want you back here in this jail. You understand me?"

Abel's young, tear-streaked face turned up to the imposing man. "Yes, sir. I understand, and I promise I'll be back." He turned and dashed in the direction the men had taken his ma, but he had gone only a few steps when he slid to a stop. Turning, he said, "Thank you, Marshal Logan." Then he spun around and dashed for the doctor's office.

Will watched the boy race away, followed by the doctor, then turned to the marshal's office. Everyone was inside. Before he stepped through the door, he glanced at the horses. Toby was lying next to Buck, apparently sleeping through all of the excitement. Two horsemen were racing out of town in the direction of the ranches. *Probably headed out to tell Cooper,* he thought. *At least I have some time to get the boy out of town.*

The marshal was behind his desk, and all of the prisoners were in the jail except for Ambrose Cooper, who leaned against the jail bars.

"Are you gonna tell me what's going on, Logan?" Marshal Snead asked.

"I'll make it quick, Snead. Red and I caught this bunch and overheard their conversation. Cooper here was passing out money and bragging on how he had killed Marshal Osborne. Then his gang laughed and mentioned he'd killed Tyler Young because he was sweet on Fran Young. He got riled, and that was when we stepped in. They also talked about rustling cattle from the Lazy Y."

He pulled several papers from his vest pocket and spread them out on the marshal's desk. "Red, I need you to sign these."

"What's that?" Red asked.

"I wrote out statements last night before hitting the sack. These two papers state what was said by the gang. I'm leaving one. It'll have my signature and yours. The other one I'm taking with me. Sign 'em both."

Red stepped forward, took the pen from the marshal's desk, and signed the two papers. He blew on them for a second to dry the ink, and stepped back.

Leaving the papers open to allow the signatures to completely dry, Will picked up one and handed it to Marshal Snead. "This is a statement signed by me as a deputy United States Marshal and Red, Bob Fleming, as to what we overheard. Also, Ambrose Cooper, just this morning, admitted to Mrs. Young that he killed her husband. He said he did it because he loved her."

The marshal stood with a pursed mouth, his head shaking as he stared at Cooper. "I cannot believe it. This is crazy."

At the word crazy, Cooper straightened up and glared at the town marshal. "It ain't crazy, Snead. She loves me and always will."

The Lazy Y cowhands started for Cooper. Before Will could stop them, Art Ramsey's voice reverberated through the jail. "Hold up! Leave him alone, dang it! Get yourselves out to your horses, and let's head back to the ranch."

The angry cowhands stared at Cooper. Will could see they'd like nothing better than to hang the man and be done with him. "Do what your foreman says, boys," Will said. "I'll get him back to Colorado, and he'll get what's coming to him."

Darcy nodded. "Come on, boys. Let's head back to the ranch. There's plenty of work to do there." He turned to Will. "Good luck, Marshal. You're gonna need it."

Red was one of the few cowhands who had not charged toward Cooper. He was watching Will. After Darcy's statement, he said, "I'd feel better if I were going with you, but you sure made a good point. I reckon I'll stay, but luck with you."

Will nodded to Darcy and Red. "Thanks, boys. I appreciate your help."

With that the cowhands trooped out to their horses, mounted, and galloped out of town, leaving a thick dust cloud hanging.

"Marshal," Will said, "it's time I hit the road. I'll be taking Cooper, but you've got the rest. There's statements here of their rustling, but the only one to watch out for is Thatcher. I'm thinking he's turning into a hard case. A little time in the lockup probably wouldn't do him any harm at all, but it's up to you what you do."

Snead looked first at Will and then at Cooper. "You'll never make it back to Pueblo. Mott'll leave your carcass for the buzzards long before you get to Colorado."

Will's big hand grasped Cooper's arm, and he gave him a hard shove toward the door. "Hope you're wrong." To Cooper he said, "Get out there and climb on your horse. We're heading out."

Cooper stumbled through the open door, caught himself on the hitching rail, straightened, and said, "I ain't goin' nowhere, Mr. Marshal. My uncle'll be in town shortly with all of our hands. They'll plant you in the ground."

Will stepped up to the younger man, poked him in the belly with the muzzle of the shotgun, and said, his voice calm and relaxed, "Boy, now's the time to listen to me when I speak, and do what I say. My job is to get you back to Colorado. The judge said to bring you back alive *if I could*. Now whether or not I can is gonna depend on you. Get on your horse."

Cooper watched the big man for a second longer, then swung under the hitching rail, unhitched his horse, and mounted.

"Come on, Toby," Will said to the dog. He climbed into the saddle, dropped the shotgun into its scabbard, and said to Cooper, "Keep it down to a trot. Let's go." The two of them trotted north out of town. Before they dropped over the first hill, Will looked back, still no dust. *Good,* he thought, *I'd like to get at least a few miles north of Las Vegas before we take to the hills.*

They continued to ride northeast, following the road. Cooper kept looking back. Will could see the hopeful look on the man's face. It was obvious he expected to see the dust of his uncle's racing horses any minute.

Reaching the Mora River crossing, they stopped to water the horses.

"I need a drink," Cooper said.

"You've got a canteen. Use it."

Cooper gave him a look that would fry ants, untied his canteen, and took a drink.

Toby lay down in the shallow river, allowing the water to rush around him, cooling his feet and belly. He lapped water as it flowed by.

"Don't drink too much, Toby. We might be having to make a run for it before long."

The dog stopped drinking and looked up at Will, then stood and shook. Water flew everywhere, a few drops reaching Will.

"Ride upriver, and stay in the water."

Cooper's head snapped around to Will. "Pueblo ain't thisaway. It's up the road."

"Keep your horse in the rocky part of the river bottom. Now, get moving."

Reluctantly Cooper started his horse forward. He took a couple of anxious looks back down the road they were leaving, before the steep banks of the river blocked it from sight.

They continued to ride northwest up the river. After staying in the river for over a mile, Will said, "All right, there's a trail up the bank off to the right. Take it, but stop just before we top out."

Cooper did as he was told, and halted his horse short of the top. Will rode up beside him, removed his hat, and eased Buck forward. He stopped the horse when his eyes cleared the bank. He was looking at pine trees in the distance and sagebrush across the basin between them and the trees. A small herd of antelope fed a short distance from them.

Heads popped up throughout the herd, and the fleet animals stared at Will. When he had made sure the countryside was clear of Mott Cooper or his men, he motioned his prisoner forward, following up and out onto the prairie.

"Head toward the thickest pines," he said, pointing. "Straight yonder."

Cooper did as he was told. "It don't matter what you do. Uncle Coop has an Apache tracker who could follow you through a dust storm. You ain't gonna get away."

"Less talking, more moving." With his last words, Will swung his reins across the rump of Cooper's horse. The animal leaped forward, and they loped across the sage-covered basin. Reaching the trees, they rode in deep enough to be out of sight from anyone on the flat, but were still able to view anyone approaching.

"Get down," Will ordered.

Cooper sat his horse and said, "Ain't you ever gonna untie my hands? I cain't hardly feel 'em."

Will pulled his binoculars from his saddlebags and scoured the valley for movement. Evening was approaching. If Mott Cooper was going to find them today, it would have to be soon. Darkness was approaching quickly. It would be impossible for any tracker to follow their tracks without light. Even if the Apache figured out they were going up the Mora, he'd have to guess where they came out. Guessing wasn't usually in their playbook without enough information, so odds were the pursuers would camp for the night.

He knew Mott Cooper would be anxious to retrieve his nephew. From everything he had heard about the man, he also knew that he would first want to make a peaceful attempt. The man was law abiding but, like many powerful men, would cross the line where blood was concerned.

Seeing nothing, he returned the glasses to the saddlebags and looked at Cooper, who still sat his saddle. "Cooper, get down, and go sit by the big pine." He nodded toward a tall ponderosa pine.

When the young fella just stared at him, he rode close, kicked his boot out of the stirrup and kicked Cooper. The boot caught him on his bicep, just below his shoulder, and knocked him rolling to the ground. Will said to Toby, "Watch him, boy," and picked up the reins to Cooper's horse.

The big white dog trotted nearer to Cooper, and a low rumble came from deep within his throat.

Cooper jumped to his feet and backed away from the dog. "He ain't gonna attack me, is he?"

"You know as much about that as I do. He and I are just getting acquainted. Were I you, though, I'd be mighty careful."

Cooper backed to the tree Will had indicated and dropped to the ground, his eyes locked on the dog. As the man moved toward the tree, the dog moved forward, keeping the same distance between them. When Cooper sat down, Toby watched him for a moment, then dropped to his haunches, his eyes never leaving the man.

Will swung down, pleased with Toby's response to his order. *Wish I knew all his commands,* Will thought. *He just might help me get some sleep.*

14

Will was up well before daylight. He had tied Cooper to the big pine and had watched his prisoner and Toby through the night. He had gotten no sleep, as he'd used this first night to test Toby. He had told the dog to watch Cooper and then to guard him and finally had given the single command *guard*. Toby seemed to understand the last command, and while Will faked sleep, watching the dog and his prisoner, the dog stayed on watch.

Early, Will dug through his saddlebags and tossed Toby some jerky. He gobbled it down and gazed at Will. "If you want anything else, you'll have to get it yourself. Go!"

Toby disappeared into the darkness. Only a short time passed before he returned with a rabbit, which he brought straight to Will. The big man took the rabbit and hefted it. "I'd love to cook it, boy, but no fire this morning." He tossed it back to the dog and said, "You eat it."

Without hesitation, Toby went to work.

"I could eat part of that rabbit," Cooper said from his tree.

"You want it raw?"

"No, but you could cook it."

"Now wouldn't that be smart," Will said. "I might as well fire off a couple of shots, along with the fire to help your uncle find us."

"Don't matter. He's gonna find us anyway, and when he does, he's gonna kill you."

"Maybe." Will walked over to where Cooper was tied. "I'm going to release you. Don't try to make a run for it. Toby will catch you before you've gone ten steps."

Cooper eyed the dog. "I ain't afraid of no dog."

"In that case, take off anytime you want." Will untied him. "Go take care of your business, and we'll be on our way."

Cooper disappeared into the darkness. "Why're you doing this?" he called, deep in the forest.

"You know why. You killed a man. A U.S. Marshal."

"Did you know him?"

"No."

"If you didn't know him, why are you risking your life for him?"

The simple answer, Will thought, *is it's my job. But is that the only reason?* He thought on the question until Cooper came out of the darkness. "Sit down," he said, and tossed his prisoner some of the cold biscuits and bacon Cookie had stuffed in the sack.

This boy, Will continued to think as he chewed on the dry biscuit, *asks a good question. I guess the answer is that us Logans have been taught what's wrong and right since we were pups. Ma and Pa were taught the same way. Uncle Floyd rides miles out of his way to help folks in need. I suppose it's in our blood whether we're wearing a badge or not.*

"Young fella, I'm sorry you have to ask, but I'll tell you anyway." He stopped to take a bite of bacon, chewed the tasty pork, swallowed, and said, "You've taken men's lives. For that, you'll be tried before a court of law and receive a verdict. It'll either be innocent or guilty. If they find you guilty, then they'll have to set a sentence. That'll also be up to the jury."

"Humph. I didn't ask for a lecture. I just asked why you're doing this."

"Finish eating. We've got to be moving."

Will stood and walked to where Toby was lying. The dog was licking his paws, removing the last taste of rabbit. Toby raised his head and allowed Will to scratch him behind the ears. "Good boy." Will stopped, pointed at Cooper, and said, "Guard."

Toby jumped up, trotted closer to Cooper, and sat, eyes locked on the man. Will watched the scene for a moment and, confident his prisoner was well guarded, began saddling the horses. Once they were ready, he led them back to the camp, picked up Cookie's sack, which was much lighter now, tied it on behind his saddle, and said, "Mount up."

"Where we goin'?" Cooper said, swinging into the saddle.

"Thataway." Will waved his finger to the northwest, deeper into the trees and diagonally up the mountains.

Cooper looked at him like he was crazy, then shrugged and started his horse forward, with Will following.

Light was breaking as the sagebrush disappeared from view, hidden from sight by the thick trunks of the ponderosa pines. They rode silently on, the horses' hooves making little sound in the pine needles except occasionally when a shoe struck an exposed rock.

The sun rose slowly, persuading the chill to melt away into a pleasant morning. A small herd of mule deer stopped their browsing and watched the two riders until determining they were no danger.

Will had been enjoying the silence of the mountains. A breeze moaned softly in the aspen tops, causing the bright green leaves to flash in the morning sun. They rode down a steep slope into a narrow valley. The cool smell of the nearby timber filled his being and sharpened his understanding of why his uncle Floyd loved the mountains so.

"What's this?" Cooper asked sharply as they came to the edge of a shallow but fast-moving creek.

"Figured you'd know this country," Will said, allowing the horses to drink. Toby had disappeared a while earlier. Now, he came loping down the opposite side of the valley, past a thick grove of aspen standing as sentinels on the mountainside. Will watched him for a moment, then stepped down from his horse. "Get down and fill your canteen."

He watched as Cooper jumped from the saddle, canteen in hand, and lay flat on the ground, drinking. He shook his head and kneeled, first filling his canteen and then scooping water with his hand until his thirst was slaked. He stood, stretched, and looked down the pass for any movement—nothing. He knew they were back there. It was only a matter of time until they caught up with them.

"Mount up."

"Marshal Logan, we've been in the saddle all morning. My rear's tired. Give me a minute to stretch."

Will looked at the complaining youth. "How old are you, Cooper?"

Ambrose Cooper had been holding his saddle while he squatted and stretched. He straightened, threw Will a defensive look, and said, "Twenty-one, why?"

"Just wondered. Now, get on that horse, and move out. Stay on this side and follow the creek."

"How long?"

"Till I say different."

The two continued along the creek through a narrow valley, mountains to each side of them. The creek made a hard right turn and hugged the western side of a steep slope. Will breathed a sigh of relief and thought, *Just like Uncle Floyd described. This has to be Coyote Creek. I guess he must have traveled all over these mountains.* He remembered his uncle Floyd describing these New Mexico mountains and valleys. He had described this one in detail, a long narrow valley that continued for miles, with the creek meandering from one side to the other.

"Break into a lope," Will ordered.

Cooper slapped his horse in the sides with his spurs, and the animal began an easy lope. Buck took up a steady lope, smoothly staying with Cooper's horse. Toby, with his long gait, ran alongside the horses, his white fur flowing in the wind.

They held the pace for about two miles, then Will slowed, Cooper following. The creek had swung to the west side of the narrow valley, and now the valley was turning northwest. Will looked up at the steep western slope. There was a ledge about fifty feet above the valley floor. The bend in the mountains provided an excellent spot to hide them from sight should any riders be following. He took a piggin' string and said, "Hold out your hands."

Cooper looked at the big marshal and slowly extended his hands. Will tied them and said, "Get down."

Will pulled his field glasses from his saddlebags and hung them around his neck. Next he slipped his rifle from the scabbard and dismounted, looping his reins around a stand of sage.

He flipped the reins from Cooper's horse around the sage as he had with Buck. He then turned and pointed to a spot away from the horses. "Sit there." Then, taking his rope, he looped it around his prisoner's body and pulled it tight.

"Hey, what are you doing?"

"I don't much like the idea of you riding off with the horses while I'm gone. Toby should stop you, but I don't want to take a chance. Slide your back up against those two stands of sage."

Cooper slid against the sagebrush, and Will ran the rope around the base of the two. Then he secured it to Cooper, testing the strength. The brush gave some, but it would hold him long enough for Will to get to the ledge, examine their back trail, and return.

"Remember, I'll have you in sight the whole time I'm gone, and I don't have to take you in alive."

Cooper, lips drawn tight, stared back up at Will. "You've told me already. Where are you going?"

Will said, "Guard," to Toby, and the dog took his position, eyes glued on Cooper. Taking one last look at his prisoner, Will started up the steep slope, grasping at the thick red limbs of the manzanita as he climbed. Only a few minutes passed before he neared the ledge. Easing onto the flat rock, he crawled along the side where the ledge joined the mountain, until he could see down the valley.

Laying his rifle carefully on the rock outcropping, he glanced down at his prisoner, who was remaining completely still under the watchful eye of Toby. Will nodded in satisfaction, checked the sun's position, a precaution against reflection, and raised the field glasses to his eyes. He examined their trail where they had come out of the branch and turned up the valley. He was just about to let out a sigh of relief when a man, on foot, trotted into view. He was following their trail. The man stopped where the creek turned north up the valley, knelt and examined the ground. Will knew he was checking their tracks. He waited.

The man stood and stared up the valley toward the ridge Will was on. He felt the man's eyes, but knew it was impossible for him to see his form snug in the brush on the ledge. Still, he could swear the man was looking straight at him.

He was definitely Indian and probably the Apache Cooper had been talking about. Will watched and waited, not daring to move. The Indian stood for a long moment, then turned, trotting out of sight, and disappeared in the direction he had come. Will waited for a count of ten to make sure the Apache was completely out of sight, crawled back to the edge, dropped over, and made his way carefully and quickly down the mountainside.

He untied the rope from around the sage and removed the loop from Cooper's body. "Get on your horse."

"I'm comfortable, Marshal. Why can't we rest here for a while?"

Will reached down and grabbed Cooper by the arm and yanked him to his feet, shoving him toward his horse. "Get on your horse."

Cooper stared at Will. "You've seen something, haven't you. They're gettin' close." He opened his mouth to let out a yell, and Will slapped him hard across his still sore left cheek.

Cooper grabbed his face, his eyes livid with hate. "Uncle Mott'll kill you for that."

"Maybe, but not before you get on your horse."

He shoved his prisoner toward the animal and waited until Cooper reluctantly climbed aboard. Toby stood tall, his big body tense and ready for action, as if he sensed something was amiss.

Will's foot hit his left stirrup, and he clucked to Buck as his right leg was going over the horse's back. They started moving up the creek. They traveled for about a hundred yards, until Will found the type of ground he was looking for. They were riding through thick sagebrush, which made it difficult to see their tracks. The ground was cut to pieces by feeding buffalo.

"This way," Will said, and rode Buck into the creek, turning back in the direction they had come. He made sure Cooper followed. They continued until they reached the rocky stream that joined the creek beneath the ledge where Will had spotted the Apache. The stream came in almost perpendicular to the creek from near due west.

Will wished he had forced Cooper ahead of him, but there was no time. He had no idea how close Mott Cooper was following behind the Apache. If they were close, Mott's crew could be up with them in ten minutes or less. They had to get out of sight, but they couldn't ride faster because it would muddy the stream they were in and be a dead giveaway they had turned off. He forced himself to keep it slow.

The stream snaked its way west, climbing into the narrow cut, which would take them to another valley paralleling the one they had been in. Finally, it turned enough for them to be out of sight of any riders in the valley behind them. "Come on," Will said, and rode out of the stream.

"That won't fool Uncle Mott's Apache."

"I don't need it to fool him long, just delay him. Get going, and stay alongside this stream until I tell you different. Run!"

The boy slammed the spurs to the horse, and Will, leaning forward in his saddle, said, "Get 'em, Buck. Come on, Toby."

It's just like Floyd described, Will thought as they galloped through the cut. Big pines lifted to each side of the narrow pass. *At its widest point, it can't be more than fifty yards. If it is the right cut-through, it should make a turn back to the left, opening into another valley.*

Sure enough, they galloped around a bend that swung left, turning back west, and a larger valley opened in front of them. Will pulled up next to Cooper, leaned over to him and said, "Turn north."

The two of them turned into the big valley and headed north. After traveling for less than a mile, Will said, "Slow down." He brought Buck to a walk, with Cooper right alongside. The big buckskin's sides were heaving along with Cooper's horse. Both horses were mountain horses, used to the altitude, but the past two days had been hard on them.

Will glanced down at Toby. The big white dog had kept up with the horses. His tongue was out, and he was panting but not nearly as hard as the horses. Will said, "Get down. We'll walk them a ways." He swung down, watching his prisoner to make sure he did the same. The two of them walked up the valley, leading their horses. The animals needed rest, but that wasn't likely to happen any time soon. Fortunately, water was plentiful in this valley.

Coming to a small stream, Will stopped, motioning for Cooper to do the same. They watered the horses while Toby waded into the middle of the stream and plopped down in it. Will watched several trout swim near the dog, slurping at his long, white, swirling hairs.

"Let's move," Will said, swinging back into the saddle.

Cooper gave a low moan. "Ain't you figgered out that they're gonna catch us? You're just wearing us and the horses out for nothing."

"Move it, Cooper."

Reluctantly, Ambrose Cooper stepped back into the saddle.

They continued north. The valley gradually narrowed, and if he had listened to his uncle correctly, Coyote Creek should be swinging over into this valley up ahead. If the Apache continued up Coyote Creek, it was possible Mott Cooper's party could cut them off where the valleys intersected. There was the possibility that Cooper's uncle would ambush them if he had the chance.

Will rode closer to his prisoner. Cooper eyed him with suspicion. "Whatcha doin'?"

"Stop your horse and hold still." Will, using a couple of piggin' strings, rigged a small harness that hung over Cooper's neck, with a loop at his chest. Will slipped Cooper's bandanna up from his neck and into his mouth, gagging him. Then reached for his shotgun.

Cooper's eyes grew large, and he jerked his head back. "Be still. I'm not gonna hurt you." Then he took the shells from the shotgun and hung the shotgun in the makeshift harness. He had to use an additional string and make several adjustments, but he finally had the triggers tied down. With the triggers tied back, nothing would stop the hammers dropping except his thumb. Should he be shot, the hammers would fall. It would be terrifying for Mott Cooper. He eared both hammers back and tried holding them back with his thumb. He lowered them to let his thumb rest as they continued to ride forward.

Cooper shook his head and tried to get loose, but Will drew his .44-caliber Remington and poked Cooper in the ribs with the muzzle. "Don't try to alert anyone, Ambrose. As you can see, the shotgun is empty, so you don't have to worry about getting your head blown off. On the other hand, if you try to give this scheme away, I might have to shoot you with my .44. So was I you, I'd be nice and quiet." Will stared at the gagged man. "Nod your head if you understand me."

Cooper nodded several times, rapidly.

"Good. Like I've told you before, I don't want to have to hurt you. But I have no qualms about it if you force me. Understood?"

Again Cooper nodded.

"Good. They may not even be there, but if I were your uncle, that's where I'd wait."

They continued forward. For now, it was just a matter of the horses, Will and Cooper all getting used to riding so close, with Will's hand on the shotgun, the muzzle under the man's chin. All the players finally got their rhythm down, and slowly the horses walked toward the possible ambush.

The horses walked closer, slowly narrowing the distance to the junction. *It's all right with me if I'm wrong,* Will thought. *I'd just as soon get this fella and me back to Pueblo in one piece.*

They were nearing the convergence of the two valleys when three horsemen rode out of the mouth and turned toward them. Will could see one of them was the Apache who had been tracking him. They were carrying a makeshift white flag—a white handkerchief tied on the end of a Winchester's barrel.

"Ummm-ummm," Cooper said.

"Is that your uncle?" Will asked.

"Umm," Cooper said, and nodded.

"Good, you stay nice and quiet and relaxed. If you do that, we'll be through this in one piece. If not? Well, we'll just have to see."

Cooper turned his head carefully, his chin just above the muzzle of the shotgun, looked at Will, fear in his eyes, and nodded.

"Good. Now stay quiet."

The two men walked their horses toward the advancing trio. Toby trotted alongside Buck, his eyes on the three men.

At twenty feet the three pulled up. Will did the same and eared the hammers back. Mott Cooper was easy to pick out from Snead's description. A big, easygoing man. Clean shaven, riding an equally big bay. The big man's face showed concern, anger, and fear when he saw the shotgun's hammers pulled back. His eyes locked on the muzzle of the shotgun and his nephew's bruised face. Then they dropped to the tied-back triggers.

15

"You'd be Will Logan," Cooper said, nodding at the badge on Will's vest.

"Yep, I'm guessing you're Mott Cooper?"

Cooper gave a sharp nod, his eyes still fixed on the shotgun muzzle beneath his nephew's chin. "Why the blazes do you have my nephew trussed up in that contraption? If you or your horse slipped, or your thumb came off either of those hammers, you'd blow his head off."

"That's what I was just explaining to your nephew. I'm glad you understand the situation, Mr. Cooper. If the fella you sent up that ridge yonder"—Will nodded to the ridgeline to his right, near where Cooper and his men had come into view and where he had seen the glint of a rifle—"gets an itchy trigger finger, it probably wouldn't be too good for your nephew."

Mott Cooper swore. "He was just insurance if you started shootin'." He stood in the saddle, turned and waved his hat toward the ridgeline. Moments later a man stood and waved back.

"Good," Will said. "Now you need to understand—"

"No," Mott interrupted, "*you* need to understand. I'm here for my boy. You've done good to get this far. That was mighty smart leaving the road and trying to cut through these mountains, but Kuruk could track you in the dark. He's a master of these mountains." He nodded to the Apache.

"For him to be able to track in the dark," Will said, "it sure took you gents a long time to catch us."

Mott frowned. "That's not the point. The point is, I'm taking my nephew."

"As I was saying," Will said, "*you* need to understand that your nephew is under arrest for robbery and murder. I've been ordered to return him for trial if possible. If not, then I'll return his body, but one way or the other I'm taking him in, either riding or lying across his saddle."

Mott Cooper's face changed color as Will talked. First, at the mention of murder, his face went white, but when Will mentioned taking the young man in over his saddle, his face darkened, and anger flashed in the man's eyes.

"Ambrose has never killed anyone, ever. I don't know where you get your information, Marshal, but you're badly mistaken."

Will moved the shotgun slightly to relieve the strain on his thumb. At the movement Mott and his ranch hand jerked. The Apache, Kuruk, sat motionless, his expression never changing.

"Be careful, man!" Mott exclaimed. "You could kill him."

"I have to admit, my hand is getting tired. You fellas should ride back the way you came 'cause I'm not moving this shotgun until you're gone." He nodded toward the man on the ridge. "And that includes him."

Mott turned and waved. Moments later they could see the cowhand begin making his way down the mountain ridge.

Will, holding eye contact with Mott, continued, "If you think this young fella has never killed anyone, then you're sorely mistaken. I heard him admit to killing both U.S. Marshal Farley Osborne and the Lazy Y owner, Tyler Young, and I suspect he killed the stranger found by the spring."

Mott Cooper's mouth opened in surprise. He closed it and stared at his nephew. "It wasn't you, Ambrose, was it?"

The cold-eyed boy looked straight at his uncle and shook his head.

"See," Mott said, "he didn't do it."

Will flexed his left hand again. "I heard him brag about it when the only people he thought were anywhere near was his gang. I'm thinking you don't really know your nephew."

Mott's eyes had jumped back to Will's hand when he flexed it. With his eyes on the shotgun, he said, "I know my nephew, and he wouldn't lie to me."

Will shook his head. "We can argue about this all you want, but when my hand gets so tired I can no longer hold these hammers back, all the argument in the world won't help your nephew. You need to pull your men out and go home. I want you out of my sight."

"Marshal, you can't kill my nephew. He's all I've got left in this world. His pa was no good. He beat the boy something fierce. Ambrose needs a chance in life. This isn't the way."

"I'm thinking he's already had more chances than he deserves. Listen to me, Cooper. My thumb is starting to cramp. It could slip anytime, and that would be the end of your nephew. It's time for you to cut bait. Get out of here. I don't want to see you anywhere near me. I can't hold these hammers back much longer."

Mott looked at the hammers and Will's thumb. The tendons in the lawman's hand were standing like stiff rope just beneath the surface of his skin. It was obvious to anyone his hand was tired. Will could see the man make up his mind.

"This ain't over, Marshal." He looked at Ambrose, whose eyes were wide, and his head was shaking so hard his hat almost flew off. Worry filled Mott Cooper's eyes. "Don't you worry, Ambrose. I'll get you out of this, just not right now."

Will watched Mott Cooper. *Here's a man I could like,* he

thought. *He's tough, and he loves his nephew. Only his nephew is pure bad, and he'll never believe it.*

The Apache had been eyeing Will and the shotgun. He leaned to the uncle and said something too low for Will to understand.

Mott leaned forward in the saddle, staring at the shotgun. "Kuruk says the shotgun's not loaded."

Will knew his situation had just gotten worse. He could feel Ambrose start to nod, and shoved the muzzle deep into the boy's throat, causing him to gag.

"He's choking," Mott gasped. "Get that shotgun out of his throat."

"I told you to pull out," Will said. "I know you're going to kill me, but this murderer won't get loose. You'll have his brains all over you. Then you'll know if the shotgun is loaded or not."

"All right, don't hurt him. We're leaving, but you'll never make it out of these mountains."

"Maybe so," Will said.

"Let's go," Mott said, and the three men yanked their horses around.

In their turn, Will caught the rapid movement of the Apache's rifle, the barrel dropping, lining up with his chest, and he threw himself to the right. The reins jerked as he attempted to pitch his body out of the path of the bullet. Buck responded by throwing his head up, right into the path of the bullet. It struck the horse in the forehead, killing him instantly.

Ambrose slammed his spurs into his horse and leaped past the shocked Mott Cooper. The shotgun jerked from Will's hand and bounced harmlessly in its harness around the young killer's neck.

Will, having used all of his leverage to clear the path of the bullet, had little left to throw himself farther, when Buck fell, landing on his right leg and trapping his leg and revolver between the horse and the ground. Toby had jumped out of the way and stood near Will, between him and the riders, a low growl issuing from his throat.

Mott Cooper had ripped the gag from Ambrose's mouth. "Give me a gun," the boy demanded. "I'm gonna kill him."

"Shut up," his uncle said. "You'll kill no one." He untied the boy's hands. Then untied the shotgun.

The Apache walked his horse near Will and sat looking down at him. Will couldn't get his rifle or his revolver out from under Buck. *What a turn,* he thought. *I love you, Deborah.* Realizing it was useless to attempt to get a weapon in play from his position, he relaxed and spoke to the big white dog. "Toby, go." The dog stared at him. "Go!" The dog spun and dashed for the timber.

"Don't let that dog get away," Ambrose screamed. He grabbed a rifle from the other rider, threw it up and fired, but Toby was racing in the midst of the sagebrush and manzanita, cutting back and forth toward the timberline, and the bullet missed. Before he could fire again, his uncle knocked the rifle up.

"Leave the dog alone."

Ambrose stared at his uncle with crazed eyes, gripping the rifle so tight his knuckles were white. Finally, he lowered the muzzle. .

Mott said, "Give me the rifle."

Time clicked by as Ambrose gripped the rifle, then reluctantly handed it over to his uncle. Mott rode forward to where the Apache watched Will, pulling up alongside the Indian. He turned slightly and tossed the shotgun in the sage. "When you get loose, you can get it then."

"You're making a big mistake, Cooper," Will said. "That boy's a killer. He's already killed at least two, maybe three men, and he'll do it again. He likes it. From here on, the blood's on you."

Mott shook his head. "Ambrose would never kill anyone, Marshal, 'ceptin' it was self-defense. Have you ever heard him sing? He sings like an angel."

Will tried to move his leg under Buck, but the weight held

him like a vise. "I'm not getting out from under here. It's your play."

Ambrose placed both hands on the saddle horn and looked across the valley. "Mighty pretty country, not a bad place for anyone to die, but I've never killed a lawman. I don't reckon to start now." He stopped and turned to Kuruk. "How'd you know the shotgun was empty?"

"Boy not scared. Mad, angry, not scared. He be much scared if shotgun loaded."

Mott shook his head. "That's not much to go on. You could have gotten him killed. The marshal sure had me convinced."

Kuruk shook his head once. "Me know boy. He not scared. Gun not loaded."

Mott looked down at Will. "Sorry about your horse. He looks like a mighty fine one."

"He was."

"Like I said, I never killed a lawman, and I'm not starting now. When you get out from under your horse, don't come back to the C Bar. If you do, I'll have to kill you. I don't have a family. I built my ranch for this boy. I'm not letting you take him."

"Then you'd better get ready," Will said, squirming slightly to try to relieve the pressure on his leg. "'Cause if it isn't me, it'll be another marshal, and then it'll be the army. You'll lose everything. No matter how much you want this to be a lie, it isn't. Ambrose Cooper is a killer, and he's wanted by the law. If you think I'm wrong, ask Fran Young what he said to her."

At the mention of Fran, Ambrose pushed his horse forward. "Please, Uncle Mott, you've got to kill him. You can't believe a word he says, but he'll never stop. Give me a gun, and I'll do it."

"No, let's go home." Without another word, he turned his horse and headed for the other riders.

The Apache hung back for just a moment, smiled, exposing strong teeth, and dragged his thumb across his throat in a cutting action, then turned and galloped after them.

Will dropped back to the ground and patted the dead horse's neck. "Buck, I'm mighty sorry, ole hoss. You saved my life, and you sure didn't deserve to die for it. You've been a fine friend." After trying to relax his back and leg, the pressure of the revolver against his thigh was becoming excruciating. The twist he had been in when Buck fell put the hammer in such a position it was digging into his leg. He knew Buck weighed at least a thousand pounds, maybe more, and it felt like all of that weight was on his leg.

Will examined his situation. He was on his side with his leg trapped under a thousand pounds of horseflesh, and was beginning to lose the feeling in his foot. The hammer of the Remington was digging into his thigh, and the haft of his knife was hurting his hip.

The thought hit him. *My knife, if I can get it out, maybe I can dig my leg from beneath Buck. At least enough to pull out from under him.* He reached across with his left arm and pushed up from the ground while twisting his right arm under and behind him. His fingers could just reach the butt.

His left bicep bulged against his shirtsleeve as he strained to lift higher. As his body thrust up, his legs were pressed deeper into the dirt. The Remington's hammer dug deeper in his leg, sending sharp jolts of pain through his thigh, but he persisted. Managing to get a thumb and forefinger around the butt, he pulled. The knife moved a quarter of an inch and stopped. The leather safety string he had over one edge of the turned-up guard to keep it from falling out of the scabbard was working. Only, this was not the time he needed it to work. He collapsed on the earth.

Maybe, he thought, *I can get to my saddlebags. I've got my Barlow in the bags, and I think it's in the left side.* Attempting to throw himself out of the line of the bullet from Kuruk's Winchester had actually caused Will to slide farther down in his right stirrup. The move might have saved him, but it had allowed the horse to fall high on his right leg, giving him very little movement from his trapped position.

He could touch the saddlebags where they lay across the horse, but only by pushing his body up with his right forearm. He strained and stretched, touched the bags, and fell back, gasping. He had to get out from under Buck. The sign Kuruk had made when he rode off could mean only one thing. The Apache would be back. Will would be an easy scalp if he remained trapped beneath his horse.

Lying amidst the sage, the smell was stronger than the pines that marked the valley edges and ran up the mountains. A robber jay lit nearby and hopped around his hat, occasionally pecking at it. "Nothing for you there, you little thief. Leave my hat alone." The bird stopped, looked at him, and deemed himself safe, continuing to hop. He left the hat and hopped near Buck's head. Will's sense of smell caught dog only moments before he felt the big tongue licking his hair.

"Hi, Toby. It's good to have you back, boy." He reached around and petted the big animal. Toby moved up beside him and sat, looking down on him. "I know. I've got to get out of here, but you need to keep a lookout for that Apache." At the word Apache, the dog looked up, and his big head searched the countryside.

Even in his dire situation, Will couldn't help grinning at the dog. "You amaze me, boy. Sometimes I think you understand human talk." He reached up and scratched the dog's head. Somehow, Toby's presence gave him a second wind. This time, he pushed himself up with all of his might, every muscle straining as he reached for the saddlebags. Close, so close, and then his finger slipped under the edge. Just a little farther. His leg and back screamed in pain, but he pushed a tiny bit farther and felt his thumb slide under the edge, allowing him to grasp the bag. He yanked as he fell back, flipping the bag over and within his reach.

Will lay on his side, gasping for breath. He allowed himself only a few breaths to replace the oxygen driven from his lungs by the contortion to grasp the bag. Twisting back around and using protesting stomach muscles, he held himself up. Once he was as high as possible, he lifted the bag with one hand and deftly unfastened the rawhide loop with the other.

Since it had flipped over, the bag was upside down. When he released the tie, the flap flew open, and everything fell from the bag and to the ground. Normally that would have been wonderful, but in his present position, on his right side, facing Buck's head, all of the contents lay on the ground behind him. He again had to twist around and, more feeling than seeing, find the knife —if it was in this side. He quickly went through everything. His stomach muscles immediately started to burn like fire. No gun. He knew his other Remington was in the saddlebag under Buck, but had hoped he'd inadvertently put it in the left side. Finally, when he thought his muscles would give out, he felt the rounded handle of the Barlow. His fingers quickly closed on it, and he fell back to his right side, relaxing again while he gasped for air.

Toby sat quietly on his haunches, watching the surroundings and occasionally looking at Will. The Barlow felt good in his hand. It wasn't much of a weapon, but it would do the job up close. At that moment, the Great Pyrenees stood and emitted a low growl. *Not yet,* thought Will, *I need more time. If it is Kuruk, he could just shoot me and then take my hair. But if he wants a good story, he might come in close. If I can just get my hands on him.*

16

Will moved, and the Remington's hammer dug into his leg. He gritted his teeth against the pain and watched Toby's eyes. The dog was gazing along their back trail. Kuruk must be approaching from that direction. He tried to turn his head, but saw nothing.

He knew Kuruk would kill Toby without a thought. "Toby, go. Go!" For the second time Toby looked at him as if reluctant to leave, but dashed back to the treeline. A shot rang out, closer than Will had thought, and then another, then silence.

He quickly opened the Barlow and tucked it under his aching leg. He lay still, listening for the Apache's approach. There was nothing but the quiet of the mountains. A strengthening breeze rustled the leaves of the aspen and pine and caused the sage to rattle lightly against itself. A southeast wind.

With the arrival of Toby, the camp-robbing jay had departed. Will felt truly alone. He missed his wife and, with the thought of her, became more determined. He lay still, waiting, listening. Almost inaudible, he heard the light swish of a moccasin gliding over the dusty ground, no clothing scraping on sagebrush, no rattling of gear, just a slight swish.

Suddenly his hair was grabbed from above and behind him and pulled tight, stretching his neck, giving Kuruk an open target. "Nice hair, white man," Kuruk said. "It will look good on my belt." Kuruk waited. "What? You no talk, no beg? Good. Make scalp more valuable."

Will saw the flash of a blade move above his eyes and sweep down for his open throat. He'd have to grab the Indian's wrist with his left arm and hang onto him long enough for a killing blow with the Barlow. If he allowed Kuruk to escape, he'd never get another chance. His left arm flashed up and clamped around the right wrist of the Apache. He heard Kuruk chuckle, still confident, still maintaining a hold on Will's hair, pulling and stretching the open, inviting throat.

The Indian, having the freedom of movement denied Will, twisted his right arm to free it from Will's grip, but the big man only tightened his grip, squeezing harder. The chuckle disappeared as Kuruk released Will's hair and began a flip that would take him out of the clasped hand and far enough away from the marshal's long arms. Then he would finish the job. But Will's size and strength came into play. Kuruk was strong, but he was a smaller man and older. He couldn't overpower Will. Now, realizing he couldn't flip out of range, he concentrated on forcing the knife into Will's throat.

Will drove his hand beneath his leg, felt the Barlow's handle, and yanked it out. He knew Kuruk saw the knife, because the Indian's moves became more desperate. The man tried to turn while throwing all of his weight against his knife, but Will with his one hand kept him off balance and drew him nearer. The Apache grabbed for Will's right hand, but a moment too late. Will had a target, but he knew it was well protected, and he had only the two-inch blade to work with, not the almost eight inches of his Bowie knife. But he knew, as did Kuruk, the two-inch Barlow could be enough.

As Kuruk grabbed for his right hand, Will tightened his grip on the Indian's wrist, exerting all the force he could muster. Kuruk pulled back, twisted, and with the twist, bones broke in his wrist. Will heard them. There was no indication of pain from the Apache except a relaxing, only slightly, of his grip on Will's right wrist. It was enough. Will drove the two-inch blade into the Apache's chest just below the sternum. He thrust it up until much of the Barlow handle disappeared into the Apache's chest. Blood gushed over Will's hand, but he managed to hang onto the knife, knowing he had found his mark.

Kuruk relaxed, and Will pulled him over, hanging onto the knife hand. He guided the man to the ground at his right side. Kuruk stared into his eyes and, as his lifeblood fled his body, said, "You Floyd Logan's son?"

"Nephew," Will gasped, trying to feed his body the air it needed.

"I thought. Floyd Logan bad medicine. He dead?"

"No. Very much alive."

Kuruk grunted and coughed, took a shallow breath, and said, "No friend." With those last words, Kuruk's head fell back. His left hand loosened from Will's wrist and dropped to the ground. Will watched him a little longer until the man's eyes began to glaze over, then, grasping the Indian's big knife, threw the body from him. He lay, as best he could, resting. His body shook from the exertion. He would kill for a drink of water, but when Buck fell, the canteen had fallen from the saddle horn and was out of reach.

Daylight was leaving the valley, and he could feel the chill of the approaching evening. He could also feel Buck's body cooling. He had to get out from under his horse. Wiping the Barlow off with some nearby grass, he laid it to the side and took the Indian's knife. With it, he began to dig under the holster. He had to get the pressure off the hammer. Slowly he dug until he felt the holster move on its own, just enough to get the hammer out of his leg. He felt around the holster. It wasn't wet. At least the holster hadn't dug a hole into his flesh. Then he began digging along his leg as far under the horse as he could reach.

He called for Toby, and in the darkness, the ghostlike form of the dog padded into sight. "Good dog." Will stretched out a hand and rubbed the dog's head, happy to have his companion back.

Toby growled at Kuruk's body and sniffed the blood. After satisfying his curiosity, he moved away and sat watching as Will continued to dig.

The work was slow, but gradually he had a shallow trench dug beneath his leg. Darkness had brought with it the chilling mountain temperatures, but the desperate effort was providing a second benefit, needed warmth. Will could even feel his trapped leg warming.

He managed to dig to just below his knee. Finally, in complete darkness, he got his left foot against the saddle and pushed while bracing with his hands and forearms pressed against the ground. Movement, but only a little. Still, the slight shift infused him with excitement, and he pushed to dig the trench deeper. One of the problems, besides his not being able to see in the dark, was the weight of the horse followed the leg as he cleared beneath it. The flat surface of the saddle fender helped spread the weight, nourishing his hope.

With his third try, the leg move perceptibly, but it felt like his boot was stuck under the horse. Will was tired. He had experienced exhaustion in his life before, and he knew he was approaching that point now, especially without water. This effort had to be over soon, or he wouldn't have the energy to continue, and with the cold of the night, he could die right here.

One last time he gave a mighty heave, and with excruciating slowness, the leg began to move. He was able to slide a little farther from the horse. He braced his arms in a new position, reset his foot on the saddle, and summoned his last bit of energy.

Slowly the trapped leg slid from under the horse, missing the boot. With his right leg rescued, he rolled over onto his back and lay gasping again, but it wasn't long before the unrelenting cold began to seep back into his body. He had to get moving.

Will tried bending the leg. Pain coursed through the limb, but he continued. It felt much like when his feet had almost frozen. Once they began to warm and the blood returned, they burned like fire for a while. Now, it was burning in the same way.

While he lay there, he pulled the Remington from its holster. He had expected the revolver to be full of dirt, but the scabbard and his leg had been great protection. The weapon was clean and ready to fire. Relieved, he slipped it back into the holster.

Time passed with him exercising his leg, extending it and then grasping behind the knee and pulling it toward his chest. With the burning in his foot diminishing, he grasped the saddle and struggled to his feet. He stood, swaying. Tentatively, he took one step. His leg held his weight. Another. Then another. The leg would be sore for a few days, but it was working. He wandered out into the sage where Mott Cooper had thrown his shotgun. In moments, he caught a reflection from the stars off the barrel. There it lay. Picking it up, he wiped it off and headed back to Buck.

Moving a short distance from Buck and Kuruk, he started a fire. *I don't think anyone else will be along,* he thought. *I'm sure they're expecting Kuruk to show up tomorrow with a scalp and a story, and I need heat.* He looked at the dark blob that was Kuruk lying next to Buck. *Ironic, the Apache died next to the horse he killed.*

Will had gotten the supplies from the sack and his saddlebags. He'd have to do without his saddle tonight. He had unfastened the cinch straps, but didn't have the strength to pull the saddle from under the horse tonight, but he could get the saddle blanket. He was also able to get his bedroll. That would do. He had Toby to keep watch tonight. Thinking of keeping watch, he looked back at Buck and said, "You've been a really good horse, Buck, a fine companion. I'm gonna miss you." He sat for a while longer, listening to the coyotes make music, occasionally joined by the deeper call of a wolf.

He said to Toby, "You've got the watch all by yourself tonight, boy. Wake me up if you hear anything." Will laid the saddle blanket across his legs, pulled his blankets up around his neck, rested his head on his Stetson, and was asleep quicker than a firefly could blink.

MORNING DAWNED GRAY AND COLD. A southeast wind howled up the valley. Will, buried beneath his blankets, woke with his chest and arms cool, but his back was warm. He realized Toby lay next to him, against his back. He welcomed the big dog's warmth. He tossed off the blankets, pulled on his moccasins, and looked at the cold fire, then the trees bending in the wind, and decided there would be no fire this morning, no matter how cold he felt. The last thing he wanted in these mountains was a fire.

"Toby, it's gonna be a cold morning." He shrugged into his coat and walked over to Buck. It was a good thing he had unfastened the cinch last night, because Buck was bloating badly, even in this cooler weather. He glanced at Kuruk and shook his head. *I don't know why you came back, but it sure wasn't a good decision for you.* He bent, unfastened Kuruk's now extremely tight gun belt, and pulled it out from under the Apache. Next, he went through the Indian's pockets. The man might have relatives who could use whatever he had on him, but there wasn't much. He found three silver dollars.

"Where's your horse, Kuruk? It would sure come in handy. He looked down the valley in hopes of seeing the man's horse, but there was nothing in sight. Moving back to Buck, he decided to try getting the saddle out from under the horse. With his fourth attempt, the fender and stirrup slid out from under the massive weight.

He had everything, but his success with the saddle was both good and bad. It was good that he had all of his equipment, but it was bad because he was the only one to carry it. He went to his bedroll, rolled it up, and tied it. He moved his saddle and rifle and laid them down next to the bedroll and shotgun, which were next to his saddlebags.

He stood looking at the pile of equipment, none of which he wanted to leave. He reminded himself that he was like the pioneers Uncle Floyd had guided west. They loaded their wagons with all of their dressers, pianos, beds, furniture, and keepsakes, only to dump them in the Great Plains or the Rocky Mountains when their teams could no longer pull the weight. He looked again at his equipment and said, "But I need all this." He tied the bedroll so it hung across his chest. With piggin' strings, he made a harness for Toby to carry the saddlebags, and slings for both the rifle and shotgun. Both of the weapons, he hung across his chest, where they rested on his bedroll and would be easy to bring into action if needed.

Toby sat looking at him. "I know it's crazy, boy, but I need your help." He bent over the saddlebags and pulled out the pack of jerky. Toby got just as many sticks as he did. After they ate, he took a swig from the canteen, hung it around his neck, and swung the saddle across his shoulder. After one last look at his horse and Kuruk, he said, "Let's go, boy. We're burning daylight." The two started back down the valley.

Mid-morning of the fifth day from the day Buck had been shot, Will and Toby rolled into Las Vegas. Early that morning Will had stepped out on the road that connected Trinidad and Las Vegas.

It was a heavily traveled road, and within the hour a wagon rolled into view, headed toward Las Vegas. It looked to be heavily loaded, but the driver pulled up when he was even with Will.

He took in the bedraggled appearance, the badge on his vest, and said, "Out for your morning stroll, Marshal?"

Will removed his hat and with the back of his sleeve wiped the sweat from his forehead. "I wouldn't say that. You headed for Las Vegas?"

"No, sir, but I am going through that fine city. I'm headed for Santa Fe and making good time, if I do say so myself. Could I interest you in a ride?"

Will gave the man a tired smile. "You might be able to twist my arm. You have room for a little dog?"

The teamster grinned at Will. "Reckon I could harness him up with my mules, looks big enough to out pull the whole lot." Growing serious, he said, "Sure, Marshal. You can put him in the back with your saddle and other gear. I'm a mite loaded, but I'm bettin' I can make room." He climbed down and walked to the back, opened it, and jumped in. "Give me a minute to do a little housekeepin' here." A few minutes later he said, "Hand me your saddle and gear."

Will unloaded, giving the teamster everything except the shotgun. Once everything was stowed to his liking, he jumped down from the wagon. "You can let him jump up in there if you want."

Will pointed to the back and said, "Go."

Toby leaped into the remaining space, made a couple of circles, and dropped to the floor, shaking the wagon.

The teamster closed the back. "Your dog looks a mite tired." Pointedly, he looked Will over. "Kinda like you."

Will nodded. "That's true. I'm riding up front?"

"Yes, sir. I'd be beholden. Haven't had a soul to talk to since my helper left me in Trinidad."

The two men climbed back up to the wagon seat, and the

teamster called to the six mules, popped the reins, and they were on their way. "Name's Josiah Watson, but most folks just call me Josey."

Will turned his head toward the big man, looking him over. "I mean no offense, but you sure don't look like a Josey to me."

The teamster laughed. "Well, my pa's name was Josiah, and as far back as I remember, he was called Josey. I was named after him, and everybody called me Little Josey. I growed up, and most stopped callin' me Little 'ceptin' my family. Why, if'n I was to go home right now, my ma would be callin' me Little Josey."

Will nodded his head. "Understandable. I want you to know I'm mighty appreciative of you giving us this ride. Both Toby and I were gettin' a little whipped. The way I figure it, we've been walking for about five days, and there's not much level ground in this part of the country."

"No, sir," Josey said. "Me and them mules'll agree with you there. They no more than start down a hill than there they go headin' back up another. Makes it plumb tirin' over a day's time, much less five. What happened to your horse?"

"Poisoned."

Josey looked askance at Will. "Poisoned?"

"Yeah, lead poisoning. A man shot him, trying to kill me."

Josey's wide face lost the easygoing look it had been carrying. His forehead wrinkled, eyes squinted, and mouth pursed. They rattled along for a while until he asked, "What happened to the man?"

Will continued to stare down the road. "He's back there with the dead horse."

The wagon continued to roll, jolt over the rocks, and sway. "Dead?"

"Yep."

Josey leaned over the edge of the wagon and shot a long stream of tobacco juice. He wiped his mouth with the back of a tobacco-stained sleeve. "I'm pretty familiar with these parts. Anybody I might know?"

Will turned and looked at his host. "You're an inquisitive sort, aren't you?"

"Yes, sir, I sure am. My ma used to say I asked too many questions, but that's been about the onliest way I could find stuff out. When folks don't want to answer, they usually don't say anything, or tell me to mind my own business, which you're sure welcome to do."

Will couldn't help but like the teamster. He was a friendly sort, and he had given them a ride, which both he and Toby sorely needed. He swung his left ankle across his knee and examined the hole in the sole of his moccasin. His feet would have been in big trouble if Josey and his wagon hadn't come along. "You familiar with the C Bar ranch?"

"For sure I am. I've hauled hay out there before. Owned by Mott Cooper." His eyes widened, and he turned to stare at Will. "You didn't kill Mott, did you?"

"No. You know the Apache who works for him?"

"Sure, name's Kuruk. Kind of a scary fella. Not somebody I'd want to cross."

"He's the one."

Again, Josey, wide-eyed, turned to stare at Will. "You killed Kuruk? The Apache?"

"That's a fact."

"He killed your horse?"

"That he did."

"And you killed him because he killed your horse?"

"No, I killed him because he was a little too intent on taking my scalp."

Josey stared at the road and his mules, then he turned and looked at Will's hair. "I can see why he'd want it, all nice and thick like that. It'd make a nice scalp." He spit a long stream over the side of the wagon again. "Cooper ain't a-goin' to be too happy about you killin' his Apache. He put a lot of store by that feller."

"I reckon he won't."

Topping the hill, Las Vegas came into view. "Where'd you like me to drop you? I'm stoppin' at the stables first. I've got some stuff to drop off, and the mules need waterin'."

"Stable's fine with me. I can leave some things there. Listen, Josey, I'm much obliged for the ride. I'd be glad to pay you. The government reimburses me, so whatever you think's fair is fine with me."

"No charge, Marshal. Just glad to help a man."

"Thanks. Do you know Cooper's nephew, Ambrose?"

"Sure I do. Most folks know of him, a little wild."

Will nodded. "More than a little wild. He killed a United States Marshal up in Colorado, and I'm here to take him back. He also killed Tyler Young, owner of the Lazy Y. What I'm telling you is to steer well clear of him. I think the boy is a little off center, so you never know which way he'll tilt."

Josey was shaking his head as they pulled up in front of the stables. "Thanks for tellin' me, Marshal. I'll steer clear, but Mott's mighty fond of that boy. He's a good man, but I'm afraid he'll fight you if you try to take Ambrose."

Will and Josey walked to the back of the wagon. Josey opened it, and Toby stretched, first his front shoulders, then his back. When he was finished, he jumped down and trotted to the watering trough.

Josey watched him go, then climbed into the back of the wagon. "That dog's got a mind of its own."

"He does," Will said, taking his equipment from Josey. He nodded to the teamster and carried his equipment to the front wall of the stable. He set it there and went back for his saddle.

"I hear the boy's fast, Marshal," Josey said, starting to unload several items from the back of the wagon. "But he ain't the onliest one. Mott's no slouch when it comes to one of them hand weapons. I hope it doesn't come to it, but if it does, you watch yourself."

Will picked up his saddle and headed for the stable. "Good to know. You take care, Josey."

"You too, Marshal."

17

As Will walked toward the stable, Bert came out and slid to a stop when he saw the lawman. A surprised, almost fearful, expression covered his face. He looked at Toby standing next to the trough, who was watching him.

"Uhh, hi, Marshal. What can I do for you?"

"You can let me store my gear until I can get a horse."

"Well, you know we rent 'em. We can also sell you one."

"Why do you mention selling me one, Bert?"

"Uhh, well, uhh, Marshal, you are carrying your saddle, and I don't see your buckskin."

"That makes sense, but Bert, you look surprised to see me."

The boy kicked at a dirt clod, exploding it into pieces. "Marshal, you did ride out of town."

"Yes, I did, but my returning shouldn't surprise you. Have you heard anything? You can tell me, Bert. I am a U.S. Marshal."

The boy thought on Will's last statement. Will could see Bert laboring over his decision. "You can trust me, Bert. I won't tell anyone what you tell me. It will be confidential."

At last Bert made up his mind. "They said you were dead."

Softly, Will said, "Who said that, Bert?"

"Otis and Levi stopped by. They said that Ambrose told them you were dead. They said Ambrose sent the Apache Kuruk to kill you."

Will patted the boy on the shoulder. "You did the right thing, Bert. Thank you. I won't tell anyone. So, you're talking about Otis Thatcher and Levi Edward?"

"Yes, sir. I don't mean to be telling tales, but that's what they told me."

"Were they with anyone else when they told you this?"

"No, sir. I was here rubbing down some horses when they rode up, all laughing and joking. They asked me to ride along with 'em, but I told 'em I had to work. I'd promised my pa I'd get the horses done." Bert had been looking at the ground as he told his story. Now he raised his head and looked directly at Will, concern covering his face. "Pa's been sickly since a fractious bay kicked him in the side. They just laughed and said it was too bad, they had an opening in their gang."

"You're a good son, Bert. Your pa is lucky to have such a devoted boy. Any idea how they got out of jail?"

Bert had warmed up to Will and was talking freely. "Yes, sir. Just as soon as you rode out of town, Marshal Snead released all of 'em. Weren't long after that Mrs. Young rode into town with her foreman, Mr. Ramsey. You know, the lady who owns the Lazy Y?"

Will nodded. "Go on."

"Well, sir, they was fit to be tied, wantin' to know why he had released those rustlers and all."

Will shook his head. He knew Snead would turn them loose before he was out of sight. "Did you hear what Marshal Snead said to Mrs. Young?"

"Yes, sir, I not only heard it, I saw it. It all happened right in front of the marshal's office. He said he was a town marshal and didn't have any juris ... uh, jur ..."

"Jurisdiction, Bert. He meant he didn't have any authority to hold them."

"Yep. That was it. Boy, did Mrs. Young light into him. She called him a worthless excuse for a marshal, and she hoped he'd saved up plenty of money, 'cause next election comes around he'd be looking for another job."

"Good for her," Will said. He pulled a silver dollar from his vest pocket and flipped it to Bert, who snatched it out of the air and examined it. "Bert, the Marshal Service thanks you for the information. Could you tell me if you have any C Bar horses in your stable?"

The boy shook his head, still looking at the silver dollar. "No, nary a one. Is this for me?"

Will nodded. "You've been a big help. Do you know if any of the C Bar riders are in town?"

"Yes, sir, I do. There's a couple of 'em down at the saloon." He pointed down the street.

"Good," Will said. "Would you mind taking my saddlebags, bedroll, and rifle inside? I'll be back for them shortly. Also, I need to buy a really good saddle blanket if you have one."

"I'd be glad to, Marshal." He looked at Will as if he expected to be lambasted and said, "The saddle blanket will be four dollars."

Will looked at the boy and shook his head. "Bert, you folks are almighty proud of your gear." Before Bert could respond, Will held up his hand. "I know. You're just doing what your pa told you. I'll take it."

"Yes, sir. You want me to keep it here with your saddle?"

"No, I want you to get it for me. I'll be taking my saddle and the shotgun."

When Bert disappeared inside the barn, Will took six shells for the shotgun from his saddlebags and dropped two into the chambers, snapping it closed as Bert returned with the blanket. He took the blanket, and with the saddle over his right shoulder and the blanket and shotgun in his left hand, he headed down the street.

He passed several buildings until he came to the saloon. Seeing the two C Bar horses, he dropped his saddle on the board-walk and examined them. Both were in good shape, but the big dun looked stronger, like a horse that could carry his weight for a long distance. Furthermore, he recognized this as the horse that had been ridden by a big fellow who was along with Mott Cooper when Kuruk shot Buck. He patted the horse on the neck and said, "You'll do, boy." Will unfastened the saddle and threw it in the dirt next to the horse. Then he picked up the blanket, smoothed it out, and swung the saddle over the dun's back.

He had just pulled it tight and shook it when a big cowhand, followed by the entire saloon, charged out the door. "Hey! Get away from my horse!" the man yelled.

Will had leaned the shotgun against the hitching rail. He picked it up, leveled it at the man and his friends, and said, "You know who I am?"

The cowhand had a difficult time tearing his eyes from the shotgun muzzle, but finally took a close look at Will. When he did, his eyes widened so far, they appeared to bulge out of their sockets. "You cain't be here. You're de—" He stopped, staring at Will.

"Dead? Is that the word you're looking for? If so, you can see I'm very much alive." He pulled a sheet of paper from inside his vest and handed it to the cowhand. "What's your name?"

The cowhand looked at the folded paper, the shotgun, and Will, finally saying, "Fletcher, my name's Bing Fletcher."

"Hello, Bing Fletcher. You should know the name of the man you left to die. I'm United States Marshal Will Logan. Does this horse belong to you or the C Bar?"

"He's my horse. I mean, he's in my string. He belongs to the C Bar."

"Good, then open that paper you're holding. Can you read?"

"Uhh, not too well, but my pardner can."

"Where's he?"

Fletcher tossed a thumb to his left. "That's him."

Will looked at the smaller man next to Bing. "Your name?"

"I'm Sandy Bateman, Marshal. Would you mind lowering that scattergun. It makes me kinda nervous."

Will nodded. "I understand, but I'm sure you'll understand, it makes me kinda nervous when a group of men charge me after shooting my horse and leaving me to die. You understand that, Sandy?"

"Sure, Marshal, real clear."

"Good, now would you read that paper for everyone to hear."

"Sure, Marshal." Bateman opened the folded document and began to read. "I, United States Marshal Will Logan, do confiscate one horse from the C Bar. This is done to replace the horse killed by the C Bar when they assaulted me and took my prisoner."

Will nodded and handed Bateman a pencil. "Now between the writing and my signature, I want you to write out the description of this dun. Then you sign it." He looked at Fletcher. "Do you understand what has been read?"

Will could see Fletcher was getting mad. The man didn't answer quickly enough, and Will barked at him, "Come on, Fletcher, do you understand what Bateman read to you?"

Angry and red faced, the man said, "I understand."

"Good, make an x or sign your name beneath Bateman's."

Will was aware of the large crowd gathering to watch the excitement.

Fletcher took the pencil, and using his friend's back, he leaned forward, gripping the pencil as if he were trying to squeeze the lead out, and with the tip of his tongue protruding between his tight lips, painfully made an x. Then he handed the paper back to Will.

"Not yet," Will said. "Bateman, write Fletcher's name beneath the x, then hand me the paper."

The smaller man did as he was told, and Will glanced at it, saw it had been filled out exactly as he'd asked, folded it, and slipped it back into his inside vest pocket. He waved the shotgun toward the other C Bar horse. "Bateman, is this your horse?"

"Yes, it is, Marshal."

"Then mount up and ride back to your ranch. Tell Mott Cooper his hired killer is dead. If he wants him, he can find him next to my horse. I came here for Ambrose Cooper, and I'm not leaving without him. If he wants to bring him in without gunplay, I'll let what happened pass. There's already one dead man, and I'd prefer there be no more, but don't test me. My patience has run out.

"Think you can remember all that?"

"I sure can, Marshal, but what about Bing here? He needs a horse."

"No, he doesn't need a horse because he's going to jail. I saw him with that bunch. I didn't see you, or you'd be going along with him."

"You cain't put me in no jail," Fletcher said.

Bateman had started toward his horse but stopped when he heard his friend was headed for jail. Keeping the shotgun on Fletcher, Will said, "Get on your horse, Bateman. There's nothing for you here. The best thing you can do is pass this word on to your boss and the C Bar riders.

"I've heard about your ranch. Everything I've heard, except for Ambrose, has been good. I know you boys ride for the brand, and I can appreciate that. But when you ambush a United States Marshal, you've stepped way over the line. I got a pretty good look at the men who ambushed me in the mountains, but, like I said, I'm willing to let that pass."

He paused and eyed Fletcher for a moment. "I'm willing to let it pass *if* you don't back Ambrose or your boss. Ambrose is a killer, and he'll kill again. He admitted it. If you don't believe me, ask Fran Young. She heard him. He's sick in the head. You boys need to ask yourselves if riding for the brand means backing a cold-blooded killer and riding the owlhoot trail for the rest of your lives. Tell that to the other cowhands." Will nodded his head toward the road. "I've said my piece. Now, go on. Get out of here."

Bateman swung into the saddle and raced out of town. Will watched him disappear and pointed the muzzle of the shotgun toward the jail. "Let's go."

Surrounded by the crowd of citizens, most he knew, Fletcher stuck his chin out and said, "You ain't gonna shoot me, Marshal, and I'm not goin' to jail." He grinned and worked his hands into two huge fists. "Unless you'd like to make me."

Will had had enough. They'd killed Buck. Kuruk had tried to slit his throat while he was trapped, and to top it off, he had just finished walking for five days carrying all of his gear. His patience was gone, and he was tired. He stood, staring at the gloating grin on Fletcher's face.

Fists ready, the big cowhand, sure now that Will wouldn't shoot him, stepped forward, knocked the muzzle to the side and swung at Will.

Will felt the jolt of action. Finally he had an opportunity to strike out at someone, but Trinidad had taught him a hard lesson. He wasn't going to smash his hands against another hard head. With Fletcher's strike, Will allowed the muzzle to swing to the side, and moved his head slightly away from Fletcher's fist. The blow slid harmlessly past the left of his head. Then, raising the shotgun high, he brought the barrel down with savage force onto the top of Fletcher's head, crushing the big man's hat. His opponent dropped like a sack of oats.

One of the bystanders said, "Marshal, you may have killed him."

"That's true," Will said. He pointed to three burly men watching the show. "You, you, and you, pick up this crow bait and get him to jail."

The three men quickly moved in, and with one on each arm

and the other carrying Fletcher's feet, they hauled him to the jail. Will saw Bert in the crowd. "Bert, how about taking this dun to your stable. Feed and water him. I'll be down later to settle up."

The boy said, "Sure, Marshal," grabbed the reins and swung into the saddle. "I'll take good care of Biscuit."

Will nodded. "Thanks." He turned to the crowd. "Show's over, folks. Might as well be about your business." The crowd dissipated quickly, and he followed the men carrying Fletcher into the marshal's office. The jail was empty, but on the wall hung a ring of cell keys. Will grabbed the ring and waited while the men pushed through the unlocked door of the jail cell.

"Drop him on the bunk."

The three men did as they were ordered, easing the big body onto the bed.

"Where's the marshal?" Will asked.

One of the men spoke up. "At least once a month, Marshal Snead rides up to the hot springs about five or six miles northwest of here. Don't know if you've ever been, Marshal, but they're mighty fine. A good soaking in one of those pools will cure what ails you."

"When does he usually return?"

"Same day," the man continued. "He just rides up there to soak out the kinks. He might stop and catch a few fish on the way back, but he'll be back here before dark." The speaker turned and looked at Fletcher bleeding on the bed. "He might be a little upset with Bing in here."

"Yeah," one of the other men pitched in, "he don't hanker to blood getting on his bedding."

"Thanks," Will said. "Why don't one of you stop by the Doc's and let him know what's happened. He's welcome to stop by, if he's a mind." Will pulled another silver dollar from his vest pocket and tossed it to the man who had explained about the marshal's whereabouts. "You fellas have a drink on your government."

All three of the men perked up and headed for the door. "Thanks, Marshal," the talker said, and all three disappeared. As the last man slammed the door, Fletcher groaned.

At least he's alive, Will thought. *I hit him so hard, I thought I might have killed him. Guess it was all the pent-up frustration. This marshaling job is a lot more than I expected.*

Fletcher groaned again, but lay still. Without raising his head, the cowhand called, "My head hurts so bad I can't be dead unless I'm in Hell."

Will, seated in the marshal's chair, had just stretched his legs and propped his feet on the desk. "You may be, but you're still alive."

"Is that you, Marshal Logan?"

"None other."

"There weren't no call for you to hit me with that scattergun."

"Shut up, Fletcher. You're talking stupid."

"Well, at least not that hard. You could have killed me."

Will thought, *Actually, I thought I had for a while.* "You would've deserved it. Leaving a man to die like that is mighty mean, Fletcher, mighty mean."

This time Fletcher rose a little, groaned, and pushed up farther on his elbows, looking at Will. "That weren't our idea. A bunch of the boys argued hard against doing that, but the boss said you'd dig out, and the walk would do you good, but we all figured you for dead. You know, out in the cold, under your horse, and that was a mighty long hike out of them mountains."

When he sat in the chair, Will had figured he would have at least a couple of hours before Bateman made it to the ranch and told Cooper that Will was in Las Vegas. Since he couldn't go to the hotel, with Fletcher locked in jail and the town marshal due back, he had hoped to get a little shut-eye in the marshal's chair. He had stretched his legs, slid his hat over his eyes, and just closed them when Fletcher started talking. Using one finger, he pushed his hat to the back of his head, uncovering his brown eyes, corners showing the wrinkles of time, and stared at Fletcher.

"I'd like to get some sleep, Fletcher. I've been walking for five days carrying all my gear."

"Yeah, too bad, and I need a doctor. I'm bleeding like a stuck hog. How'd you get out from under your horse?"

Will shook his head. Obviously, there would be no sleep unless he hit Fletcher over the head again, and he couldn't think of any reason to justify that action, so he asked, "When did Mott send Kuruk back for me?"

The cowboy jerked up, hitting his head on the upper bunk frame. Immediately he grabbed the bloody side of his head and moaned. "Marshal, I really need a doctor." Then he swung his feet over the side and sat on the edge of the bunk.

"I've sent word to the doctor. Answer my question."

"Kuruk came after you? Mott ain't said a word to Kuruk since leaving you. He was pretty mad at the Apache. Don't know if it was for trying to kill you or shootin' your horse, so the Injun and Ambrose rode together when we headed back for the ranch. They was talking, off and on, but Mott never talked to him, not at all."

The cowhand paused, head lowered toward the floor in thought. Suddenly he jerked his head up again. "The kid sent him. That's what had to have happened. Like I said, after we had ridden for a ways, he and the kid started talking, and then Kuruk just peeled off and disappeared into the trees. Nobody thought anything of it 'cause that Apache comes and goes as he pleases."

18

Will looked at the bloody cowhand. "Are you sure Mott never talked to Kuruk?"

"I swear, Marshal. I was riding right behind him. He ain't hardly said a word to anyone, including the kid. He was pretty steamed. I think he was worried too. You don't go leaving a U.S. Marshal in the mountains without some consequences." He gingerly felt his scalp, then looked at his bloody, bent hat. "You ruined my hat. It was almost new. I ain't had it more'n six months."

So Mott was upset and worried, Will thought. *His nephew has put him in a corner. He's figuring out what kind of bad apple he has for a relative. Now he has to decide what he'll do. A man like that, it's hard to tell which way he'll jump.*

His thoughts were interrupted by the door banging open. A husky man with a fully bearded face and a strong smell of alcohol stepped through the door. He was carrying a small bag. "I'm Doc Bradbury. Who's hurt?"

Will sighed, unfolded his long legs from the desktop, and stood. "Marshal Logan, Doc. That would be the fella bleeding in the jail cell."

Doc Bradbury nodded at Will and eyed Fletcher while Will unlocked the cell door. "What'd you hit him with?"

Will nodded to the shotgun leaning against the cabinet by the desk.

"Better check your shotgun. Fletcher's known for having a hard head."

"Now, Doc, there ain't no call to be talking about me like that. Especially since I'm bleeding so bad. I could bleed to death, and you smell like you've been dunked in a barrel of mash."

Will stepped aside and watched as the Doc pushed through the cell door. "Just got back from cutting open a fella on Tanner's ranch. Had to get him pretty soused up. To thank me, he puked about half of it all over me. You'll just have to live with the smell, and you're not going to bleed to death, Fletcher." He yanked Fletcher's hand away from his wound, looked at it, glanced at the hat, then looked back at the wound. "It's a good thing you had that hat on, otherwise, I'd be forced to put some stitches into that." He took a rag from his bag and dabbed around the cut. The bleeding had slowed almost to a stop. "Hold this rag on your head until the bleeding stops."

Fletcher, who had been sitting on the edge of the bunk while the doc examined his wound, shook his head when Doc Bradbury stepped back. "Whew-wee, Doc. You stink somethin' awful. Why, you smell worse than the bunkhouse after a Saturday night dance."

The doctor closed his bag, looked at Fletcher, and said, "Stop complaining, or I'll charge you," and started for the cell door.

"Is that all you're goin' to do?" Fletcher asked, almost in a whine. "It still hurts pretty bad."

"Quit whining," Doc Bradbury said. "You'll be fine. Try to keep the wound clean. From the looks of your hair, that'll be a lost cause." As soon as he was out, Will locked the door.

"How long you keeping him?" the doc asked, filling a chair as he sat.

"Up to him."

"Word's all over town you're here for Ambrose."

"That's right, Doc. I get him, I'm out of here."

"Mott Cooper's a good man," the doctor said, staring at Will, who had again taken the seat behind the town marshal's desk.

Will leaned forward. "What I keep hearing, Doc. But that good man left me pinned under my horse to die in the mountains. If it hadn't been for Buck, who took a bullet fired by one of his men that was meant for me, I wouldn't be talking to you right now. Doesn't sound like much of a good man to me."

Will examined the man sitting across the desk from him. He didn't look anything like any doctor he had ever seen. He was as husky as a coal miner and had a beard to put any old prospector to shame. Bright blue eyes gazed back at him from a heavily wrinkled face.

"He's in a bad place. That nephew he took in is damaged goods." The doc stopped for a second, held his head back, and scratched at his beard beneath his chin. "It isn't the boy's fault. His mother died when he was little, and his father has somehow managed to keep from stretching a rope for all these years. According to Mott, he constantly beat and starved the boy. When the kid was eight years old, Mott took him. Word is he threatened his brother that if he ever showed up on the C Bar, he'd kill him."

"Doc," Will said, "that's all too bad. I mean it. No boy should have to grow up like that, but nowhere in there can I find an excuse for killing other men. He shot Tyler Young in the back of the head."

"I heard. You're right, there's no justification for that kind of action. The point I'm making is that Mott is a good man, and his feelings toward that boy are those of a father. He's being forced into a hard decision." The doctor stood before saying, "I just wanted you to know that."

Will leaned back in his chair, folded his arms, and stared at the doctor. "Doc, believe me, I know what you're telling me. I've heard it from almost everyone I've talked to, but it's out of my hands. I'm taking Ambrose Cooper or his body back to Pueblo."

Will's statement hung in the room like a deadly fog. The doctor walked to the door, opened it and, before exiting, turned to face Will. "Marshal, you've got to understand, I don't think there is a soul in this town who will lift a hand to help you. You'll be on your own. You'll be alone."

"Not the first time I've been in that situation, Doc. But what you and this town have to understand, if I'm killed, there will be more marshals showing up, or even the army. Ambrose Cooper is going to face justice, either now or later."

The doctor, eyes sad, gazed at Will for a moment longer, nodded and stepped out the door.

Will glanced over at Fletcher, who was watching him. "If you have anything to say, Fletcher, say it now. I need some sleep."

The big man shook his head and carefully stretched out on the bunk.

Will again stretched his legs across the desktop, found a comfortable position, and pulled his hat down over his eyes.

IT FELT like he had just fallen asleep when a voice boomed into his sleep-fogged consciousness. "What the blue blazes is going on here?"

Sliding his hat back, he saw Snead standing in front of the desk, a string of trout in one hand and a rod in the other. The man was glaring down at him.

Will looked up at Snead and said, "Well, now. It looks like you had a successful fishing trip, although the magic waters of the hot springs didn't do a lot for your attitude."

Snead glared at him. "I want to know why Bing Fletcher is bleeding all over my clean bunk. You know how much a new mattress is gonna cost me?"

"Reckon it's not going to cost you a thing. The town will pay for it. Now why don't you calm down, go take care of your fish, and come back with a little better disposition, and I'll fill you in on what's happening."

Snead glared at him for only a second, spun around, and headed out the door.

Fletcher chuckled from inside the jail cell. "Sheriff Snead likes a clean office and fresh fish. But he'll be back."

"I expect so."

Will walked to the small stand that supported a washbasin, pitcher, and water. He tipped the pitcher into the basin and rubbed his face with the cold water. After several applications, he felt the webs of sleep gradually dissolve. He stretched, went back to the shotgun, and checked the loads. After assuring himself the shotgun was fine, he drew his .44-caliber Remington, checked it, and dropped it back in the holster. Through the windows of the office, he could see the sun drifting lower. If he was coming into town today, Mott Cooper should be arriving soon. Satisfied with his weapons, he left the marshal's chair open and settled into the chair across the desk, the one the doc had sat in. If it was strong enough to support the doctor, it should carry his weight.

He had no more than relaxed when the marshal walked in. His grim face lightened a bit when he saw his chair vacant. "Now talk."

Will, though tired of the rough talk from the town marshal, let it pass. "Mott Cooper and some of his crew ambushed me five days ago." He went on to tell the story up to the doctor's visit to Fletcher. The irritated expression on Snead's face never changed.

"So what do you plan to do if Mott comes loaded for bear?"

Will had expected some kind of response to Cooper's ambush and killing of Buck. When instead, it looked as if Alton Snead was going to stick with what he had earlier said, his temper began to rise.

"I'll tell you what I'm going to do. I'll arrest Ambrose Cooper while the law in Las Vegas sits on its rear and does absolutely nothing."

Will watched Snead's face turn red. The man's ears absolutely glowed.

"I've already told you where I stand," Snead said.

"You sure have, and when a fellow lawman comes under fire and is left to die, you'll continue to ignore the guilt of both Coopers?"

"If you hadn't come to town, none of this would've happened."

"No," Will said, leaning toward the desk and Snead, "if Ambrose Cooper hadn't killed a U.S. Marshal and Tyler Young, none of this would have happened. You'd better start thinking straight and figure out who's the bad guy here."

Snead looked down at his old hands. The skin was beginning to wrinkle across the back of the scarred and sunbaked skin. "I've been in this business nearly my whole life. Tried my hand at storekeeping, but never managed to make a go of it. The wife's been trying to get me to quit for years. It's hard on her. The last few years I've hung on, trying to get a little nest egg saved, but there's always something that comes up."

He looked up at Will. For the first time, Will could see the age showing on the man, the wrinkles in the forehead, companions at the corners of the eyes, a few going up and around the thin mouth. He hadn't noticed it before.

Snead continued, "I didn't get into it for the money. It just seemed like the right thing to do. I was fairly quick with a gun and needed a job. Managed to always make the right decision. I reckon I've stayed too long."

He had been sitting stooped in the chair, but his shoulders suddenly straightened, and his head came up. He turned his chair and nodded at the shotgun. "Reckon you'll need that if Mott brings his crew into town."

Snead stood and pulled a ten-gauge shotgun from the gun

cabinet, breaking it open. Reaching for an open box of shells, he dropped a shell in each of the double's chambers, snapped it shut, and laid it across the corner of the desk, then picked up a few more, which he stuffed into his vest pockets. "How do you plan on taking them?"

Fletcher had been listening. He stood and walked to the bars of the cell, gripped them, and stared at Snead. "Are you crazy? You cain't go against the C Bar, Alton. That ain't even a little bit smart. You'll get cut down just like this feller's goin' to. You'll be through, finished."

Ignoring Fletcher, Snead said to Will, "I took a mighty fierce tongue-lashing from Fran Young when I let them boys go. Reckon I've been looking the other way too long. Like I said, do you have a plan?"

"The only person I've wanted from the start is Ambrose. However many ride in, I'll meet them and give them one more chance to turn him over. That's the only plan I have."

"All right," Snead said, "I guess it's settled." He looked out the window. Shadows were beginning to crawl across the street as the sun approached the peaks of the western mountains. "Gettin' close to suppertime. Callie's fixin' up those trout. There's way more than two people can eat. Care to join us?"

"I'd like that, Marshal," Will said.

The two men stood and, with shotguns in their hands, started for the door.

Fletcher shouted, "Alton, you're crazy! You can't do this! You owe your job to the C Bar!"

Will turned to Snead and nodded his head at Fletcher. "Is he always this loud?"

"That's not loud," Snead said. "You should hear him when he's drunk."

Will pulled on the door latch, but the sound of the click was lost in the pound of hoofbeats.

The two lawmen stepped onto the boardwalk and watched

five men yank their lathered horses to a stop. Mott Cooper was in the middle, two cowhands to each side of him. Ambrose was nowhere in sight.

Will cut Cooper off as he was about to speak. "Cooper, I'm guessing you rode into town to tell me where your nephew is."

"He's gone, Logan, well away. You'll never catch him."

"Then I guess you're under arrest for helping a murderer. I might even add on horse killing and attempted murder."

"You listen to me, Logan. I didn't send Kuruk. I don't know who did, but I didn't." He turned to Alton Snead. "Alton, you don't belong here. You go on home to Callie. I'm sure she's got supper set for you."

Will, pleased with the change in Snead, listened as the town marshal spoke. "Mott, you and I have been friends for a few years now. We both know something's been off with Ambrose since you took him from his pa. He's a dangerous man, and he'll kill again. You just tell us where he's headed, and all the rest will be forgotten." He turned to Will. "Is that all right with you, Marshal?"

Will nodded and said to Cooper, "Kuruk took it upon himself to shoot Buck. He came back to kill me. I'll release you and all your men from any responsibility if you tell me either where Ambrose is headed or where he's hiding."

A rider next to Cooper turned to him and said, "That's what Sandy told us, boss. We know how much you care about that boy, but it don't make any sense to protect him now. He's turned killer."

Will watched Mott Cooper, knowing this was a brutal decision for the man to make. He could give the boy more time to escape by sacrificing his life and those of the men who were devoted to him, or he could stop protecting the lad who had become a killer of men, of neighbors.

Will waited. *Let him think it out,* he thought. *Maybe he'll finally see he can't protect the little boy turned killer any longer.*

A door slammed across the street, and a young boy dashed

through the empty street. He was quickly followed by his mother racing after him, shouting, while glancing at the grim men facing each other, fear in her eyes. "You come back here right now, Jacob!" The boy's black and white mutt ran, jumping alongside him, anxious to play. The three disappeared down an alley.

The last shadows stretched across the street. A cool evening breeze drifted past the buildings. Clucking chickens could be heard nearby, returning to their coop and protection for the night.

Seconds passed as Will waited. The cowhand who had previously spoken said, "Boss, it ain't worth it."

Mott Cooper swung down from the saddle and looped his reins over the hitching rail. He looked at each of the hands, still mounted. "You boys ride on back to the ranch. I'll be along shortly."

"We can wait, boss," the talker said.

"No, you go ahead." His voice hardened. "Go on. Move out."

The four men nodded, wheeled their horses, and walked them out of town.

Mott turned back to Will. "Now, Marshal, we've got business." But instead of stepping up on the boardwalk, he began to back into the street.

"Don't be a fool, Mott," Marshal Snead said. "He's not worth it. You've got folks who depend on you. Don't do this."

"I've got no one, Alton. If that boy hangs, I've got no one. He's been through more hell than any two men should have to go through. I can't let this man take him."

Will sighed and handed the shotgun to the town marshal. "This is the wrong way, Cooper. You can't change that boy or what he's done. If you kill me, there'll be other marshals coming for him. They won't stop until he's caught." He stepped off the boardwalk and angled into the street, moving to take the buildings out of the line of fire.

Cooper continued to back away, himself now moving in such

a way to clear the buildings. "There may be more coming, Logan, but if I stop you, it'll give Ambrose time to get away. That boy's my life. He deserves another chance, and I can give it to him."

Will's mind raced. *Would it end here in the dusty streets of Las Vegas, New Mexico? At this time of day, Deborah was home fixing supper, probably worrying about him. And here I am about to kill a man.* He mentally shook his head, clearing his mind of all thoughts of Deborah or anything else except for the man growing dimmer in the fading light in front of him.

"Cooper," Will tried one last time, "Ambrose is going to kill again. He's already left Fran without a husband. The United States Marshal he killed, Farley Osborne, had a family. The next man he kills could have a family. What about them? You've got a chance to save people's lives. Take it."

Cooper had stopped moving. Will could see the man's chest expand as he took a deep breath. *He's gonna do it,* Will thought.

Snead must have seen it, too, for he shouted, "Don't do it, Mott."

19

Will watched Mott Cooper's hand flash for his six-gun. The man was fast. A light, shining through a nearby window, glinted on the barrel as it cleared the holster. On Cooper's face, Will saw regret. In the twilight of the evening, the flash from the muzzle of Will's Remington lanced into the street and rattled the windows, followed by Cooper's discharge. Will hardly noticed the snap of the bullet whipping past him. He was watching his opponent's body trying to stabilize after the hammer blow from Will's shot.

The bullet had entered Mott's chest low on the right side, turning him. The shock jerked his arm and hand to the right and down.

Will knew to continue shooting until his opponent was down, and then to keep a close watch on him. Many a death had been brought on by a dying man. But Will didn't want to shoot this man again. He knew he had hit him hard. Cooper might even die from the one shot, but he would surely die if Will shot him again. *Give him a chance,* Will thought. He watched as Cooper regained control and brought his revolver back up to fire. Will shot once more, seeing, in the dim light, the vest jerk where the lead slammed into his body.

This time, Cooper's arm dropped to his side, and he stood there, head down. Someone's clock chimed four, five, six, and Cooper's head begin to rise. Will, in the cool air of the night, heard the man say, "You can't take my boy." Each word came out strained, forced, while his weapon slowly rose.

Will could see the struggle on Cooper's face, his determination. He watched, Remington ready, as Cooper's arm and hand shook from the effort but, jerking unsteadily, continued to rise.

Don't do it, Will's mind screamed.

The muzzle continued to lift until reaching near level. Will thumbed the hammer back on his revolver, steadied, and Cooper collapsed, gun dropping from his hand. Will and the sheriff rushed to him and knelt at his side.

Cooper was gasping in short, rapid breaths. His body trembled, and blood flowed from the wounds. His eyes searched and found Will's face. Between gasps, he said, "I had . . . to do it. He's . . . like my . . . own son."

"Relax, Mott," Will said, placing his arm on his shoulder. "I understand, blood's blood."

Four horsemen rode from between the buildings. Snead passed Will his shotgun. Though near dark, there was enough light cast into the street for the movement to be clearly seen.

"Don't shoot, Marshal," one of the riders said. They rode up and dropped from their horses. "How's the boss?"

"Hit hard," Snead said.

"Dad-blame it, let me through," Doc Bradbury said, shoving his bulk through the growing crowd. He dropped next to Mott Cooper and ripped his shirt open, then his long johns, pulling them wide. He quickly examined the two bullet holes and called to the crowd, "Two of you men find a board to put Mott on," and went back to work.

Will and Snead had moved out of the way as soon as the doctor arrived. They stood to one side, watching him work. He gently rolled Cooper over to look at his back. Will could see the two exit wounds. Blood was trickling from them both, but it wasn't shooting out, and there was no froth from his lungs, both good signs.

Will said, "You think he'll make it, Doc?"

Doc Bradbury stood as the men brought the board up. "Slip him on the board, and get him to my office." The men did as he ordered, and he turned to Will. "Hard to say. That .44 packed enough punch to drive all the way through. He could die from either shot, but he's a tough man. I'll clean out the wounds, and it'll be in the good Lord's hands then. Only time'll tell." He turned and followed the men toward his office.

The C Bar cowhand who seemed to be the leader said, "We tried to talk him out of it. After Sandy told us the lowdown, the rest of the boys said they'd leave afore they'd back a killer." The man spoke while watching his boss disappear in the shadows. "Ambrose got really mad. I thought he was going to draw on Sandy, but Mott stopped him. Told him to pack up his gear and head south. It about broke Mott's heart when that boy rode out. Why, I swear there was tears in his eyes, and I ain't never seen such from him."

"Yep," one of the other men said. "He surely loved that worthless kid. You'd think that boy would do one good thing and turn himself in to save Mott."

The first one said to no one in particular, "What'll happen to the ranch now, if Mott dies?"

Another spoke up. "Reckon we'll be back on the grub line, boys."

Marshal Snead looked at the crowd milling and talking amongst themselves, and said, "Go home, folks. It's over."

"What'll we do, Marshal Logan?" the cowhand asked.

Will said, "Do any of you know where Ambrose is headed?"

"Reckon we all do, Marshal. Mott told him to head to El Paso and from there Mexico. The boy speaks the lingo real good. Once he leaves El Paso, he'll disappear. Though was I you, I'd look up his pa. He might know more."

"Anybody know his first name?"

"We all do. Mott's folks named him George Washington Cooper, after the president. Now, ain't that a hoot, him being named after a president."

"Thanks, boys," Will said. "Here's what's going to happen. Tell all the hands who were involved in that little fracas in the mountains to forget it. I have."

"I agree," Marshal Snead said. "You fellas head on back to the ranch, and I'll be out in a couple of days."

The cowhands nodded. The one who had done most of the talking stepped up to Will. "I saw it all, Marshal Logan. You did your best to talk him out of it, and then you gave him every chance."

"Thanks," Will said.

The four men swung into their saddles and turned their horses to leave. One of the men who had said nothing up to now said, "Marshal, he wasn't alone. Ambrose. When he rode out, I saw him join up with another rider. Couldn't tell for sure who he was, but he rode like Otis Thatcher. He may be young, but he's a bad hombre. Those two just seemed to fit good together."

"Thanks," Will said.

The four men turned and rode slowly out of town.

Will and Snead watched them go, then headed back to the office.

"What now?" Snead asked.

"I'm headed for El Paso after I get a decent night's sleep. I do need one more thing from you, other than letting Fletcher go."

Reaching the office, Will pulled out the paper he'd had Fletcher and Sandy sign. "How about putting your signature on here? That'll make it a little more official. I'm not a horse thief and have no desire to be called one. I just figure Cooper owes me one."

Snead read the paper, signed it, and handed it back to Will. "Seems fair to me." While he was talking, he grabbed the keys and unlocked the cell door. "You can go home, Fletcher."

Fletcher, dejected, had stretched out on the bunk. "Bert came in here just after the shooting. Told me what happened. Mind if I sleep here tonight? I don't feel much like riding."

"Sure, spend the night. If I was you, though, I'd get on out to the ranch come morning. You never know about Mott. He's a tough man."

"Thanks, Marshal. I'll do that."

Will started for the door, Snead right behind him.

"You still up for a good supper?" Snead asked.

"Kinda lost my appetite."

"I can understand that, but you come on down to the house. Callie'll be anxious. Having a guest will perk her up."

"Marshal? Marshal!" The call stopped both men, and they turned toward the voice. Marching toward them was a man, an older version of Abel, with Abel reluctantly in tow. He marched the boy up to the two men and stopped, shoving him forward. "You tell Marshal Logan what you know."

Abel looked down, saying nothing. He took too long gathering his thoughts, and his pa smacked him hard across the back of the head with his open hand. "You listen to me, boy. If you ever want to see your ma again, you tell the marshal right this minute what you told me."

The boy had grabbed the back of his head and stumbled forward, Will catching him.

"You have something to tell me, Abel?"

"He sure does," his pa said.

Abel, holding the back of his head, looked around at his pa, as if to say something, thought better of it, and looked up at Will. "Coop . . . I mean Ambrose, ain't goin' to El Paso."

The boy had Will's attention. "Do you know where he's going, Abel?"

"Yes, sir, I sure do. He and Otis are headed for the mountains. Mr. Cooper has a cabin in the mountains not far from the springs." He turned to Snead. "You know where it is, Marshal, reckon you've stayed there before."

Snead nodded. "Several times, Abel, but what makes you think Ambrose won't go to El Paso?"

"He told us, you know, Finn, Levi, Otis, and me, that he'd never go back to El Paso 'less it was to kill his pa. He ain't goin' there no matter what Mr. Cooper said." Abel grew more confident. "I saw Otis getting his horse ready. He told me he's going with him. Levi and Finn ain't gonna go. I ain't either."

Will extended his hand to the boy. "Thanks for telling us, Abel. That'll save me a long ride I wasn't looking forward to." After shaking the boy's hand, he extended his hand to the boy's father. "Thanks for bringing Abel. He's been a big help."

Gene Rogers took his hand. "Marshal, he wasn't brought up like this. He fell in with the wrong bunch. We thought Ambrose was a nice fella. He'd come over to the house and sing for us. You know, you'd listen to him and think what a nice boy." He shook his head. "Who would've thought."

"Don't beat yourself up, Mr. Rogers," Will said. "We always look for the best in folks. Sometimes we get fooled. That's not our fault. It's theirs." He looked down at Abel. "Listen to your ma and pa, boy. Ambrose is a really bad person. Now he's gone and gotten his uncle shot up, maybe killed, and he let him do it instead of riding in and giving himself up. Stay away from folks like Ambrose, and you'll grow to be a good man. Your telling me this is a big step on the right path." He looked back at Gene Rogers. "How's your wife doing?"

"Good, and thanks for asking. Doctor says she just got a little too excited when she heard about Abel and Ambrose. She's doing fine, but we'd best be getting back. Sure don't want her worrying."

Abel and his father started walking off.

"Abel?" Will asked.

The two stopped and turned back.

"Do you have any clothing or anything that might have Ambrose's smell on it? I'm going to see if Toby can track him."

Abel shook his head. "No, sir, I sure don't." He thought for a second, then looked up, excited he could help, and said, "But you might check with Bert down at the stable. I know Ambrose used to leave clothes there so he wouldn't have to ride all the way back to the ranch."

"Thanks, Abel," Will said, and walked with Marshal Snead toward his house. The big white dog trotted alongside.

WILL HAD STAYED the night in the hotel. With Toby trotting alongside, he stopped by Doc Bradbury's office. "How's he doing?" he asked the bleary-eyed doctor.

"Still alive. That's about the best I can say." He took the small, wire-rimmed glasses from his wide face, wiping them with the end of the blood-spotted apron he wore. Clean, he placed them in a metal case and dropped the case into a large pocket on the front of the apron. Lifting his eyes from the task, he looked at Will. "What'll happen to him should he live?"

"He'll have to stand trial. I could come back and get him, or have the prisoner wagon pick him up. If that happens, he'll be tried in a federal court, which means a long sentence, but I've already talked to Marshal Snead. If Cooper lives, the marshal will arrest him, and the trial will be here in Las Vegas. So I guess it'll depend on what the jury here decides. He did try to kill a U.S. Marshal. Reckon that can't go unpunished."

The doc nodded. "Thanks, Marshal. I don't imagine a jury here will be too hard on him." His teeth showed, among the whiskers, in a faint grin. "After all, you are a stranger." He quickly grew serious. "But it's a shame about Ambrose. For such a talented lad, he's a real demon. I still can't believe he killed Tyler Young. What kind of crazy act was that."

Will glanced out the front window, anxious to be on his way. "I think you hit the nail on the head, Doc. Crazy's the word. I'm no medical man, but I think the boy is really twisted. He doesn't think like a normal person. He told Fran he killed her husband because she loved him, Ambrose." Will shook his head and asked, "You're a doctor, does that sound like a sane man to you?"

"No, Marshal, it doesn't." Their conversation was interrupted by a moan from the other room. "I've got to check my patient." The doctor turned.

Will said to his retreating back, "See you, Doc." He opened the door and stepped outside. Toby lay on the boardwalk, soaking in the morning sun. He looked up at Will. "You feel like a trip to the mountains, boy?"

The dog pushed up into a sitting position and stared at Will.

"I guess that's a yes. Let's go." They walked to the stables and found Bert working on a bridle. The boy looked up. His face brightened when he saw Toby.

He dropped to his knees, and the big dog, tail wagging, trotted to him. With Bert on his knees, he was looking Toby right in the eyes. Bert grabbed the dog and vigorously rubbed his face and neck while Toby gave Bert's face a tongue bath. Bert, laughing, glanced up at Will and, self-conscious, stood. "Sorry, Marshal, what can I do for you?"

"Looks like you two get along."

"Yes, sir, we sure do. Eli and I used to run around together. Toby was always along. We had a lot of fun."

"I can see," Will said. "I'm here for Biscuit and to settle up."

"Yes, sir." Bert pulled out the small notepad he carried, flipped a couple of pages, and came to some figures. Adding quickly, he said, "That'll be six dollars and seventy-five cents, Marshal."

Will, still amazed at the amounts they were charging in Las Vegas, but determined to say nothing more, counted out the money and dropped it into Bert's hand. "There you go."

"Thanks, Marshal," Bert said, noticeably surprised Will had said nothing about the pricing. "I'll get Biscuit. By the way, he's a fine horse. I'd say you made an excellent . . . uh . . . trade," the boy said awkwardly.

"Kuruk killed my horse, Bert. It was a fair trade, and I've got the paper to prove it." Immediately Will thought, *What am I doing justifying my actions to this boy?* Then he said gruffly, "Where's my tack?"

Also happy to change the subject, Bert said, "Tack room," and ran to get Biscuit.

With Biscuit saddled and loaded, Will swung into the saddle. "Let's go, Toby."

The big white dog watched Will, but remained stationary by Bert. Will rode a few steps, but the dog didn't move. *I guess a dog needs a boy,* Will thought. "Can you take care of Toby, Bert?"

The boy dropped down and threw his arm around the big dog's neck. "Oh, yes, sir, I sure can, and Pa likes him, too. He'll be just fine here."

"What about Nasty Ned? He could cause you or Toby some problems."

"No, sir. He won't cause us no problem at all. Pa's gettin' better, and he'll whip Mr. Fairburn three ways from Sunday if he tries anything."

"All right, Bert, you've got yourself a dog." Will sat a moment longer watching the huge dog. The animal sat, tongue hanging out, watching him. *I swear that dog is smiling at me.* He shook his head and bumped Biscuit in the flanks, saying only loud enough for the horse to hear, "Let's go, boy, before I turn maudlin."

Will rode out of Las Vegas, feeling the morning sun warm on his left side. He'd ride north for a ways before taking the trail toward the springs. Alton Snead had given him good directions.

He'd be at the springs in a few hours. The cabin was only a couple of miles past them.

The dun moved along with an easy stride. "Hopefully he and Otis are at the cabin, Biscuit. I'm ready to get back to Deborah. This lawman business is lonely work."

They reached the trail that turned west from the main road. Will applied slight pressure with his left leg and laid the rein across the right side of the horse's neck. Turning left, Biscuit made his way into the hills toward the hot springs. Will's eyes were constantly on the move, watching for a possible ambush. Being forever on the alert had become a way of life, though his mind drifted back to Cooper. *Odds are good, with Doc Bradbury taking care of him, Mott Cooper will survive. He's a good man put into a tough situation. He took responsibility for a boy who was already broken when he got him. All of the man's good intentions have gone by the wayside. Now, if he lives, he'll probably end up in prison for several years. What will happen to his ranch, all of his work? All because of a wayward nephew he took in. But what else could he do?*

Hearing the sound of a fast-moving horse coming up behind him, he turned in the saddle, spotted Snead, and pulled Biscuit to a stop. Fishing rod flopping across the back of his saddle, Alton Snead waved. Moments later he pulled up alongside Will.

"After all the excitement, I thought I'd go fishing up this way. Fancy running into you out here."

Will nodded at the town marshal. "Yes, sir, mighty pretty day to go fishing. I expect, though, there might be some lead flying around the fishing hole."

Snead jerked his head back and, with wide-open eyes, tried to feign surprise. "You don't say. I'd get mighty riled at someone shootin' up my fishing hole."

Will bumped Biscuit in the flanks, and the two lawmen rode side by side.

"Thought you had town duties to take care of today," Will said.

"They'll still be there when I get back."

The hours slowly drifted by as they climbed into the timber. Big, solid ponderosa pines rose high, reaching for the bright blue sky. Sprinklings of green, white, black and brown rose from the scattered aspen groves dotting the mountains. A herd of elk fed in a small park. Their heads were up, watching, when the two horsemen rode into view, but seeing no threat, heads dropped, and they went back to feeding. From overhead on the limb of a pine, a tufted-eared squirrel barked at them until they were well past, his bark muffled by the trees. The smell of the pine and pine needles filled Will's nostrils, and he took a deep breath. His soul sang with the air of the mountains, clear, crisp and filled with life's promises.

Those promises would end for someone today, maybe him, maybe the fugitives. No one knew the future. *Least of all me,* he thought. His mind raced over his past. Deborah, and the war wound that took his memory for so many years. Cuba, his imprisonment and the unceasing sugarcane chopping. Finding Deborah again, and then almost losing the Texas ranch. The deaths of Wade and Liam, war survivors, friends and partners in the ranch. No, of all people, he certainly had no crystal ball.

With Snead at his side, he continued riding toward the cabin, Ambrose and Otis, and then, hopefully, home.

20

They reached the huge red boulder, bigger than a small house. Almost bisecting the rock, from side to side, was a wide yellow streak. The boulder was a landmark Snead had told him about. From here, the cabin was less than five hundred yards ahead. He dismounted and pulled his rifle from its scabbard, partially worked the lever to ensure there was a round in the chamber, then pulled it shut. Snead did the same. With rifle in one hand and reins in the other, the two men began slowly climbing toward the cabin.

His first indication they were nearing the cabin was when Biscuit's nostrils began to flare in preparation of a whinny. He clamped his hand over the horse's nose. "Easy, boy." Biscuit shook his head, but stayed quiet.

The house was well built, but had no windows. It faced east, or down the slope in the mouth of a narrow box canyon. The canyon end could not be seen through the pines, but Snead knew this country well and had described it to Will. A stack of firewood lay haphazardly tossed against the front cabin wall, next to the door. To the south, or left of the house, from his position, was a small barn. Built of logs, it too was sturdy, providing good protection from the cold for the animals inside. Its door, barely wide enough to pass a wagon through, was pulled closed. From inside he could hear hammering, metal on metal.

They faced a dilemma. He had been told there were at least two men. If that was the case, was one in the barn and the other in the cabin? What was the chance they were both in the barn? Were there more than two? Should they split and each take a building, or should they both attack one and warn those in the other building? If they went together, which should they take first, the house or the barn? He didn't like either building. Both had a single access. Opening the door would make them easy targets for either man, or men.

"You cover the house, and I'll take the barn," Will, making up his mind quickly, said to Snead. "There's a good chance, if there's shooting, whoever is in the house will bolt outside for a horse. If they do, you've got 'em."

Snead nodded his agreement. "That's probably Otis hammering. His pa is a wheelwright. Don't know why the boy didn't stick with his pa. The kid's good at it."

The hammering continued. Will slipped cautiously toward the barn. Reaching the door, he examined it. It was a solid, wide, single door, with a pull latchstring that could be retracted from inside. Fortunately it was hanging out. He would have to pull the latch, push the swinging door open, and once past the door, step to the side. He waited for the next hammer strike.

At the clang, he yanked the latch and shoved hard. The heavy door swung easily on well-rigged hinges, but with a loud squeal. Rifle ready, he leaped to the side. Sure enough, it was Otis. He was bent over an anvil with a horseshoe gripped in tongs. His shirtsleeves were rolled up, and the veins in his flexed and sweating biceps stood out. The hammer was lifted high.

"Hello, Otis."

The boy stared at Will, eyes wide with surprise. "What?" Then he glanced at the back stall of the barn, alerting Will.

"Whoever else is in this barn, step out, nice and easy, hands empty. You're not in bad trouble right now, but if you make a sudden move, I'll be forced to shoot you. You boys are way too young to die."

While he scanned the barn, Will spoke to Otis. "Drop the hammer, boy, and then the gun, nice and easy. It's time you head back home while you still can."

Otis slowly lowered the hammer and dropped the tongs, leaving the shoe on the anvil. His six-gun hung from his right side, the holster barely visible to Will.

Will raised his voice to reach whoever was hiding in the barn. "I'm not telling you again. Throw the gun out, and stand up, hands empty."

Slowly a head appeared above the back stall. It was Finn Peterson. Will knew the boy wasn't much older than Abel Rogers.

He spoke in a quivering voice. "I ain't got no gun, Marshal. It's inside the house with Levi and Ambrose."

Otis spun on Finn. "Shut yore stupid mouth, kid."

Will said, "Shut up, Otis. Finn, get your hands up high, where I can see them."

The boy's hands shot up, palms forward, empty and shaking.

"All right, step out in the open. Otis, I said to drop the gun belt."

Surprise had long since left the face of Otis. His eyes were squinted, nostrils flared, and lips pursed in a flat line. His fists clinched and unclinched. Head tilted slightly down, bushy eyebrows drawn together, he looked hard, determined, more like a grown man in his thirties than one just breaking into his twenties, barely old enough to be packing a gun.

"Just relax, Otis," Will said, "and drop the gun belt."

Otis stared at him.

"Boy, I see you have a real itch to draw that gun, but the bullet from this Winchester will tear you apart long before you can get that hogleg out of your holster. Now drop it!"

Besides his shaking, Finn didn't move. His wide, childlike, blue eyes were locked on Otis, waiting.

From outside came the yell of Snead. "Hold up, Levi. Drop the gun and move over by the woodpile."

A shot rang out, and there was a scream, then a desperate cry, "I'm shot, oh mama, I'm shot."

At the sound of the shot, Otis made his move. Will had known the boy wanted to draw, even against such terrible odds, but he had hoped the moment would pass, and sanity would prevail. Unfortunately, sanity was nowhere around when it came to Otis. With his inexperience and constant practice, he felt bulletproof. Only, he wasn't.

Will waited, watching the boy's hand whip down to the revolver. He was fast for a wheelwright, but nowhere near fast enough to be a gunfighter. Will knew he should never wait. Waiting could get a man killed, but he hoped the boy would have a sudden change of heart. There was still time. He might change his mind. There was always time—until there wasn't.

When the muzzle of the six-gun cleared leather and started to turn toward Will, time ran out for Otis. The 1866 Winchester Yellow Boy roared in the confines of the small barn. Though held at waist level and pointed by instinct, the muzzle was centered on the boy's left side, which was facing Will. The Yellow Boy bucked in his hands, sending the big hunk of lead blasting toward Otis.

It ripped first through the boy's left bicep. The bicep that only moments before had been providing the power to grip the tongs holding the horseshoe, but now instantly turned into bleeding shards of exploded flesh. After passing through his bicep, the bullet tore through his left lung, turning it into pink froth. From there it continued, ripping into the strong, resilient heart, cutting short its projected three billion beats, and, energy expended, came to rest under the skin of his right side.

Otis staggered toward Finn, the gun dropping from his hand onto the hay-covered floor. His face shocked, dismayed, telling the story. In his last moments, he realized he was not the strong, fast, unbeatable gunhand he had imagined himself. He was just a young man, with skills to become an excellent wheelwright, whose body was now ripped and torn and would never grow older.

The instant he fired, Will worked the Winchester's lever, throwing the empty case out and driving a fresh round into the chamber.

"Don't shoot, Marshal," Finn screamed. "I swear I ain't got no gun. Please don't shoot."

Will, regretting having to shoot Otis, swung the barrel of the Winchester to cover Finn. The boy stepped clear of the stall, arms thrust high, and there was a dark, wet splotch expanding down his legs.

"I'm not going to shoot you, Finn. Just stay where you are. You'll be fine." He moved to the fallen Otis, who had been dead on his feet and now lay crumpled in the sawdust and manure covering the floor. In death, Otis still had a look of surprise on his face. Blood covered his upper body.

Will picked up the revolver and motioned for Finn to move to the door ahead of him. Finn stepped wide around his fallen friend, eyes hardly leaving the body. Tears flowed down the boy's cheeks.

"Stop at the door," Will ordered. He moved close to the door and called, "Alton, you all right?"

"I am, but Levi's crumpled up over by the woodpile, and I think Ambrose is inside."

Will said to Finn, "Is there any other way to get out of the cabin?"

"Yes, sir, Ambrose showed us the tunnel Mr. Cooper built at the back of the house. It ain't rightly a tunnel, but there's a door in the floor, beneath a cabinet, that opens to some stairs going down to the cellar. The cellar has an outside door. It's hidden behind a big pile of brush."

Will called, "We're coming out." He motioned to Finn. The boy stepped out of the barn and looked around until he spotted the town marshal.

"Go sit by Levi, Finn, at the front of the cabin," Snead ordered.

Finn looked at Will, who motioned him to move, and walked around to the front of the house. Will followed.

When the boy saw Levi, he whimpered and said, "Oh no," running to his friend.

"Relax, Finn," Snead called. "He'll live. Sit down beside him."

Will walked over to Snead and said, "I think Ambrose is gone. Finn said there's a back exit out of the cabin."

"No, there can't be. I've spent a bunch of nights in that cabin. I can tell you there ain't a door anywhere."

Will nodded toward Finn. "The boy says it's under a rug and cabinet that sit against the wall."

"Why, that old rooster," Snead said. "I never could imagine building the cabin without another way to get out. I looked around, couldn't find one, and assumed he was just in a hurry. He sure fooled me." His face turned grave. "Otis?"

"Dead." Will sighed and shook his head. "I had the drop on him, but when you shot Levi . . . The crazy kid tried to draw on me. I guess he figured he was fast enough to beat a leveled rifle."

Snead shook his head. "All of this can be laid at the feet of Ambrose Cooper, including his uncle. These boys were a little wild, but never into any serious trouble until Ambrose came around."

"Speaking of Ambrose," Will said, "I'm going inside. He's probably gone, but we need to know for sure."

He handed his rifle to Snead and pulled his Remington. As he walked by the boys, Finn said, "He's long gone, Marshal. He had his horse tied in the back, not far from the cellar door."

Will stepped past the boys toward the door. He knew he could be stepping into big trouble. The day was bright, and his eyes were adjusted to the bright light. Inside the dark cabin, they'd have to readjust. He'd need time, and the only way to get it was to distract Ambrose, if he was in there. He picked up one of the split logs for the fireplace and threw it hard into the dark cabin. It banged off the back wall as he went in low, somersaulting across the floor and slamming against the opposite wall. No gun roared. A quick look around the cabin showed him it was clear. Along the back wall he could see where the cabinet and rug had been pushed aside, and the cellar door gaped open. Ambrose was gone.

Relieved, Will stood. If Ambrose had been here, the boy would have put lead into him. The only question would have been where, and if he could've killed him first. Dropping the Remington into its holster, he said, "All clear. Ambrose is gone."

Snead walked in and looked at the cabinet. "I'll be durned. I never thought of moving that cabinet. Sometimes I thought it was mighty stupid of Mott to put his rug under the cabinet instead of the table, but it was his place, and I reckoned he could do as he pleased. I just appreciated him letting me stay here on occasion. Guess it was me who was stupid."

Outside again, Will gazed down at Finn and Levi. The second boy was gripping his bleeding left hand in his right. He turned up a tear-streaked face to Will. "It hurts mighty bad, Mr. Marshal."

Will squatted down and took the damaged hand in his, dwarfing it. "I reckon it does, boy." The bullet had taken off the boy's little finger as cleanly as if a butcher knife had been used instead. The finger was completely gone, and the white bone of the knuckle glistened in the light. "You're lucky."

The boy had been holding the damaged hand, and Will gently placed it back in the youth's hand.

"I ain't feelin' too lucky, Marshal Logan."

Will looked at the pained face. "You've just found out how bad a bullet wound hurts, and it only cost you a little finger. Imagine how it would feel if that ball had torn through your belly instead."

"Oh," Levi said, thinking on Will's statement. "I see what you mean. I guess I am lucky."

Snead said, "Finn, go help Levi wash up that hand, then we'll wrap it up."

"Yes, sir," Finn said. He helped Levi to his feet, and with his friend leaning on him, they walked to the well.

"Think they've learned anything?" Snead asked Will.

"I'm not much at predictin'," Will said, "but my guess is those boys have seen the last of the wrong side of the law."

"I'm bettin' you're right. You're goin' after Ambrose, I'd guess."

"Yep. When I catch him, I'll not be coming back to your town. I'll be headin' straight for Pueblo. You'll take the boys and Otis back to town?"

"I'll do that," Snead said. "I don't much look forward to telling Otis's folks. They're good people. Old Mr. Otis works hard as a blacksmith and wheelwright, has a good business. This'll tear 'em up, but at least they have other children. Those kids will help keep their mind off their dead son, if that's possible."

"It's not worth much," Will said, "but I'd appreciate it if you'd tell them I'm mighty sorry."

"I'll do it."

Will, shaking his head, continued, "I gave that boy more time than I've ever given another man. If I'd waited another second, as slow as he was, he would've been standing over me."

Snead nodded. "Sometimes this is a hard job. It pulls at a man, but you just do your job and move on to the next."

"I need to talk to them and see if they know where Ambrose will go," Will said, watching the boys return.

Snead pulled off his bandanna and wrapped it tight around Levi's hand. The pressure halted the bleeding, but Levi was still in a great deal of pain. The boy wasn't crying out, but occasionally a tear would escape from his brown eyes.

"Do either of you know where Ambrose may go?" Will asked them.

Levi spoke up through the pain. "Yes, sir, reckon I do. He said he had some friends in Santa Fe, and if we got split up, we was to meet him at the Bucket of Blood Saloon."

"That's right," Finn said. "He said we would be one of the most famous stage-robbing gangs ever known. Said them eastern writers would write stories about us."

"Did you believe him, Finn?"

Finn looked at his feet, then looked up at the big marshal. "Yes, sir. I reckon I did, then."

"Do you believe him now?"

Finn shook his head violently. "No, sir. Them was all lies. I knew Otis when he wasn't a bad sort, and he's dead now. If'n he hadn't listened to Coop, he' be alive today." He looked down at Levi's hand. "And Levi would still have his finger. No, sir. I don't believe him at all."

Will looked at the sky. The sun sagged toward the western peaks. "I'd best be on my way. There's a good chance I can catch up to Ambrose long before he gets to Santa Fe."

"You take care," Snead said, "and thanks for everything."

"Yep," Will said. He nodded to the boys, picked up his rifle, and headed for Biscuit. Walking back to the horse, Will's mind slipped back to his deceiving of Fran Young and the Lazy Y hands, the shooting of Mott Cooper and the killing of Otis Thatcher. It weighed heavy on his mind. He worked on puzzling out the problems of being a lawman.

The goal was to protect the public and put away those individuals who thought it easier to let the honest man work for a living and then steal what he'd earned. It made it even worse when the thief killed to accomplish his goal. He decided everything he'd done had been ethical. Yes, he'd lied to Fran and her cowhands, but it had been necessary to find Ambrose. If he had ridden into Las Vegas and told them the real reason he was there, the kid would've been gone. But then, he was still chasing him. But the lying still didn't sit right with him. He'd have to study that out some more. Both Mott and Otis had been righteous shootings, though killing either of them turned his stomach. *I sure hope Mott doesn't die,* he thought, *but whether he does or not, I'll be carrying the weight of those shootings with me for the rest of my life.*

Reaching Biscuit, he slid the Yellow Boy into its scabbard and swung up into the saddle. Biscuit was ready. He rode to the back of the cabin and examined the ground. Ambrose had left a trail an eastern dude could follow. He turned Biscuit south and started the chase again. *This kid is tough to hold on to,* he thought. *But the next time I catch him, he's going to stay caught.*

21

W ill, sitting a tired Biscuit, looked down on the lights of Santa Fe. The kid surprised him. Several times he thought he would catch him, but Ambrose managed to slip away. He knew he was being followed, and Will felt sure he knew who was following him. He had to figure Ambrose was getting desperate. He felt sure he would find the young killer in Santa Fe, probably among friends.

Riding into town, the smells struck him first. Wafting on the cool evening breeze, the odor of human waste mixed with the smell of goats, cattle, dogs, and sheep reminded him he was back among people. He had grown used to the clean smell of the mountain country, so the odor was especially offensive, but Will was no simpering wallflower. He had smelled this and worse.

But the sweet smell of rose blossoms dulled the more offensive smells, bringing a scent of pleasure, even of anticipation. His mouth began to water as the previous smells were overpowered by the enticing aroma of tortillas, frijoles, and tamales. Hot peppers added their spice to the air and brought a smile to his lips. There were bad smells in a town, but good smells, too. He caught the scent of a woman's perfume and thought of Deborah, felt her cheek against his, smelled the unforgettable scent of her hair. "Ah, Biscuit," he said, "many more thoughts about Deborah, and I'll be tempted to turn around."

A man standing at the door of a hacienda he was passing said, "Ah, señor, you must have Spanish blood, for you speak of a señorita?"

Will, embarrassed he had been overheard speaking to his horse about Deborah, cleared his throat while pulling Biscuit to a halt, and said, "No, señor, I speak of my wife."

"Ahh, your wife. Then you must truly be in love."

Will, thoroughly embarrassed because he did not speak of love to other men, cleared his throat again and said, "Well, yes, but I am not usually overheard."

Immediately, the man stepped from the shadows of the hacienda gate. "Permit me to apologize and introduce myself. I did not mean to intrude on a man's private thoughts, and since you were speaking them out loud . . . but so, I am Luis Renato Noguera Bolivar, at your service." The man swept his large sombrero from his head and gave a deep bow. Will inclined his head to the man.

"Señor Noguera, it is I who must apologize for my rudeness. It is a pleasant night, and the scent of a woman's perfume brought to mind my beautiful wife, and thinking myself alone, I spoke to my horse . . . I am William Wallace Logan, but I go by Will."

The man stepped closer, and in the light from the hacienda, Will could see the white hair.

"Señor Logan, please step from your fine steed and come into my poor abode. I am sure you are hungry and tired from your long ride. It would be my pleasure to show you a little hospitality in order to repay you for my effrontery."

"It isn't necessary, Señor Noguera. I am dirty from many days in the hills and would not want to bring this dirt into your home."

The man turned and spoke quickly in Spanish. Another man

leaped from the darkness. Will's hand whipped down to his Remington.

"No, señor. Tsk-tsk," Señor Noguera said, "we are starting so badly. This is Juan. He will take care of your horse, give him water, feed, and a good rubdown. He means you no harm."

Will grinned, his teeth flashing in the hacienda's light, and swung down from Biscuit. "I reckon you are a man who doesn't accept no."

The older man smiled. "You are correct, Will, and please call me Luis. I detest formality. You may leave everything on your horse. It will be brought to you."

Will watched Biscuit being led away, and thought, *I'm either getting shanghaied or meeting a fine fella. We'll find that out soon enough.*

He turned to the older man and, in fluent Spanish, said, "Thank you, Luis. I appreciate your hospitality."

"Ahh. You speak Spanish, and I detect . . ." He paused, a finger to his cheek, thinking. At last a smile graced his wide face, spreading the salt-and-pepper mustache and showing bright white teeth. "I detect a hint of the islands."

"Very good, Luis. Yes, I learned your language in Cuba. I was involved with sugarcane."

"Ahh, a grower?"

"No, a slave."

His host's eyebrows rose. "Umm, Will, please come in. I sense a long and interesting story, which I'm sure my family would love to hear."

A servant led them into a large courtyard, where separate rooms opened from a wide flagstone walkway.

"Please, go with Rafael. He will show you to your room, where there will be a bath for you and clean clothes. My son is about your size, and he is in Mexico. He will not mind your use of them."

"That's not necessary, Luis," Will protested. "We just met. You have no reason to be so generous to a stranger."

"But I do, Will. I cannot let a man who has the language of love on his lips and a U.S. Marshal's badge on his vest continue into my city without showing a little hospitality."

"Señor?" Rafael said, and motioned to one of the rooms.

Giving in, Will nodded to Luis and followed Rafael into the bedroom, where a large tub sat steaming, with towels, soap, and a washcloth on the stand next to it. *I don't know how I fell into this,* Will thought, *but that bath looks too good to turn down.* Will switched to Spanish and said to Rafael, "Thank you."

The man smiled and nodded. "I can help you, sir, or if you prefer, I'll be outside. Just call me when you're finished."

"Thank you, I'll call you."

The man nodded, turned, and disappeared from the room, pulling the door closed behind him. But not so quickly that Will missed the female voices and excited laughter drifting in from the hallway. He grinned and thought, *This might be an interesting evening, and for a while, I can take Cooper from my mind.*

He stripped quickly, dropping his dirty clothes in a pile next to the tub. The hot water, almost burning hot, soon relaxed tired and aching muscles. He lay in the slant-backed tub for a few minutes, enjoying the wonderful comfort of the hot water. Reaching to the small side table, he grasped the square of soap and held it to his nose. A flowery aroma emanated from the square, nothing like the lye soap he was used to. It reminded him of the soap Deborah brought from the east. He slid down in the tub, his head disappearing beneath the sudsy water, and scrubbed dirt from his hair. He couldn't believe how good it felt. After cleaning his dirt-encrusted hair and scrubbing every inch of his body, days of dirt were left floating on the surface of the water. He stood and splashed water over his white legs to make sure none of the grime from the water's surface stuck to him.

Drying, he couldn't help but see his reflection in the large full-length mirror. The dark brown of his sun-baked hands and face contrasted with the gleaming white of his body. Wide, muscled shoulders filled the mirror, and heavy biceps stretched the towel. A peppering of white was scattered throughout his light brown hair, which hung almost to his collar.

The streak of white hair, on the right side of his head, marking the old bullet wound that stole his memory for so long, gleamed in the flickering lamplight. The towel wiped over puckered skin in his left leg where, in the same battle, a bullet had struck, breaking his leg.

He grinned at himself in the mirror. *I've got more holes in me than Ma's old pincushion.* His eyes travel to the bayonet wound in his right side and the bullet wound in his left bicep, but turning, his smile disappeared. Reflected in the mirror, scars laced his back from the vicious strike of the Cuban overseers' whips in Cuba. The sight brought back to his mind concern for the Cuban friends who had risked their lives to rescue him and get him safely to an American ship.

Still thinking about his friends and the convoluted turns his life had made, he slipped into the clothing laid across the bed. Since his long johns were in the pile of dirty clothes, he first slipped the undershirt and light underpants on. Both were soft and cool to his freshly scrubbed body, still hot from the bath. He slipped the shirt over his head, smelling the pleasant, aromatic fragrance from the soap it had been washed with. It fit well except for the tight stretch around the shoulders. *Señor Noguera's son must be a big guy,* Will thought. *Hope he doesn't mind me borrowing his clothes.*

Will pulled on the black trousers, which also fit well except for being a little loose in the waist and tight in the thighs. He was relieved to see a pair of clean moccasins. It would be a shame to wear his dirty, beat-up boots with these fine clothes. He had dressed similarly, for a while, when he was in Cuba, until he had been captured by the Spanish soldiers. He cleared his head of those thoughts of the past.

Opening the door, he found Rafael standing outside, waiting. In Spanish, the servant said, "Señor Logan, I will take your clothing. It will be washed and ready for you in the morning, along with your other clothes. Clothes dry quickly in Santa Fe's dry air."

Also in Spanish, Will said, "Thank you, Rafael, you are too kind."

The man inclined his head and held out his arm toward the dining room, down the hall. "Come, Señor, you are expected." He led Will to the entrance of the dining room and stepped aside, disappearing along the hallway toward Will's room.

Señor Noguera sat at the head of a long engraved wooden table. A large, but regal-looking woman sat at the other end, while two young women sat on one side, with their backs to him, one near her mother and the other near Luis.

Will entered the room, inclined his head first to Luis, then to the lady at the end of the table, and, in Spanish, said, "Thank you very much for your hospitality. I had expected to be eating in much less pleasant surroundings."

The lady at the end of the table smiled and gave a slight nod of her head in acknowledgment.

Luis stood, made a slight bow, and said to Will, in English, "We all speak English here, my friend." He then turned to the woman Will presumed was his wife. "This is a weary and poetic traveler I met this evening. He also happens to be a United States Marshal, Marshal Will Logan."

Will smiled and nodded. He could smell the aromas escaping from the kitchen, and his mouth immediately started watering, and to his chagrin, his stomach let out a long, low growl, heard throughout the room. The girls covered their mouths as they broke into uncontrolled giggles, greeted with a stern look from the lady at the head of the table.

Will saw the look that passed between the woman and the girls, and it promised no good for the young ones. He said, "Sorry, folks, I've been on the trail for a while now. Guess my stomach knows good food when it's smelled."

The girls couldn't control themselves. In spite of their mother's warning looks, they started giggling again.

"Come," Luis said, "sit by me, and please disregard my impolite daughters. It appears all of their training has been wasted."

At their father's comments, the laughter disappeared from the girls' faces. The older of the two said in a soft lilting voice, "We are sorry, Papi." She looked up at Will. "Please accept our apologies, Mr. Logan."

Will smiled at the two of them. "No problem. Reckon I thought it was pretty funny myself."

"Do not encourage them, Señor Logan," the lady said.

From his end of the table, Luis held out his arm toward the lady. "This is my lovely wife, Dolores Rosa Cuellar Parilla."

Will smiled to his hostess and said, "It is a pleasure to make your acquaintance, Señora Cuellar."

"As it is mine, Señor Logan, but please, call me Dolores."

"Thank you," Will said. "I am flattered by your kindness. I am Will."

"Yes," Luis said, "and these two are Teresa and Rosaria. Teresa is the oldest, but sometimes it is hard to tell." He motioned to Will's chair. "Please, sit." Immediately he clapped his hands, and food began to arrive.

The girls smiled shyly at Will. Teresa said, "We are so sorry, Señor Will."

"I have a bunch of brothers and sisters, and I've heard a lot worse."

He watched as servants placed large portions of beans, a salad, thin-sliced beef covered with melted cheese, and ladled a spicy-smelling sauce over the beans and meat.

"Rosa, please bless our food," Luis said.

The youngest daughter quickly bowed her head and gave thanks.

"Now," Luis said, "eat up."

Will tried to eat slowly, but the seasoned taste of the beef and peppery beans drew his fork quickly between bites. The tomatoes, cucumbers, bell peppers, lettuce, and corn of the salad, also drizzled with a spicy sauce, provided a wonderful contrast to the meat and beans. Before the others were nearing half finished with the food they had been given, Will was done, and the servants were back with more. He glanced at his hostess, who was smiling and nodding.

"Please, Señor Logan, eat. There is plenty. It is a pleasure to see a hungry man eat."

"Thanks, ma'am," Will said. "This is mighty good food."

His plate was reloaded, and the food quickly disappeared. Finishing the second plate, he called it quits. He could eat more, but it was time to stop. Placing his fork on his plate, Will leaned back in his chair. The girls were smiling at him. He gave each a smile and turned to look down the table at his hostess. "Dolores, I don't know when I've eaten so much. Thank you for your generosity to a stranger."

She waved a hand in the air, dismissing his thanks. "You have not finished, Will. It is time for dessert."

"Rosaria, Teresa, are you ready for dessert?"

Both girls clapped their hands, eyes locked on the kitchen door. Even as Dolores spoke, the servants stepped out bearing loaded plates. The smell of cinnamon and warm caramel filled the air.

Rosario squealed and said, "Churros with caramel sauce. Oh, I love them."

A plate of three was set in front of each person. The girls obediently watched their mother. When she cut into the first one, they followed suit. Will glanced at Luis, who was beaming at his daughters.

Will's first bite melted in his mouth. The fried sweet dough, covered with sugar and cinnamon, with the added taste of the caramel was heavenly. He couldn't help but smile at the taste. He had eaten churros before, but these were exceptional.

Will said to Luis, "These churros are definitely the very best I have ever tasted."

Luis nodded, waiting to speak until he had finished his bite. "Yes, our cook has been with us for a long time, and many friends have tried to hire her from us. I believe you say hijack."

Will laughed. "I can certainly understand why. The lady is quite a hand with cooking."

"She is," Luis said. "Now, Will, it is time for you to sing for your supper. Perhaps you could tell us the story of how you ended up in Cuba, working in the sugarcane fields as a slave, if you wouldn't mind."

"It is long, and I fear it would be boring," Will said.

Rosaria, almost jumping in her seat, said, "Oh, no, Señor Will. Papi told us what you had said about your Spanish. We would love to hear your story. It would be exciting for us."

Dolores cleared her throat. "Not too exciting, I hope. It's almost bedtime for you girls."

Teresa's face turned pouty and sad. "Please, Mami, we have a special guest. Let us stay up and listen. We promise to go straight to bed when Señor Will is done." She turned her pleading large brown eyes to her father. "Papi?"

Will observed Luis look to his wife, who smiled and nodded. "Yes, my daughters," he said, "you may stay up and listen. But tomorrow, you must jump out of bed when your mami calls."

They both nodded their heads vigorously, saying in unison, "Yes, Papi, we will."

He turned to Will. "Señor?"

"I will be glad to, Luis, but I am trailing a killer. His name is Ambrose Cooper. A young man in his early twenties. I'd like to make sure he's in town. My information is that he has friends in the Bucket of Blood saloon. He has a beautiful voice and might even be singing there. If you had someone—"

Luis held up a hand. "Say no more, Will. I will send Juan and his brother to investigate. They will find out for you." Luis called Juan, explained to him what was needed, and the man was gone.

"In that case," Will said, "let me tell you how I managed to land myself on the island of Cuba, slapdab in the middle of a righteous insurrection." Will started the story with his waking up in the hospital in Washington, DC, and seeing Deborah. He kept the family enthralled for almost two hours until finally ending with his marriage to Deborah in Pueblo.

"And that's pretty much the full story of my adventuring years. I'll have to say again, I was really lucky in getting my memory back, and especially finding Deborah."

Both girls, tired as he could see they were, sat entranced with his story. "Oh, Señor Will." Teresa sighed. "That is such a romantic story. I am so happy for you and Señora Deborah."

Dolores stood, prompting both Will and Luis to rise, and said, "An amazing story of trials, love, and good fortune. I am sure you thank God daily that you found your Deborah."

"Ma'am, I certainly do."

She smiled at him, then turned to her daughters. "It is bedtime. Say goodnight to Señor Will."

Both girls rose, curtsied, and thanked him before wishing him a good night. They then hurried from the room, their skirts rustling and shoes clicking on the tile. Dolores started to follow, but stopped and turned back when Will said, "Ma'am, I am very grateful for the bath, the excellent supper, and the opportunity to share your wonderful home."

"It is my pleasure, Will. I have gotten used to my husband occasionally ambushing unknowing travelers. It gives our children the opportunity to learn of other peoples' lives. We were very enriched by you and your story this evening." She inclined her head and was gone.

Moments after she departed, Juan and his brother came into the room, hats in hand. "Jefe?" Juan said.

"You have information?"

"Yes, Jefe. This Ambrose Cooper is in the Bucket of Blood. He was telling of Señor Logan following him and saying how he will kill the marshal."

Listening closely, Will said, "Did he indicate when he might leave?"

Juan shook his head. "I don't think he plans on leaving, Señor. There was a girl holding tightly onto his arm. He looked as if he has plans for the evening."

Luis said, "Will, would you like for me to have someone keep an eye on him?"

Surprised, Will said, "That would be real nice, Luis. I need a good night's rest. I'll pay whoever you get a five-dollar gold piece if they'll watch Cooper tonight and come get me if he starts to leave."

Juan spoke up. "Jefe, I can do this if you do not mind."

"Good," Luis said, "keep an eye on him, and let us know if it looks like he might be preparing to leave."

"Yes, Jefe," Juan said, and hurried, with his brother, from the room.

22

A faint knock on his door brought Will awake. He palmed his Remington and eased to the door.

"It is Juan, Señor."

Will slipped the cold barrel of the Remington between his back and his waistband and opened the door.

"It is five o'clock, Señor. There is no sign of movement in or around the cabin, but the town will soon awaken. If you would catch him, this might be a good time."

Juan handed him his clean clothes.

"Give me a minute."

He quickly dressed, slung his gun belt around his waist, checked his Remington, and followed Juan out of the house.

Luis was waiting with several men. They were all armed. "We are ready to help, Will. We have enough of this kind in our town. We do not need more."

He looked at the men, all experienced, with determined faces.

"How far is it?" Will asked.

"Better to ride," Luis said. "We will be noticed, but traveling by horseback, we will arrive before anyone can warn him."

"Good," Will said. "Let's go."

The men followed Juan and Will to the saddled horses. Everyone climbed aboard their horse, and Will nodded to Juan. Five minutes later, they pulled up in front of the Bucket of Blood. Lamps were still lit inside, and the lonely sound of the piano carried into the street. *Five o'clock,* Will thought, *and they're still going at it.*

"It is better to leave our horses here, Señor," Juan said.

Will dismounted along with Luis and the other men. With Juan and Will leading, they entered the alley paralleling the north side of the saloon. Sitting about fifty yards behind the saloon, a small shanty stood by itself except for an outhouse a short distance away.

Nearing the front of the house, Will stopped the group and whispered, "Cover me. Don't let any of his friends near." He headed for the door, Luis and Juan alongside. He stopped and said to Luis, "Sorry, but I need to do this. Thanks for your help. Wait for me here. If somehow he gets past me, try to stop him without killing him."

Luis, disappointed, nodded and spoke to Juan. The man nodded and stood with his boss. Will slipped toward the shack. Reaching the door, he found the drawstring pulled inside. There was no chance he could get that latch open without the drawstring, and even if he did, the door was probably barred from the inside.

He stood thinking. After a moment he raised his six-gun and pounded on the door with the butt, yelling, in a high voice, "Coop, Coop, that ranger just rode into town. If you're a-gettin' out of here, it'd better be now!"

Cursing, scrambling, and yelling came from inside. Added to the yelling was the sound of crashing furniture and stomping feet. Within moments, Ambrose Cooper burst from the shanty, hopping on one foot while trying to pull a boot on the other. His hat hung down his back on its string, and his shirttail was hanging over barely fastened pants. His gun was in the holster, leather loop safely over the hammer, and the belt wrapped around the holster. He had it tucked awkwardly under his arm. With his head down, working diligently to get his remaining boot on, he hopped straight up to Will, who hit him lightly in the chest, stopping the gunman.

"Howdy, Ambrose. You looking to go somewhere?"

The boy's mouth dropped open, and still hopping, he would have fallen if Will hadn't grabbed his arm. Dismayed, he looked around at the armed men behind Will. His eyes blinked like a raccoon caught in lamplight. He stood there, boot in one hand, looking like a boy caught in some mischief.

Will said, "Put your boot on."

Ambrose bent over, with Will bracing him, pulled his boot on, and straightened.

"I'll take that gun belt," Will said.

Surprise slowly turned to anger and frustration.

Will, in the dim light of morning, watched the boy's expressions change. He reached out and yanked the gun, holster, and gun belt from under the killer's arm.

Over the boy's shoulder, Will saw the dawn light illuminate the dance hall girl who had provided Ambrose with what would probably be his last female companionship. She was a fragile-looking thing. Probably about the age of the killer. Blonde hair hung to her waist. She clutched a worn-thin cotton housecoat to her frail-looking body. Hollow eyes, blank in the morning light, watched the proceedings.

"You coming back soon, Coop?" she asked, not yet grasping what was happening.

"No, ma'am," Will said, "I don't imagine you'll be seeing Mr. Coop again."

She looked at Cooper's back and then caught the glint of the marshal's badge on Will's vest. Her face changed from fragile to hard as she said to Will, "You're lucky you didn't give him a fair fight, lawman. He'd a killed you, dead."

Will touched his hat and said, "Have a nice day, ma'am." He grasped Cooper's arm and started walking back to the horses. "Let's go, Ambrose. You've got a date with a judge."

This time when the boy looked up at Will, the swagger was gone, and so was the brief flash of anger. There was no frustration, no hate, not even the tiniest bit of fight remaining. The wide yellow eyes were filled only with fear.

WILL WAS WORN OUT, but his heart soared as he rode into Pueblo with his prisoner. It had been a long haul from Santa Fe, through Las Vegas, Trinidad, and finally home.

They had stopped to check on Mott Cooper. Will was surprised to see Fran Young there, and Mott was doing much better with her nursing him. It seemed the two of them were enjoying the new relationship.

Snead had told Will he was waiting to jail Mott until he got better. Will didn't mention it to Snead, but he doubted if Mott would ever see the inside of a jail, and truthfully, he didn't care. He found it hard to blame the man for what he did. He was protecting his family, in a twisted sort of way.

Leaving the horses at the stable in Las Vegas, Will had a chance to see Toby. Bert and the big white dog appeared to be inseparable, but Toby was still glad to see him. He was surprised at how pleased he was to see the big dog. A lot had happened since Toby had decided to stay with Bert, and it had pushed the dog from Will's mind, but when he saw him again . . . It was funny how a man could get so attached to a dog.

On the trip, Will had learned firsthand how well Ambrose could sing. After the first day on the trail, Ambrose relaxed and started singing. Like everyone had told him, the boy had a beautiful voice, and Will never got tired of listening. He knew Ambrose had an ulterior motive. The boy hoped Will would lower his guard, and if he did, Ambrose, with the angelic voice, would pump Will full of lead, but he had never gotten the chance, and now it was almost finished. He had only to turn Ambrose over to his boss, U.S. Marshal Benjamin Morgan.

Riding along the main street, Will noticed several people looking at him and then whispering. *Understandable,* he thought, *Ambrose Cooper has become a known man, but I'll be rid of him soon.*

He passed Doc James's office and considered stopping in to see Deborah, but decided against it. The first thing he wanted to do was throw Ambrose in jail and forget him and all the baggage that went along with him. He'd gone over in his mind, time and again, what he might have done differently to keep from killing Otis, but it always came out the same way. He'd done the only thing he could do. On one occasion, when he was angry at Will for tying him at night, the boy laughingly told Will how he had convinced Otis of how fast on the draw he was. Then he had said, "Otis would make a terrapin look fast." Will had never struck a bound man, but at that moment he was sorely tempted.

He pulled Biscuit up in front of the town marshal's office. He could leave Ambrose here and find out the whereabouts of Marshal Morgan. "Get down," he said to Ambrose.

The boy stared at him and lifted the corner of his lip in a sneer. Will restrained himself. He had been known to kick a man out of the saddle, and this boy deserved it, but not today. He was feeling too good. He'd soon see his lovely Deborah.

He swung down, tied Biscuit, walked around to Ambrose, reached up, and clinched long fingers around his arm, then physically dragged him out of the saddle. Still holding the arm, the boy wincing from the pain, Will marched him into the marshal's office. To his surprise, and from the look on his face, his also, Marshal Morgan was sitting behind the town marshal's desk.

Morgan looked first at Will, then at the diminutive Ambrose. Recovering from his surprise, Morgan said, "You caught him."

Will nodded. "Yep. Shot up a couple of folks to do it. One of 'em's dead, but I caught him. Found him in Santa Fe, thanks to the help of Señor Noguera."

"Know him," Morgan said. He stood, walked to the wall adjoining the cell, removed the jail keys, and unlocked the cell. Will shoved Ambrose hard into the cell.

The young man stumbled through the door, finally steadying himself against the back wall. With the locked jail door between him and Will, his bravado returned, and he said, "Good thing you didn't draw against *me*, Marshal. You'd be the one with dirt in your face."

Ignoring Cooper, Will and Morgan walked to the desk, Morgan returning to his seat behind the desk and Will dropping into one of the chairs in front. It creaked with his sudden weight, but held.

Will stretched his long legs, leaning back in the chair.

"It's good to be home. I'll take care of the horses, then I'm gonna mosey on down to Dr. James's office and see if there might be a pretty girl looking for me there."

Morgan's face had held concern since Will walked in with Ambrose. "You haven't heard?"

Will felt a chill creep through his chest. "Heard what?"

"Blake Foster and his gang escaped. Foster shot Sheriff Fletcher in the getaway. He's got Nash and Fisher with him."

"How's the sheriff?"

"Doc James seems to think his odds are real good."

"Good," Will said. "When did this happen?"

"Two days ago."

"How'd it happen?"

"Look, Will," Morgan said, leaning forward, his forearms on the desk, "that ain't important right now."

Will's brow wrinkled in puzzlement. "What is, Marshal?"

"Do you remember Foster grabbing your wife's arm after she doctored him?"

Will gave several slow nods. "Yes, so what?"

"He took her."

Will was on his feet in an instant. The rush of adrenaline drove every semblance of fatigue from his body. His fists clinched. Eyes narrowed, and in a low voice, he said, "How did he manage that?"

Morgan was not surprised at the fierceness of the question. He understood the stock Will Logan came from. "When he broke out of jail, the best we could tell from the tracks is that he headed straight to your house. It was late in the evening, almost bedtime. He evidently just charged in and grabbed her."

"I don't believe that. She keeps a Cooper five-shot double-action revolver next to her bed. Anybody charging through her door unannounced at that time of night would find a mighty unfriendly greeting."

"They did. The gunfire is what alerted everyone, but by the time anyone could get there to help, the gang was gone. However, there was a lot of blood on the sitting room floor. One of the folks who heard it said it sounded like a war, and she heard a scream. Couldn't tell if it was a man or woman."

Will, his heart racing, said, "Who was shot?"

Morgan shook his head. "We don't know. It looks like whoever's carryin' the lead was bleeding mighty bad when they rode out of town."

"Have you notified the ranch?"

"A rider rode out the same day, two days ago."

Will nodded and said, almost to himself, "Good. Whoever's coming should be riding up soon." He reached to his vest, yanked the badge off, and slammed it on the desk in front of Marshal Morgan. "I resign."

From the jail cell, Ambrose said in a falsetto voice, "Whatsa matter, Logan? Is the missus in trouble?"

Will spun to face the man. He was no longer the calm marshal. His wife had been taken by killers who had already killed an older woman. The face Ambrose saw was totally different from the one he had looked at over the past weeks. The mouth was set in grim, determined anger, jaw muscles stood like cords of steel. His brown eyes had turned almost black and promised pain and death to the foolish man who made the mistake of getting in his way or goading him.

The boy shut his mouth. His face turned pale, and he said, "Sorry, Marshal, I meant nothing. Don't know why I said it."

Will turned back to Morgan, who had stood when he saw the look on Will's face. He picked up the badge and handed it to Will. "Keep it. I want those boys brought in alive. It's up to the territory to hang 'em, not you."

Will looked at the badge in the marshal's hand. He didn't want the law backing him when he went after those three. As badly as he had felt about killing Otis, right now, he could blast the life from the body of the three kidnappers without a second thought. If they physically harmed Deborah, they would be better off being caught by a Comanche rather than Will.

"Take it, Will. The law needs to come to this territory if we want statehood. You can be an example." He held it out farther. "Take it."

Will stared at the badge. It represented law and order, the right way to handle disagreements. But he wanted to punish the men who had and were putting his wife through goodness only knew what.

A cloud had drifted across the sun, and as Will looked at the badge, the sun slipped from behind the cloud and shot a beam straight through the window, turning the badge into a tiny silver halo with a bright star in the middle.

At almost the same moment, Marshal Morgan said softly, "It's the right thing to do, Will."

Will watched as his arm reached out, and his fingers closed around the badge. He felt the warmth from the sun on the back of his hand. He didn't want to pick it up. He wanted vengeance, but deep inside his mind, it was like Deborah was speaking softly to him. Reminding him how great her respect was for him and his family.

Finally, he said to Morgan, "I'll do it. I don't want to, Morgan, but I'll do it. I can't promise we'll bring them back alive, but I'll wear this badge."

"Good," Morgan said, and clapped him on the arm. "Let's get you ready for the trail."

A sudden blast of wind rocked the building. Pulling their hats tight, the two lawmen walked outside in time to see Dr. James and his wife, Abigail, hurrying toward them.

Nearing Will, she said, "Oh, Will, what is going to happen to my sweet Deborah?" She continued forward and threw her arms around the big lawman, sobbing on his chest.

Dr. James, his silver-white hair standing almost straight up in the wind, since he had ventured outside without his hat, brushed down the hair with one hand and patted his wife on the shoulder with the other. "Now, now, Abigail, don't burden Will with your sadness. I'm sure he has sufficient of his own."

She stepped back, unconcerned with what the wind was doing to her hair, composed herself, and said, "You are right, Louis. I am so sorry, Will. I know you must be suffering great pain. Are you going after them?"

"Yes, ma'am," Will said, grabbing his hat as a gust almost sailed it down the street. He pulled it tighter and continued, "I need to swap horses, but I'll be on my way soon. I'm expecting some help from my family. They should be arriving anytime. If they make it here soon, we'll leave together, but if not, I'll take off myself. They'll catch up. Either way, Abigail, I'm going to bring your niece back, don't you worry."

Squinting against the wind, her eyes tightened more. "And those evil killers?"

"Yes, ma'am, I'll be taking care of them, too."

"Good. God bless you, William, and keep you safe." She

turned back to her husband the doctor. "Louis, get me out of this wind, right now."

Dr. James said to Will, "Good luck, son. You be careful. I saw you bring in that other man. I know you must be tired. You take care of yourself." He grasped his wife's elbow and guided her back to his office, both trying to hold their hair in place in the high wind.

Will pulled his hat tighter on his head and swung into the saddle. Morgan handed the reins of Ambrose's horse up.

He took it. "Don't know where this wind came from," Will said to Morgan.

The marshal shook his head. "Just came up. It's been calm for the past few days. Don't know if it'll help or hinder."

"As long as it doesn't blow away any tracks, we'll be fine." He turned the horses for the stable. *Smokey should be ready to run,* he thought. Biscuit was all right. He was a good horse and more than willing, but he just didn't have the strength and speed Buck had. Biscuit would fit well at the ranch. He'd make a good cattle horse, but he'd have to find a replacement for Buck. Turning into the stable barn, he saw Floyd galloping toward him, with Jeb Campbell at his side. *Now try to hide, Foster,* Will thought, a wolfish grin breaking out on his face. *With Floyd you could be a light-footed spirit and he'd still track you across the clouds.*

23

Shorty and Morg rode close behind Floyd and Jeb. The four men pulled their lathered mounts up, walked them to the watering trough, and dismounted. Morg took the reins of the others' horses and waited while they drank. Floyd, Jeb, and Shorty moved quickly toward Will.

Floyd extended his hand to his nephew. "Good to see you, boy. How you holdin' up?"

Will first shook his uncle's hand, then that of Jeb and Shorty, nodding at Morg. "I'm fine, Uncle. I'm glad you showed up. As soon as I get Smokey saddled, I'm after the lowlife who took Deborah." Seeing no other riders, he questioned his uncle. "Where's the others?"

Floyd said, "The rider Morgan sent caught us at a bad time. All the boys are up the north valley, working cattle. I don't expect them back to the ranch house for several days. By the time they get back, we'll have these coyotes trapped and skinned. Even Kate's up with 'em, so there ain't no way to let 'em know till they get back."

Will looked at the four men. The youngest in the bunch was his uncle Floyd, and he was fifty-seven. Jeb was probably the oldest. His body looked strong, but his face and hands had the texture of old boot leather with valleys for wrinkles. Though he was starting to stoop a tad, he still carried wide shoulders and a slim waist. "How you doin', Jeb?" Will asked.

"Mighty fine, boy." He patted the big Bowie knife hanging from his belt. "Reckon I can still handle a few half-pint varmints."

Will nodded, his face grim. His uncle's friends, all real-life, dyed-in-the-wool mountain men, had never backed down from anything except maybe a grizzly, and they all had the scars to prove it.

"When we leavin'?" Shorty asked.

Morg, who was standing at the trough with the horses, said, "Shorty, you're gettin' about as hard of hearing as that old woman what works down at Lockwood's General Store. The boy said he's leavin' as soon as he gets his tack switched."

Shorty turned on his friend. "Don't you go callin' me deef. I could hear better than you when I was twenty, and I still can." He shook his head and said to anyone who might be listening, "That old man's getting more cantankerous than a birthin' grizzly."

Floyd and Jeb followed Will to where he was switching his equipment to Smokey. Jeb asked, "You know which way they're heading, son?"

"Marshal Morgan said they took off up the road towards the Springs."

Floyd and the two older men nodded. "Good," Jeb said. "You stay on the road, and we'll split out on each side, catch them if they split off. You know any of the tracks?"

Will tied on his saddlebags and said, "The marshal said they're riding their own horses. Whoever slipped them a gun also had their horses saddled for them. He also said they took Deborah's mare, so we all know her tracks."

"Good," Floyd said. He glanced at the badge on Will's vest. "What you plannin' on doin' with 'em when we catch 'em?"

Will stopped what he was doing and turned to his uncle. "I'll tell you what I'd like to do. I'd like to give them a little Comanche medicine, but I promised Marshal Morgan I'll *try* to bring them back for trial."

Jeb, a big chew of tobacco in his mouth, moved it to one cheek and spit. A long brown stream shot across the barn. "I ain't made no promise. A varmint messes with a woman don't deserve no trial."

He turned and walked out to the trough, taking the horses from Morg. The tall old trapper strode over to Will. "Sorry about your wife, boy. We'll get her back."

Will shook the man's hand. "Thanks for coming, Morg."

Will motioned toward their horses and said to his uncle, "You going to ride those? They're pretty lathered up."

"They'll be fine," Floyd said. "This first part will be nice and slow. They'll get rested. It'll be a while before we come up on them fellers. These horses, even after a run, are better than anything in this stable."

Shorty nodded, jumped up to the stirrup, and swung into the saddle. "That's gospel if I've ever heard it."

"Good enough," Will said. "Let's head out." He swung up on Smokey, the other three mounted, and they headed out of town.

Marshal Morgan, standing in front of the sheriff's office, waved and called, "Luck," as they rode by.

If an easterner had seen the five men riding out of town after the kidnappers, he would have pronounced failure on the group. With the exception of Will, they all looked like escapees from an old folks home. What the same easterner wouldn't know is that the youngest at fifty-seven had acquired the long scar along the left side of his face at the age of sixteen, from fighting an Indian brave to the death, armed only with a knife. Each of the grizzled men had similar stories he could tell. What they lacked in youth, they made up for in toughness and hard-earned experience.

Leaving Pueblo, the four mountain men spread wide, two on

each side of the road, scanning for tracks while they walked their horses toward Colorado Springs.

Will was in the road, Floyd riding nearest, to his left, on the west side. He said to Will, "I don't expect they'll ride far before turning off the road. They don't want anyone seeing them, especially with a woman. The longer they stay on the road, the better their chances of being spotted."

They continued north, toward the Springs. An hour out of Pueblo, Morg, who was the far west rider, called, "Tracks, and one of them is Deborah's mare." The four men swung toward Morg, each riding wide, keeping clear of the outlaws' tracks.

Like Will had told Morgan, the wind, so far, had been no problem. The tracks in the dirt were protected by the sage, where the wind's full force hadn't yet reached. Plus, the moan it made through the brush and trees covered what little noise they were making, allowing them to slip closer to their quarry.

They continued riding, halting every now and then to give their horses a break. Since leaving the roadway, the terrain had slowly climbed. Ahead, along the steepening grade, the dark tree-line waited. Tracking would be harder there. Light would be muted by the treetops, and the riders would be out of the sand and dirt, into the pine needles.

Only a sharp eye could pick up the bent or bruised pine needles. Unless completely dry, the needles, after being compressed by the weight of a horse, would gradually spring back to their original shape. But the tiny needle would be ruptured, and there would be a mark, faint, but large enough for a good tracker's sharp eye. In this group, there were older eyes but no bad tracker.

"They're gonna have to go to ground soon, or turn north," Jeb said. Will listened to the mountain men's discussion. The five had dismounted at a small stream, allowing the horses rest and water in the steepening terrain.

"Danged right they are," Shorty said. "If'n they don't, they'll be into the big canyon country, and I'd bet a dollar to a pine knot those boys don't know this country well enough to navigate their way through them canyons."

Everyone nodded. Will, impatient to be after his wife, said, looking at his uncle, "You about ready to get started again?"

Floyd glanced around at the other mountain men. "Son, we'll need to be stopping real soon. It'll be getting too dark to follow their tracks in the moonlight. Not much of that light'll filter down here to the ground. We got water for the animals here and a bit of grass. This'll make a good stopping place."

Will knew his uncle was right, but he felt a chill in his spine. Stopping would mean another night for Deborah in the company of those animals. His fear for his wife drove him to push on despite the darkness, but he knew his uncle was right. This was a good spot. The horses could rest, water, and feed. Plus it would be useless to try to follow them in the coming night.

Jeb spoke up. "Floyd's right, Will. Ain't no sense stumbling through these trees in the dark. No tellin' what might happen. Worst case, we could break one of these animal's legs, and then where'd we be?"

Resigned, Will took a deep breath, shook his head, and said, "I know y'all are right. But it don't make me like it."

Morg started unsaddling his mount. "It's tough, boy. You got yourself a fine woman there, and it's hard not to just keep riding, but she's a strong woman, too. She'll come through this. You mark my words."

For one of the few times in their long partnership, Shorty said, "Morg's right, Will. She's mighty tough. Those fellers don't have no idea what they got themselves into."

Floyd had unsaddled his horse and was laying his saddle on a soft pad of pine needles. He kicked several pinecones out of the way. "The boys are tellin' you straight, son. Deborah reminds me of Leotie." It was growing darker under the trees, and the faraway look in the old mountain man's face was hidden from all of his companions except Will, but they all grew quiet. Each knew the strong bond between Floyd and his Indian wife had never been broken, even by her death and these many years.

He continued, "Leotie went through hell. Boy, I'm not saying Deborah will. I'm tellin' you she's just as tough, and no matter what happens, she'll come back from it. I ain't much on predictin' a thing, but I promise you this. We'll get her back, and you two'll be fine."

Following Floyd's statement, Will and the others went quietly about their duties of taking care of the animals and setting up their camp. There would be no fire tonight, no flickering light to give away their position. Jerky and dry biscuits would be their fare, and for these five hardened men, it would be no sacrifice. Each had lived on less. In the silence, thoughts of past experiences, nights in their beloved mountains, battles fought, won and lost. The atmosphere was almost tangible enough to touch. In the fading light, a lone squirrel barked thrice, softly, as if hesitant to disturb the men below him. A lone wolf tuned up far back in the mountains, his forlorn call lightened by the sound of coyotes barking.

THE MEN, silent, determined, and deadly, rode out of camp as soon as it was light enough to follow a track. Only two outriders were sent out, to prevent any surprises. They were on the tracks. Old eyes picked out the bent or broken needles, the overturned or faintly scratch rock, an occasional piece of hair from a horse. They worked their way slowly through the mountains, moving from pine to aspen, to meadow, and into pine again.

Slowly they rode, deciphering the meaning of each turn or change of direction of the tracks. They found the remains of an old camp. The kidnappers weren't concerned about their camp being found. No attempt to hide it had been made. It was left a mess. Nothing had been done with their fire, allowing it to burn even as they rode away. Driven by the wind, grass and needles had caught, and the fire had burned until it reached a patch of clear ground, fortunately too large for it to jump.

Will shook his head. "We could've been facing a forest fire with the wind we had yesterday."

Floyd nodded. "They don't care. Probably would have liked a fire, figuring it would stop anyone following them, but we already knew this was a worthless bunch. Taking a woman who helped 'em . . . that's about as low as you can get."

"Look here," Shorty called.

The men, still mounted, looked toward where Shorty was pointing. Several bloody rags lay on the ground. Will said, "There was a sight of blood in our house. I'm hoping Deborah managed to get off a couple of shots when they broke in." Though he knew what they were thinking, that it could be Deborah's blood, no one said anything. He continued, "Counting here and what was at the house, I'd say that fella isn't long for this world. Although, it looks like someone, hopefully Deborah, is trying to fix him up. That'd be the nurse in her."

Floyd climbed down from his horse, knelt, and closely looked over the ground. "Looky here." He pointed to small indentions in the ground. "These are knees, where the person knelt to patch up this no-good."

The men eased their horses closer, leaning to get a better look.

Will felt his heart leap. He had been worried the person shot might have been Deborah, but rationalized they would have left her to die if she had been wounded.

Shorty said, "Them is mighty small knees. Knees that size could only be a woman."

Morg nodded. "Yep, likely so, unless one of those boys is a mighty small man."

Shorty spun in the saddle to face his friend. "Cain't you keep yore face shut for once. You know that's Deborah."

Morg, unfazed by Shorty's remark, nodded again. "Most likely, but it still could be a tiny man."

Jeb stared at the indentations a moment longer, stood, the sound of his arthritic knees popping was heard by all the riders, but no one said anything, for all of the mountain men suffered the same problem. Too many days wading in icy beaver streams in their early years had done the damage. He swung into the saddle and said, "It's Deborah all right. I've been reading sign too long not to be able to tell a women's knee prints."

Shorty stared at Morg and gave a sharp nod. "That settles it."

Morg winked at Will to let him know he was still poking at Shorty, and said, "Maybe."

Floyd turned his horse to the trail. "Let's get after them varmints. I'm ready to put 'em all in the ground."

Will rode next to Floyd. Knowing the answer but unable to resist asking, he said, "You think we'll catch up with 'em today?"

Floyd shook his head. "Not a chance unless they go to ground."

The tracks' direction drifted left. Floyd nodded at the tracks. "It looks like they've headed northwest." He turned to Jeb. "You thinkin' what I'm thinkin'?"

"Mebbe so. It's still a ways, but it looks like they're turnin' for Oro City."

Shorty piped up. "Oro sure ain't much of a place, store, couple of beat-up saloons. That's about it. They's been rumors a few brigands are makin' it home. Maybe they got 'em some friends there."

"I've heard of it," Will said. "The town's in a valley, up in the high country."

"That's the place," Morg said. "Cain't call it much of a town now, though. Hit gold up there in the sixties, but it ain't lasted long. They had trouble gettin' the gold out 'cause the country was riddled with black sand."

Floyd nodded. "That's some rough riding. If that's where they're heading, it'll take us a couple more days."

The pursuit had given Will plenty of time for thinking—too much. He couldn't push the worry for Deborah's safety from his mind or the thought that had been nagging him. "Boys, you're not going to believe this. The fella I just brought in was all messed up in his head about a woman whose husband owned a ranch near Las Vegas. He's a fine singer. I reckon he's good enough to sing in one of those musicals back east, but she had a piano, and since he was interested in learning, she tried to help him."

He paused and looked around, making sure everyone could hear him. "Now she's a fine-looking woman. Much older than him, but that didn't seem to make any difference to that crazy kid. Because she invited him into her house and tried to help him, he figured she wanted him, so, to expedite matters, he ups and kills her husband. I was down there chasing him because he'd killed a U.S. Marshal, but I discovered his murder of the lady's husband while I was investigating."

"How's she doing?" Jeb asked.

"It's a long story, which I'll tell sometime, but she seems to be doing mighty good."

The horses continued across a valley, scattered pines at the edges, while Will composed his thoughts. The other riders remained silent. Entering the treeline, Will continued, "So I bring this fella to the jail in Pueblo and turn him over to Marshal Morgan, to find out *my* wife has been taken by another sick kid, only this one has most of his hair and half his face burned off." He shoved his hat to the back of his head and looked around at his friends and uncle. "Does that make sense to any of you?"

Jeb shot a stream of tobacco at a tumblebug, wiped his mouth with his sleeve, and said, "Nary a bit, boy, but let me tell you. In my time, I've run into a few crazy ones. We all have."

Floyd and Morg nodded in agreement. Shorty said, "Danged

peared to more promising goldfields. A few heads turned as they rode through the narrow street.

A large, filthy, dust-covered tent, braced with framing around its sides, had a temporary sign proclaiming "Saloon," hanging by a frayed rope to entice the locals into the dank interior.

They reined their horses to the hitching rail and stepped down. Loud voices, glasses clinking, and an out-of-tune piano banging flowed outside from the thin walls and open tent flap. Will, with Floyd to his left, and Jeb on his right, stepped inside, followed by Morg and Shorty, Henrys resting in the crook of their left arms. The tinny piano gradually faded, and sound ceased. All faces turned toward the five grim-looking men.

"Can I help you gents?" the bartender asked. He was a heavily built man, muscles bulging under a tight, stained white shirt, red garters stretched over bulging biceps. Sallow from years behind a bar, sporting long sideburns, a mustache, and black goatee, he looked like every other rough bartender in run-down mining towns.

Will, scanning the mostly down-and-out clientele, said, "I'm United States Marshal William Logan, and we're looking for three men and a woman. One of the men has been burned badly, and another has been shot."

"Can't help you," the bartender said, picked up a glass from the tall stack on the bar, and began cleaning it. Standing behind the bar, which was nothing more than a long board atop three whiskey barrels, he scowled at Will.

Floyd, without warning, strode to the bar, put one moccasined foot against one of the barrels, and shoved. The barrel flipped over, rolling into the bartender and taking the bar top and glasses with it. The crash of the barrel, board, a shotgun that had been hung beneath the bar and breaking glass sounded throughout the saloon.

"Mister," the bartender said, his open hands raised, "there was no call for that."

Floyd followed the barrel and bar top until his face was no more than six inches from the bartender's. A strong browned hand came up, and he grasped the bartender's goatee, yanking the man's head from side to side. "My nephew asked you a question. The woman he's talking about's his wife. She's been taken by a bunch of skunks. Now he may be sportin' a shiny badge that makes him operate within the law, but I'm not. You tell me what you know, or I'll drag you by this handy goatee up your fine main street 'til every hair is gone." He gave the goatee another hard shake, then released it.

The man's hand flew to his chin, rubbing the skin and goatee vigorously. "I didn't know the woman weren't their own. Blake Foster said they needed a place to stay. He looked mighty bad and said she was his nurse. He paid me, and I let him have my place."

"How's the woman?" Will said.

"She looked fine. In fact, she was tryin' to take care of Early. Looked like he'd been shot. He was looking almighty pale. Reckon he must've lost a lot of blood."

Will nodded. "Where's your place?"

"Fourth house after the buildings. A tent, but a mighty nice one." The bartender's voice took on a pleading tone. "Don't hurt my tent, Marshal. A wagon, this bar, and that tent are all I've got."

Will, eyes black and hard, said, "You should have thought of that before you offered it to Foster and his crew." Relenting, he said, "But we'll keep it in mind."

The bartender's face showed slight relief. "Thanks, Marshal. There's something else. Two other men joined up with Blake. He met 'em here."

"Thanks," Will said.

"They're bad, Marshal, real bad. One of 'em's known. He's hard on women. A big feller, goes by Gus Klagel. Other one is Hollis Mercer. Mercer's fast like lightning with that six-gun, and he don't need much proddin' to use it."

The bartender smoothed his goatee, and Will watched the

man, standing with both of his hands still up, while they backed out of the saloon. They mounted their horses and turned up the street, more an improved trail than street.

The piano went back to banging, but several men followed out into the dirt and black sand in front of the saloon.

Jeb pulled up and turned his head toward the men, keeping his mount pointed toward his friends, who continued slowly up the street. His icy-blue eyes swept over the men. "I'd make it a point to hang around this saloon for a while, fellers. It'd be mighty sad if we was to take you for one of them varmints." He nudged his horse forward.

Even with the strain of the moment, a slight grin drifted across Will's lips as he heard one of the men respond to Jeb's back, "Who does he think he is?"

Another in the group responded, "He don't think, he knows. Why, that there is Jeb Campbell, and I'm bettin' the other one, up front by the younger feller, is Floyd Logan. I ain't messin' with the likes of them no matter how old they are."

Nearing the bartender's tent, the moment of humor fled. They tied their horses at a hitching rail in front of the last building and continued on foot. They could hear loud voices coming from inside the tent. Will recognized the first as Blake Foster. "You ain't touching her. She's helped me and Early. She ain't a-gonna be harmed, not by you or Mercer."

Another voice, gruff and loud, said, "Boy, don't you know she ain't never gonna like you. You're just a boy. She needs a man like me. A woman like her don't want no shrively burnt-up piece of a man like you."

In a rush, Will started for the tent flap. He felt the vise grip of Floyd's hand on his arm. The older man leaned over and said in a low voice, "We can't rush in there, Will. If guns start blazing, anybody, including Deborah, could get shot. Just wait it out."

Foster's voice sounded, "You don't want to mess with me, Klagel. I'll kill you."

The other voice, deep and gravelly, answered from inside the tent. "Boy, you don't scare me. I've faced faster men than you, and I'm standing here while the worms eat their bones."

"This has gone far enough," Will said to Floyd. "I don't want any shooting inside that tent."

Jeb had moved to cover the back of the tent while Morg and Shorty covered the sides. Floyd was with Will, in the street, but near the front corner of the structure.

"In the tent!" Will called. "This is United States Marshal William Logan. We have you surrounded. Let the woman out of the tent *now!*"

"Marshal," Foster called, "you ain't takin' me in again."

"Your choice," Will said, "but think about how much Deborah has helped you and Early. She doesn't deserve to be inside that tent. Send her out, then we'll transact our business."

"She ain't comin' out," Klagel yelled.

His yell was immediately followed by a single gunshot, and Deborah dashed through the tent opening. She saw Will and raced to him. He hugged her for only a second and pushed her toward the buildings. "Run," he said.

"Oh, Will, be careful." She ran her fingers lightly along the side of his face, turned and dashed for the nearest building.

Jeb, Shorty, and Morg had moved near the ropes securing the tent, knives in hand. They looked for a signal from Will. He nodded. Three knives flashed in the fading sunlight, ropes parted, and the tent began leaning in the opposite direction. Slowly at first, and before it fell, a man bolted out, hunched over to clear the falling tent.

Will didn't know him, so he had to be either Klagel or Mercer.

The gunfighter saw Will and went for his gun. Wrong move. Four guns blasted, driving their .44-caliber chunks of lead deep into his chest. Surprised, he looked from Will to the side of the tent where Floyd, Shorty, and Jeb stood, guns smoking. His mouth opened to say something, but he collapsed facedown in the dirt.

"Don't shoot, Marshal. We're coming out," Foster said from under the tent.

"Hands high and empty," Will responded, smoke slowly curling from the muzzle of his .44 Remington.

Jesse Nash was the first of the men to push from under the tent. As soon as he cleared the tent, his hands shot up, and he stood motionless, eyes shifting from the Remington in Will's hand to the Colt held by Floyd. Will motioned him toward Floyd and Shorty with the muzzle of his Remington. He nodded his understanding and stepped toward Floyd, hands still high.

When he was close enough, Floyd said, "Drop your iron, boy. I'd just as soon put another of you lowlifes in the ground as look at you."

Nash dropped his hands to his gunbelt.

"Easy, boy. Use your left hand to unfasten that belt, nice and slow. Don't make this old trigger finger jerk with any of those sudden movements."

"Yes, sir," Nash said, raising his right hand again, and slowly unfastening the buckle before letting the belt, holster, and weapon ease to the ground.

"I'm coming out," Foster called from inside.

Will could follow the man's form under the fallen tent as he pushed along the canvas. Before Foster reached the tent flap, Will said, "Hold it there for a minute."

Foster's form stopped.

"Where's the other man?" Will said.

"Dead," Foster replied. "When Deborah . . ." The young gunman paused before continuing, "Sorry, Marshal, when your wife headed for the door, Klagel grabbed for her. I shot him. I guess you fellers killed Mercer. Reckon neither one of 'em was as fast as they thought. All right if I come on out?"

"Come out," Will said, "but keep your hands high. These

fellas out here are pretty protective of me. I wouldn't want them to shoot you by mistake."

"I'm coming out. Hands up and slow."

The flap pushed away, and Blake Foster stepped into the open. Will had not seen him for several months. Though Will kept his face clear of the shock he felt, it was difficult to believe this was the same handsome young man he had knocked into the fire with his bullet. The boy's long, brown silky hair was gone. There was an area on the right side of his head, in front of his ear, that had not burned, a patch of the thick hair remained, making more ghastly the devastating burns surrounding it. The rest of his head and the left side of his face were crinkled, pouty red skin. A few scattered hairs curled out from his head, overwhelmed by the burned area. His left ear was almost completely gone, as was a portion of his nose, grossly enlarging the left nostril. But of all the destruction the fire did to the boy's face, around his left eye was the most ghastly.

The eye stared out, like a brown marble floating in a sea of red. The eyebrow was completely gone, blending in with the proud flesh flowing down from his forehead. Part of the eyelid had melted away, leaving the eye to appear much larger. When Foster blinked, the eyelid failed to completely close.

"Not pretty, huh, Marshal?" Foster asked.

Will said nothing, for there was nothing to say. The boy's appearance had been destined to change the moment he pulled his six-gun on Will.

"You did this, Marshal. It was your bullet that put me in that fire. If you hadn't shot, I'd still be my old self. Women would still like me. I'd feel them running their fingers through my hair. They liked my hair, Marshal. Did you notice it hung past my shoulders? My ma used to brush it and tell me it was mighty pretty, that I was going to be a really handsome man when I growed up." Foster, his hands still high, had walked to the middle of the street while he was talking.

"Yes, sir. A right handsome man. That's what I growed to be, until you came along."

"Foster, I'll not deny by killing poor Mrs. Ketchum in her front yard for no reason, you brought down some mighty harsh vengeance on yourself. But when you came to our home, the home of a woman who had done nothing but help you, and took her in the middle of the night . . ." Will stopped. He could feel the anger rising in him. He knew he wasn't perfect, and unfortunately, this was one of his imperfections he had had to deal with his whole life. Pa had warned him about it, and explained that he didn't know why, but for many of the Logans it was their cross to bear. But it was there, and he felt it now.

Will took a deep breath, momentarily tamping the anger down.

"You've got to understand, Marshal. I knowed she was really nice to me, and I liked her. I wanted someone around me who treated me nice, like the girls used to do. You understand, don't you, Marshal?"

"Enough of this, Foster," Will said. He remembered Early. "Where's Early?"

"Dead. Your wife shot him when we, uh . . . broke into your house. She nursed him all this way, but he finally died just a while ago."

"Listen closely, Foster. If you haven't already figured it out, you're under arrest. I'm taking you back to Pueblo to stand trial. Lower your hands nice and slowly. Use your left hand to unbuckle your gun belt and ease it to the ground. Make no sudden movements, or you'll never see the sun set."

Blake Foster turned his head to look across his right shoulder. The sun was slipping behind the peaks. Speeding shadows dashed across the valley toward him. "Marshal, I'm lowering my hands." Slowly he lowered them, allowing them to hang relaxed at his waist. "Don't you worry about me, Marshal. If you'll give me a fair fight, it'll be you who won't be going back to Pueblo. I heard you was fast. How fast are you?"

Will looked at the boy with the fried face and knew the young man would never voluntarily go back to civilization. Thirty feet away, the gunman stood relaxed, confident in his ability, yet there was a resignation on him, an acceptance of what was coming.

Nash called, "Don't do it, Blake. We're friends. We're still alive. Don't give that up. If you beat the marshal, these other fellas will either gun you down or take you back. You won't stand a chance."

From his burned and pucker lips, Foster turned his head and gave Nash a crooked grin. "You're a good friend, Jesse, but you don't have to live lookin' like this. I ain't goin' back." He looked back at Will. "It's up to you, Marshal. You can shoot me again with your drawn gun, or you can give me a chance, 'cause I'm drawin' on you."

Will knew it was time. There was no more arguing with this killer. He dropped his Remington back into its holster. Speaking to his companions, he said, "If he should get me, and he drops his gun, take him in so he can stand trial. I promised Marshal Morgan I'd bring him in if I could."

Floyd nodded. "We'll honor that promise, boy. You do what you've gotta do."

"Foster, you can still drop those guns, but if you're dead set on dying here today, then get it done while we still have light."

The sun had disappeared beneath the mountains, and shadows enveloped them. Darkness would follow quickly. The piano from the saloon down the street had fallen silent. A lone bull elk's call echoed through the mountains, followed quickly by two others challenging him.

A dog barked at the bugling elk, and Will felt his anger dissolve. He realized he too had two loves, his wife and this mountain country. He watched Foster, waiting for his first move. He could no longer make out the man's eyes. Of all things, he could hear Deborah's excited breathing at the corner of the nearest building. If it got much darker, he wouldn't be able to see the gunman's first movement when he drew. It was crucial. He had to see the hand, or he could lose precious seconds.

"You gonna draw, Foster, or is it daylight you're waiting for?"

He had hoped his voice would shock the gunman into drawing. It did. He saw the right hand make its initial movement toward the gun butt. Without any conscious thought, his brain sent the needed signals to his hand and arm. The hand gripped the butt of the revolver and lifted while the thumb went unerringly for the Remington's hammer. Once clear of the holster, his wrist began to tilt the barrel up, toward his opponent's chest. His thumb, at the same time, ratcheted the hammer back into its cocked position, while his subconscious calculated distance and angle.

He watched Foster's weapon slide smoothly from the holster. *Close,* he thought, *it'll be close. The boy's fast.*

Muzzles flamed nearly at the same time. Will felt the sting of a slug at his left shoulder, but ignored it, for his thumb had already engaged the hammer for the second time, pulled it back, and he was sending another shot toward the staggering gunman. Foster's muzzle flamed again, bright in the darkness, and Will felt the sting of a bullet in his neck. His third blast rapidly followed Foster's, moments before Foster fired for the third time, but this time the bullet sailed off into the darkness. Night was approaching quickly. Will strode toward the gunman. He had only one round left in the Remington. He wanted to be close. This one had to be a killing shot, or Foster would have him. Relief flooded the lawman as Foster dropped to a kneeling position, the muzzle of his gun resting on the ground, his head hanging.

"You beat me, Marshal," the boy gasped. "You beat me fair and square. I didn't think you could." He took another ragged breath. "You're too old."

"You were wrong," Will said.

Foster took a labored breath. "Thanks, Marshal. I didn't want to go back and have people eyeballin' me. I can't live like that."

"You won't have to."

"You're sure right there." The boy's head dropped lower, and his hand fell limp, the revolver resting in it.

Will heard running steps and turned in time to scoop up Deborah as she leaped for him. He felt the warmth of her body against his, and the tears, cooling in the night air as they flowed down her face.

"You're safe. Oh, thank God, Will, you are safe. I was so afraid I'd lose you. All those boys could talk about was how fast Blake was. He—"

Deborah's body jerked in fear at the roar and flash of two guns just behind them. Will, one arm clutching his wife to him, protecting her, spun, bringing his Remington to bear on the body of Foster sprawled on the ground with a large hole just over his right eye.

Will looked at his uncle standing within arm's reach, his smoking Colt still pointing at the dead man.

"Boy," Floyd said, "ain't you ever gonna learn? A snake ain't dead until you cut off its head."

"Thanks, Uncle. I guess you saved my life, again."

"Why," Floyd said, chuckling, "I guess I did. You're gonna have to keep me around just to protect you."

The other mountain men broke out in laughter, slapping Floyd on the back, and ignoring the body of the dead young man lying on the ground.

Shorty said, "I reckon, with yore nephew there wearing a star, you could have a full-time job." This brought another paroxysm of laughter.

Will smiled at Deborah. "Since I need protection, do you think there's room in our house for Floyd?"

She smiled at the mountain man, her white teeth glistening in the night. "There will always be room in our home for not only

Floyd, but Jeb and Morg." She paused for a moment and winked at Shorty. "And even Shorty." Turning businesslike, she said, "Now let's see how deep those bullet wounds are. They can't be too bad, as tight as you're holding me."

Her comment to Shorty had started the men laughing again. Floyd dragged Blake Foster out of the street and dropped him unceremoniously to the side. "We'll pick up what's left in the morning."

Morg said, "I need a drink." He turned to Nash. "Come on, boy. You're our prisoner, so we have to take care of you. You feel like a drink?"

Nash, surprised, stared wide-eyed at Morg. "Yes, sir, thanks," and walked along ahead of the men.

They all headed toward the saloon, for Deborah needed light to work by. She leaned into Will's side, under his protective arm. "Are you planning on remaining with the Marshal Service?"

Will gazed across the skylighted peaks. "No, ma'am. I plan on dropping this badge on Marshal Morgan's desk as soon as we get back."

"What are you going to do then?"

"The first thing I plan on doing is making up for all that lost time with my wife."

"After that, if you're not too tired?"

Ignoring her little hint, Will said, "Reckon there'll be plenty of work around. Then come spring, we'll head to Texas, round up those cattle, and head for Wyoming." He grew serious. "Honey, I'm really tired of killing. I've been shooting people since the war began, and I'm ready for it to end. I need peace in my life."

She stopped, took his hat off, and ran her hand along the deep scar in his head. "I love you, Will, and I know all you want is some peace. Let's build a ranch, make babies, and make a wonderful life together. Someday, I want to do like your mother is doing, and sit on a wide veranda, looking over a ranch where cattle graze and children work and play. Except, I want you to be there with me."

Will reached down and gathered her to his chest, inhaling the smell he had longed for. He kissed her neck, pushed her back slightly, and said, a grin on his face, "Then we'll have kids until you cry uncle."

Her small hand slapped his thick arm. "We'll see who cries uncle first."

AUTHOR'S NOTE

I hope you've enjoyed reading *Tortured Season,* the sixth book in the Logan Family Series.

Upon beginning *Forgotten Season,* there were no plans to write three books about Will Logan. My goal was to tell the story of what had become of the lost brother and bring him back to his family. With his return his story would end, and I'd move on to another family member. But as sometimes happens, Will had more story to be told than could be contained in one book, as demonstrated by his three books in the Logan Family Series.

If you have any comments, what you like or what you don't, please let me know. You can email me at: Don@DonaldLRobertson.com, or you can fill in the contact form on my website.

www.DonaldLRobertson.com

I'm looking forward to hearing from you.

BOOKS
Logan Mountain Man Series
(Prequel to Logan Family Series)

SOUL OF A MOUNTAIN MAN
TRIALS OF A MOUNTAIN MAN
METTLE OF A MOUNTAIN MAN

Logan Family Series

LOGAN'S WORD
THE SAVAGE VALLEY
CALLUM'S MISSION
FORGOTTEN SEASON
TROUBLED SEASON
TORTURED SEASON

Clay Barlow - Texas Ranger Justice Series

FORTY-FOUR CALIBER JUSTICE
LAW AND JUSTICE
LONESOME JUSTICE

NOVELLAS AND SHORT STORIES

RUSTLERS IN THE SAGE
BECAUSE OF A DOG
THE OLD RANGER

Made in the USA
Monee, IL
10 March 2023

29575064R00152